ACHERON BOUND

Acheron Bound

a chaos novel - book two

Millie Leigh

MayhemNovels LLC

reading order:

book one
acheron ride

book two
acheron bound

dedicated to the brother i didnt know i needed, kyle

go follow him on twitch
espirituzambo

one

Sev's face turned blue as he grabbed the needle from his nightstand. Stars appeared in his eyes. Two minutes before he would black out. His breath came out as a soft wheeze as he pried the cap off with his teeth and stabbed himself in the thigh.

The injection of the purple substance forced a sigh of relief. His vision came back gradually. At least he wasn't dizzy anymore. Air filled his lungs, and he took slow, deliberate breaths.

He stopped his ticker from beeping. Thirty minutes late. It had been years since he'd slept through that alarm. Should've known better than to stay up so late but his new project kept him busy. He threw the needle into the trash and rubbed his leg until it wasn't sore.

take this.

A note on his nightstand next to a small round pill. He popped it before tossing the note away. Superior always had tests for him. Foods to try. Medicines to make him better. Stronger.

Sev ran around to get ready as he pulled his black uniform on and secured his weapons to his body. Three blades at varying lengths strapped to his inner thigh. A Lightning Zap on his belt. A Nin Spin on the opposite side. The switchblade in his heel was hidden until he pressed a release on the side of the boot. Only the Guard and Superior were allowed guns. Sev agreed with that law. He preferred a knife anyway.

Early on, he learned to always be prepared. Especially for a guy built like him. Small. Frail. But he could outsmart any opponent he faced. Beside the door, he stopped to check his attire in the mirror.

A row of six thick black buttons ran up the left side of his chest. One for each Valley Superior overthrew before Sev was born. Three pins were clasped to his chest for the lethal strikes he'd taken for Superior in the last two decades. He glided the lint roller over his shoulders as he flattened his collar with his palm.

Lynch leaned on the doorframe as he waited. He slid into step beside him as they walked the hall. His short, greasy blond locks hid beneath his dark cap. His uniform was a shade lighter than Sev's. More charcoal gray than midnight black. Third in command was a tougher gig, especially for a man in his late forties. Running around the dark secret passageways was tough on Sev's lungs now. He couldn't imagine doing it in twenty y ears.

"Thought you were standing me up." Lynch pulled a toothpick from his pocket. Before he could place it between his teeth, Sev plucked it from his fingers and flung it behind them.

Lynch rolled his eyes and took his place three steps behind him. Sev checked the cameras as they walked by and verified the red light blinked on each one. Superior wasn't kind to mistakes. And Sev would be punished if he noticed one.

He winced at the memory of that red chair in the deepest room of the basement. Padded walls kept those screams from his past locked inside.

The first time Superior strapped him in, he'd just been a boy. But he needed to build his strength. Sev couldn't be physically strong, so he had to be mentally strong. Superior made it so.

Sev pressed his thumb to the scanner, and the doors opened. Three attendants stood on the other side of the room in their usual brown dresses with white aprons. They kept the mansion clean for Superior. Did anything he asked. Yet their silence unsettled Sev.

Superior sat at the long table in the middle of the room as he finished his breakfast. His mustache, a perfect line above his thin upper lip. His wrinkles settled on his forehead. He dyed his hair dark every other month to keep the grays from coming in too fast. Couldn't have Ashbury Valley thinking Superior was getting too old to stay in charge.

"Ah, my sweet Dragon. You were almost late." The corner of his mouth ticked up.

Superior would never miss a chance to call him out. Being late was Superior's favorite infraction to punish.

"Apologies, Superior. Handled an issue early this morning. Mission?" Sev spoke in a clear and concise tone. He raised his voice once. Never again. He learned lessons fast in these walls.

"Lynch, fetch me the male twin of Team Wrath." His eyes stayed on the table as he picked up the last grape and popped it into his mouth. Sev didn't flinch when he threw the empty bowl at the attendant by the doorway. The metal clattering echoed on the tall ceiling. "And if the girl puts up a fight, just bring them both."

The woman in brown bent down to retrieve the bowl. The hood over her head fell, and she quickly pulled it back over herself before Superior noticed. Sev turned his attention away. He wasn't in the mood to murder an attendant this early in the morning. Plus, he was sure that one spoke. One of the last, he figured. A couple years ago, he heard an attendant speak. Superior had ripped that poor girl's tongue out right in front of her sisters.

"Sir?" Lynch said. Recognition crossed his face. Knew the mates on the team if Sev had to guess.

His words brought Sev back to the present. He shot a glare at his Third. "You question Superior?"

Lynch's eyes returned to steel. "No. Of course not." Cleared his throat as he turned back to Superior. "Description of the wanted?"

"Neither are wanted. No price on their heads. I just need to speak to them. Understood?" He took a sip from his glass and raised it. An attendant came and filled the glass before she disappeared again.

Lynch bowed his head an inch and shut his eyes before Superior spoke again.

"They're darker skinned. European maybe. Built. They're identical. So you can't fuck it up. They should be at their garage on 42nd and 283rd. Bring him, or don't bother coming back at all."

"Sir." He clicked his heels, winked at Sev and headed out the door.

"Dragon, wait for the boy, or the twins, in the library. I'll be needing privacy. Understand?" His brow raised as he looked up at Sev.

"Understood." Sev bowed his head and turned, but before he reached the door, Superior called him back. "Sir?"

"Entertain a bit for me. I might need to run an errand."

The two attendants opened the door for Sev to exit, and he went right to work.

The library was at the other end of the mansion. He would need to inspect all the weapons and equipment before Lynch brought them in. His curiosity prickled, but he pushed those thoughts away. Those thoughts were not allowed.

The library was one of the largest rooms in the estate. Stacks of books lined the shelves floor to ceiling, and six large chairs sat in the center of the room. A mahogany desk was at the heart of the large window, looking out at the back of the property.

Once he reviewed the area, an attendant brought his invention tablet. He pressed his thumb to the scanner and keyed in the nine-digit passcode to open his latest project. The creature would be magnificent.

Sitting at the desk, he grabbed his Lightning Zap and rested it beside Superior's. His first invention when he was a child. Smaller than his pinkie yet held a massive punch. Superior's worked with his fingerprints, so it was no threat sitting out like this.

Sev tweaked his personal one, of course. It came out green and could reach almost a hundred yards. While every other model was bright blue and could only reach about thirty.

Today, he would work on his Belvedeer. Thorns with low-dose venom. Eyes that slid back and forth from the bottom of the head to the sides. More angles to be seen. Legs so thin they looked like yarn. But they extended so it could be raised. Great for crushing skulls on the track.

The door creaked, and Sev locked the tablet and stood to await the arrival. An attendant took the tablet back to his room. The Lightning Zap was back in the holster on his belt, and he left Superior's on his desk. It sat there as a reminder. Superior was in control.

Lynch strolled into the room and saluted before he exited the room. Two sets of footsteps came from the hall, and Sev went around the desk to observe them closer.

A woman about his age walked inside. Long black hair pulled up into a ponytail. Her hair was raven, whereas Sev's was chocolate. He couldn't help but wish his was thin and straight like hers instead of a batch of curls sitting on top of his head. Her skin gleamed, and grease covered her arms. The tank top she wore barely kept her chest contained while her shorts showed off her muscular legs. She glared at him. Fire in her eyes.

Sev didn't speak as he waited for the other one to catch up. He was an inch taller than her. His dark hair was a wild mess. Brushed to the side so it covered his left ear. Grease and dirt were all through the strands that almost touched his shoulder. His jaw wasn't set like his sister's. His eyes wandered all over the room. Taking in all of the leatherbound books

Superior kept. The mural of Ares on the ceiling was to remind everyone who he was: a God of War.

Did the boy know who the mural depicted? He couldn't seem to keep his gaze off it. Until he found Sev in the room.

His dark eyes locked on Sev's. Sweat dripped down his forehead, and he wiped it off with the back of his hand. The tank he wore showed more skin than his twin's. Half of his chest was on display. His arms were more than triple the size of Sev's. He wore dark jean shorts, but Sev kept his attention away from them.

His body was everything Sev wished he could have. If only his lungs didn't restrict him. They would never allow it. Superior would never allow it either.

"Why the hell are we here?" the girl spat at him. Sev gestured to the cream leather chairs in the center of the room. "I'm not sitting. I want to know why this asshole picked us up out of the blue before the first race to come talk to Superior. We have bikes to prepare. We've never even seen the guy outside of the news. Now he's beckoning us like his dogs?"

"I'm unaware of your situation with Superior," Sev said.

The girl laughed. "You hear that Mason? *Unaware of your situation.*" She mocked his voice. The boy didn't respond. His eyes were glued to Sev. He wasn't sure what he was looking at. He didn't like it. "You sound like a damn robot."

"What's your name?" Mason asked and plopped into one of the chairs beside Sev. His large frame overtaking the chair instantly.

Mates usually knew who he was. Superior enjoyed mates in fear. Especially when they feared his weapons. And Sev was his favorite to wield.

"Seventeen."

Mason stared up at him. His eyes were a rich brown, more amber, with flecks of light. They went well against his darker olive skin. Superior was right. Had to be European. Rare in Ashbury.

The boy's sister went wide-eyed. "Wait. I've heard that name. No way, that's you."

So, they had heard of him. Must not pay much attention to Superior's news clips of Sev killing mates on the street.

"I assure you, I am the only one," Sev said.

She whistled and looked down at his little body. He studied her as she formed her opinion of him. "Ruthless killer? The one who shot some poor schmuck in the eye with a Lightning Zap? The one Superior chose out of a group of one hundred?" Her disbelief rolled off her tongue.

"Ninety-six," Sev corrected. Her expression didn't convey fear. More excitement.

She laughed again. "This guy is a trip, man." Her hand bounced off her brother's shoulder in a playful slap.

"Maia, leave him alone," Mason told her. "Not his fault God himself wants to speak to us nobodies before our first race."

"Our first year, and day zero, we get called into the principal's office." She scoffed.

Her brother chuckled. "Well, at least we know we're not getting expelled this time."

"Man, I told you that was an accident." Her voice became shrill. The heat came off her in buckets.

"All four times?" He squinted at her, and they both laughed. The anger left her just as soon as it came. "Sunset Cove wasn't for us."

"Neither is Ashbury Valley." Her eyes trailed the room. The books and art were quick to leave her interest. However, the desk behind him held her attention. "You'd think this guy would be here by now."

Sev stood by to observe their interaction. Their hands moved the same way as they expressed themselves. But where the girls' features were sharp and pointed, the boys were soft. They were so similar yet different in every way.

Lynch walked in and saluted Sev. "We have a problem."

"Speak," Sev directed.

He didn't have to. A drunken wail came from the front entrance.

Sev glared at Lynch. Grit his teeth. "What do they want?"

Lynch's eyes landed on the twins.

The girl laughed. "Us? We're nobodies."

"You're in the race. You're somebody," Lynch told her. Her posture straightened. Mason got up from the chair and strolled behind the desk to look out the window. He didn't seem phased.

Sev thought through every possibility. The amount of traffic going in and out of the mansion that morning. "They followed you here."

"I saw him," Mason confirmed.

Imbecile. Superior would ring his neck. Sev cocked his head to Lynch. "Your mission as Third is to protect this mansion. Understand? Superior ordered you to pick someone up. That is with the trust that you will do so discreetly. Not allow some vagrant, too drunk to even stand, be able to follow you."

A commotion came from the hall. Lynch grabbed his baton handle with a questioning glance. Sev nodded once.

Lynch stepped out to the hall. Within seconds, the silence returned.

"You can get scary real fast," Maia said.

"How did you know they followed you?" Sev asked Mason. Ignored Maia's comment.

"Mase is a magician. He can feel people around him." Maia stared at Sev, waiting for a reaction that would never come. "Man, you don't react to shit."

"Lynch messed up when we left the garage. The man was waiting in his car. Crouched behind his wheel. I didn't say anything. Figured he'd take care of him when the time was right." Mason stared out the window as he spoke. Sev walked over to see what he was looking at. Seemed like he was searching for something. His eyes scanned the perimeter. "Can't believe people live like this here."

Sev looked out at the yard he grew up with. It was all he knew. The maze. The trees that lined the fence. Twinkling lights along the edge of the property. Fire pits for the race parties Superior hosted. "Like what?"

"Royalty."

Sev understood his perspective from up here. It seemed magnificent and inviting. Until you crossed the threshold. The maze was his favorite, of course. It made you wander for hours if you didn't know the map like he did. The white flowers bloomed all year with a light, sweet scent. It was rare he got an opportunity to walk through it now.

Maia's jaw dropped when she joined them at the window. "Shit, can we go down there?"

"No," Sev said. Mason's shoulders caved slightly, and he spoke without thinking. "If you get through the first race, the after-party is held at the mansion. You wouldn't be noticed going through the maze. Fair warning, most get lost. Some have even perished inside those floral walls."

"Sounds like heaven," Mason murmured.

It had been a long time since Sev enjoyed something. For some reason, he imagined he would enjoy a stroll through the maze with this rider a whole hell of a lot. He shook his head. That thought was not allowed. He had no such luxury.

"Count on it, baby bro. We'll go through it," the girl promised.

"Superior must not know of your intentions," Sev warned them.

"Thank you," Mason said.

Sev hardly heard that phrase. The genuine words coming from this rider were the last place he expected to hear them.

"Seventeen, you might have a heart after all. Letting my brother see some flowers." Maia smiled at him as she sat in one of the chairs in the middle of the room. She draped one leg over the armrest and kicked her foot as she waited.

"Sev," he corrected.

"You have a nickname?" Maia laughed and shook her head in disbelief.

"You really don't know why we're here?" Mason asked.

Sev shook his head. Placed his clasped hands in front of him and took a step away. He hadn't realized how close he'd been to the rider. The grease on his skin pulled him closer.

"What time is it?" Mason asked, looking down at Sev's wrist. But it wasn't a normal watch strapped to him.

"Half past twelve," Sev replied, knowing the time anyway.

The boy grabbed his hand, and Sev tensed. Mason's brows furrowed. Sev yanked his hand back and took another step away from him. The twin smirked at him with a glint in his eye. He'd seen the numbers counting down.

A footstep in the hall announced an arrival. Sev went to position by the desk and Mason sat down across from his sister. Sev locked eyes with him before the door opened.

Superior walked in. Hair freshly slicked back. His uniform was pristine in a deep red shade to show his love of spilling blood. Sev knew what kind of man he was. All too well. Not that it stopped him from doing what needed to be done. Sev knew his place.

"My Dragon." Superior smiled wide at Sev, and he bowed his head in acknowledgment.

"Dragon?" Maia asked. Shot Sev a glare. Most likely assuming he lied about his name.

Sev kept his gaze down. Hated the nickname. Instantly brought him back to that day twenty years ago.

"Oh, he didn't tell his story? I figured with all the time in here, he would've allowed you the luxury of hearing it firsthand." Superior widened his grin. Sev hated that smile. Meant something was on the tip of his tongue. "Seventeen, do tell them."

He was not in the business of storytelling. Something was going to come of this. Clearing his throat, his words came out steady. "Ninety-six of us all had a task to complete. A mission to show our strength. Only a select few survived. Each of us had to defeat a creature of Superior's excellent making." He could hear the creature roar if he tried hard enough. "My creature was a dragon. I defeated it in seventy-three seconds."

"Whoa." Maia gaped.

"How old were you?" Mason asked.

"Eight," Sev responded. His eyes fell back to Superior's, and he held his position.

"Glorious. Thank you, Seventeen. A memory I'll never forget. You were the lucky winner that day." Superior grinned as he sat down in the biggest chair. The back was taller than the rest and the armrests wider. He waved his hand, and an attendant came with a drink tray.

"Yes, sir." Sev bowed his head.

"What did you win?" Maia asked and picked up a glass as Mason glared at her. She rolled her eyes and put it back down. Sev didn't miss the quick middle finger she flashed him. Mason didn't react.

"He won his position at my side," Superior filled her in. He waved his hand at Sev, and he bowed his head once more before receding to the door.

"Later, Dragon Bitch," Maia called after him. Superior chuckled.

"Don't call him that," Mason scolded.

Sev heard them bickering as he shut the door behind him. He headed to the basement and entered his room again. Wondered why it was he who entertained the twins for the few minutes Superior needed. However, he would never question Superior.

To enter the secondary lab, he pressed his chin to the small tray as it scanned his retina. The door unlocked, and Sev stepped inside. Found his tools scattered on the floor from the night before. He lowered himself to the floor and got right to work.

Spikes were aimed at his head charged with blue lightning. The razors coming out of the animal's back were almost done being placed correctly. Sev struggled to adjust the mouth and decided to add sharp teeth to the design.

Riders would talk of his creations for years. He didn't necessarily love killing riders. That was just a side effect, as they said. He thoroughly enjoyed designing these creatures, not becoming a murderer. Now it was ingrained into him. How to make the creatures better at killing the mates. Faster. More challenging to escape from.

The test button willed the tiger to stand on its six paws. Each had three talons as long as the stylus in Sev's hand. The razors gleamed as it rose, and its red eyes bore into Sev's lilac ones.

He forced the creature to shoot a spike into a plastic model across the lab. The incineration was immediate. Death would surely come to the riders who had to face this beast.

two

Lynch found Sev elbow-deep in the metal tiger stomach hours later. He assisted him in the clean-up before they were called to the main entrance of the mansion.

"You gonna say anything about my fuckup?" Lynch asked as they sped up their pace to meet Superior.

"Don't do it again," Sev supplied. Lynch smiled at him in the dark.

They rounded the last corner, and a member of the Guard cried on his knees in the foyer. The gun Sev designed was in Superior's right hand. Aimed at the Guard's forehead. The gun spat darts of poison into the bloodstream to guarantee a slow and painful death. Exactly what Superior enjoyed.

"Say it again," Superior commanded.

"They stole it. I swear. Have Seventeen check the cameras." He pointed at them at the end of the hall, and Superior shrieked at the ceiling. His face turned as red as his uniform.

"Dragon! Go check the tapes." Spit flew from his lips. Fire behind his eyes.

"Sir." Sev bowed his head and headed to the surveillance room on the third floor. He took the stairs two at a time and was out of breath by the time he sat down behind the computer. Damn Pulmonary Respiratis.

He typed in the passcode and opened the video archive from the library. He wasn't sure what he was looking for, so he fast-forwarded from the time Sev left the room until Mason stood from the chair. Even without audio, he could tell Maia was the focus of the interaction. Which interested Sev. Wasn't Mason the one Superior wanted Lynch to pick up? Mason didn't seem like a talker, though. He slowed the surveillance recording down when Mason headed to the window.

Maia was in a deep conversation with Superior as Mason walked around the desk. He smirked at the camera as he pocketed the Lightning Zap.

Shit.

Little thief.

Sev joined Lynch at the foyer and found Superior standing above the Guard's dead body. His blood pooled towards the center of the hall. An attendant stood waiting for the command to clean it up.

"I'll retrieve it." Sev clasped his hands behind his back in his ordered stance.

Superior wiped his hands slowly down his chest. Took long breaths in his nose and out his mouth. Bit his upper lip. A hair fell from his moustache when he released. Yanked it out with his teeth.

"Who took it?" Superior asked. His anger faded.

"The twins, sir."

"Go alone. Can't have any mistakes." He glared at Lynch. They both nodded. Sev took the secret passageway out to the main road and hopped on his bike.

Black as midnight with secret buttons for weapons mates could only picture in their nightmares. It took him weeks to adjust to his standards. Thin and sleek. All the components were hidden. One wheel in the front while two were in the back an inch apart. It gave him more support and added weight, considering his body wasn't enough. He extended the handlebars and leaned forward to go faster.

Less than fifteen minutes later, he arrived outside the garage and killed the bike down the street. He walked up to find a fire blazing in the yard. The smell hit him before he could see the orange of the flame.

Mason sat in a T-shirt and jeans on the grass. His arms wrapped around his legs casually. Maia was in the lap of a Black man across the fire with her tongue down his throat. Two blond men, older than the twins, sat around the fire on logs, tinkering with a small object they tossed back and forth. They looked too similar to not be related. Jokes and stories were being told between them.

Sev waited in the dark for the right moment. Maia laughed with the group of boys as Mason laid back in the dirt. He reached into his pocket and pulled out a small silver item the size of a bullet. It gleamed when the light from the fire bounced off. Sev could feel his fury boiling. Like a bull seeing red, he charged him. The younger of the blonds stood and yelped as he approached. Mason sat up just in time for Sev to attack. In seconds, Sev had Superior's Lightning Zap in his spare holster and a knife to Mason's throat.

Maia screamed at him. Sev was focused on the mission. Nothing would stop him. Certainly not a girl not even twice his size. He had no doubt she could hold her own. However, against him, she would definitely fail.

"Hey." Mason smiled at him. Why was he smiling?

"Sev!" Maia screamed again. Mason held his hand up to stop her.

"What is going on?" Clearly the eldest. His wrinkles more set on his forehead.

"That's Seventeen," Maia said behind him. Sev's blade still at her brother's throat, he straddled him. Sev would wait for his answer.

"What the hell did you do, Mason?" the younger one shouted. Wild eyes. Fists on his hips. Scolding the rider like a child.

Mason whispered up to Sev, "I knew he'd send you to get it."

Sev pressed harder into his neck, and Mason winced as a line of blood fell to his shoulder. His smile didn't fade. "He killed a Guard for this. For what you stole. His blood is on your hands."

"That's okay. I think you still have me beat," he said.

That was true. Years of making creatures and weapons for Superior to use in the races and the Guard to keep on their hips. Even if he didn't kill mates with his hands, he had a part in their deaths.

"What do you want?"

"I want you to walk me through the maze Friday night. At the party."

What did he say? This rider had a death wish. "What?"

"You said people get lost for hours in there. Somehow, I doubt you do. So, I'd like you to join me."

This rider was mental. He wanted to walk through the maze so bad he stole from Superior to have this chat. How did he know Sev could walk through it without a problem? Had he been watching him? Impossible. Sev needed to keep his distance from him.

"I'll be guarding Superior all night."

"Then I guess I'll just have to think of something to get you out of it," he said. A smirk played on his lips.

Get him out of guarding Superior? Maybe the rider was planning on an attack against Superior. Or an attack against Sev. The smile was what had him second guessing his theories.

"What do you want?" Sev leaned toward him.

Maia and the man she was clinging to watched silently beside the blonds.

Mason slowly raised his hand to Sev's that held the knife. He eased his hold as Mason slid it from his grasp. Sev eyed the twin carefully as he returned the blade next to its brothers on his thigh. A jolt of electricity shot from his leg up his spine. He'd never felt anything like that before.

This feeling was not allowed. Whatever it was. Forbidden. Absolutely forbidden.

Yet he couldn't look away.

"Will you be at the race?" Mason asked. He gripped the side of Sev's thighs with his large hands. His fingers dug into the spot he stabbed himself every day with medicine. He didn't flinch. The pain mixed with pleasure, and that was new.

"I go where Superior needs me."

"You'd take a bullet for him, wouldn't you?" he asked.

"Yes." Without a doubt.

"You don't think that's a bit ridiculous?" Mason asked. Sev got off the boy and stood beside him. The group stared at them in horror. Amazed their friend was alive.

"It's the least I can do. He allowed me this life."

Mason leaned closer. Tilted his head towards Sev to whisper, "he's got you on Prophilac. That's not a life. That's torture."

He didn't want the rest of the group to hear. Sev appreciated that. Wasn't sure how he guessed that. Just from his countdown? This rider knew too much. Which meant he was dangerous. Superior wouldn't hesitate to kill him based on rumors of such things.

"Don't test Superior. You will not win," Sev warned him, his eyes turned to slits.

"I don't know. Right now, I'm feeling pretty good." Mason grinned at him.

Sev felt his blood rushing as he looked at the group. The younger man stood shirtless with grease covering his torso. The older man had small scars down the left side of his neck as if from broken glass. Both had blue eyes. Must be brothers.

The man Maia was holding on to was the opposite. Black skin and dark eyes, skinny, with a bald head. A gold ring on his thumb.

"Like what you see, pretty boy?" The younger of the brothers sneered.

"Don't, Reid," Mason snapped.

"Don't let your brother do anything stupid like that again. He'll be killed next time. There are no second chances when it comes to Superior," Sev spoke to Maia, and she nodded.

"What'd he take?" she asked.

"Superior's Lightning Zap."

"It was just sitting there." Mason shrugged.

He didn't look at his sister. His eyes were still on Sev. Maia thanked him as he walked back to his bike along the road. The yelling started immediately. Reprimanding her brother for being so foolish.

Sev couldn't stay any longer. Superior would send Guard if he wasn't back in ten minutes. He made it in nine.

three

Sev's thoughts kept wandering to Mason since he'd seen him last night. The way his eyes gleamed at him. His smile. He'd held a blade to his throat, and Mason hadn't even flinched.

Superior will probably have him killed within the next few weeks. He knew that. It was realistic. And probably his fate. When he thought harder, he realized it would be himself to kill Mason. He hoped it wasn't until the second race. Mason in a suit was one thing he wanted to see.

His thoughts trailed back to Mason's words. What had he meant by the *drug was torture*? Sev had been on it since he beat the dragon. That was his prize. He got to live. He got the medicine every day as long as he served Superior. So, that's what he did, and he would for the rest of his life. And he would be the best. No other option. Mason's smile came back to the forefront of his mind.

He had to stop this. It was fantasy. Mason wasn't in his future.

Only one way to stop this nonsense. He would have to kill him. Make sure Mason died in the first race. It was the only answer. The logical step for him to break this constant flow of false narratives. These forbidden thoughts would not be his downfall. Sev tightened his jaw. The rider would have to go.

Sev would get rid of him.

Later.

Today, he had a mission to complete for Superior. His orders were to retrieve the stolen Guard handgun from a mate and bring it back to Superior. If he fights back, instant execution. Easy.

Sev dismounted his bike in the middle of town. Mates walked by and stared at his familiar face. He was getting more well-known after each attack. Mates recorded everything these days. Plus, all the videos Superior forced the media to spit out to fear the two of them.

Today, the screens in town played the videos of Superior Matthews last year in the ChaosMotors Championship. Graves Valley made sure to share the photos of his teammate riding on the back of his bike. Superior immediately updated their rules. He wasn't about to allow that in his Valley.

Matthews worse than Covington: BRUTAL

The headlines read different versions for weeks until all mates understood. The photos and videos showed Superior Matthews killing other riders on and off the track. One he threw against a tree at Covington Manor. Another video showed him fighting after the last race, attacking Guard before murdering Superior Covington to become Superior himself. Sev had seen the footage. Matthew's fighting skills were impressive. He relied on his strength. Could use more speed.

His suspect was in the center of town. Mates called it Fountain Square. The large fountain was the center of all the shops and restaurants. The cafe was the busiest spot. Coffee and pastries were in everyone's hands.

Sev slowly tracked his suspect. Predator and prey. Sev pulled out his phone and double-checked with the checkpoint profile and photo Superior sent.

Sev put his phone away as Santiago sat down outside the cafe. Sev was about to make his move when another mate tapped Santiago's shoulder and sat across from him. This mate had broad shoulders and a stiff leg. Hair so gray it looked white went past his ears. Sev stuck to the shadows to listen. The strong coffee scent around him made him gag. He hated that mud water Lynch tried to feed him.

The man handed Santiago a cup and took a sip from his own.

"I hear you got it," the man said.

Chatter from the mates around the cafe became loud as they walked in and out. Crinkling bags to get to their pastries. Everyone heading to work.

Santiago nodded. "You heard right."

"Give." The man held his hand out. Palm up. Eyes locked on Santiago.

"Not here. You follow me to the alley to our right once you hand over the money. Win-win. I get out of the Valley, you get the gun."

"Deal," the man said.

Sev sighed at the confession of the weapon. He followed them into the alley beside the cafe. The man pulled a short blade from his waist and cut Santiago's throat. The gun now in his hand, he turned to see Sev and froze. He dropped the limp body and ran. Shoved the gun into the back of his pants and sprinted around the building.

Sev couldn't run. His lungs wouldn't allow him more than a couple of yards before seeing stars. He thought of the map of the town. Which way was he most likely to go? Calculate how fast the man would run and—

Sev turned and walked five blocks. Waited three seconds, and the mate came running. He would've run past him if Sev hadn't tripped him. The man hit the pavement hard and slid a couple feet. Mates screamed as the man pointed the gun at Sev's face.

Guard guns only worked by fingerprint. He should know. Sev created them himself. He made swift and kicked the mate's arm, stepped on his wrist to keep the gun pointed away. Pressed his longer blade to the man's chest.

"How did you hear about the weapon? How did you know Santiago had it?" Sev asked. His tone harsh and his intention clear.

"Mates talk in the mailroom. Trying to change the Guard weapons for us to use against them." His voice changed to a whisper. "Letters get by without Superior's knowledge."

The man would have to die. The mail was read daily by mates watched by Guard. Spreading these rumors would not be good for Ashbury Valley. Superior would appear to be a fool. Now, he would have to investigate the mailroom gossip. If Superior didn't already know, of course.

He slid the tip of his blade up to the man's neck and jabbed hard. He watched as life left his eyes in a flash. Superior would be proud. Sev took the gun and holstered it to his hip. He'd have to reconfigure it. It would only take a few hours, but it meant more work for him.

Sev returned to Superior with his report, keeping the gossip to himself. Superior didn't have to know what he would handle. Sev was dismissed to his lab. He took apart the gun first and fixed it back to its original settings. Whoever had it before Santiago really messed with it. Clearly, they were inexperienced. All anyone would have to do is change the fingerprint scan setting to off. Only an expert would know how to accomplish that. Only Sev would know.

Lynch appeared in the doorway with a damn toothpick between his lips. Sev glared at him until he chuckled and took it out. He tossed it in the bin by Sev's computer and joined him at the long table in the center of the lab.

The room was simple but filled with lights that were too bright. And no sound. Every metal clang echoed off the high ceilings and white walls. The glass room in front of him was covered in shields he designed in case one of the creatures had an error and tried to attack.

"No missions for you today?" Sev asked.

Lynch kept his voice low. Swayed on his heels. "Not yet. I was sent out of the room. Superior is having another meeting with a different set of riders. I think he's up to something."

"Lynch," Sev warned him. They knew the laws inside the mansion. Whatever information they learned was strictly confidential. Never to be discussed. Not even between Superior's Second and Third.

"Seventeen." He locked eyes with him and sighed. "You must know something."

Sev stayed silent. After a minute, Lynch hit the table with his palm and groaned heavily. He left him to his creatures and weapons. Sev preferred it this way.

Alone.

Lynch had been there since day one. The day he was sent to the Valley for the Medicine Trials. His parents forced him inside for the opportunity. Two options: die in Sunset Cove from Pulmonary Respiratis or go to Ashbury Valley, enter the Trials with the other ninety-five children, and fight for a chance. He remembered hardly being able to breathe without his oxygen mask until the day he agreed to enter the Trials. They gave each child a sample of the new cure to be able to fight. Most of his memories from that time in his life were hazy. He was so young.

Ninety-six children. Either all of them got a few months of the daily shot until it ran out, and they all eventually died. Or one lived and received the cure for a lifetime.

Sev helped produce more inside of the Valley after the Trials. Gave his blood willingly anytime he was asked. Anything to help save the newborn children with the disease. His parents didn't know what to do with him when he got worse. Which is why they agreed to let him go.

Nobody thought Superior would keep the winner as a personal assassin. He wondered what his parents would think if they were still alive out there. Did they even know *he* was alive? What would they think of Superior's Dragon?

Another two days passed, and Sev hardly left his lab. His thoughts of the race overcame him. He'd have to figure out a plan for the rider's demise. Sev had suffered too many minutes of wasted fantasies. Sev knew his future. And the handsome boy would not be in his. He'd come this far to allow a rider to ruin his life.

His ticker beeped until he gave himself the shot. Sev reset the timer. Twenty-five hours maximum. Twenty-seven hours was the longest he'd survived so far. That was just another one of Superior's tests when he first arrived.

Sev prepared himself on race day and beat Lynch to the foyer. Superior was right behind him. Sev led them to the car, and Lynch drove to the arena. Superior's Third didn't open his mouth once.

"I suspect everything is in order, Dragon?" Superior wiped his mustache with the tips of his fingers as he sat beside him in the back seat.

His machines were in place. Guard would be armed and ready throughout the arena and one stood watch outside the control room. Had to keep mates out. All the computers activated the creatures as they watched from the stands.

"Yes, sir." Sev handed Superior a glass of his favorite blue wine and watched as he gulped it in three. Drops rested on the corners of his mouth until his tongue stole them with a quick trip around his lips.

They were the last to arrive, as usual. Fifty teams were ready at the start line. Superior took his seat in the stands. He didn't like sitting in the box. He wanted to experience it like the rest of the Valley. Wanted to see the blood and destruction he created. With Sev's help, of course.

Superior stood on his seat, and the crowd hushed.

"May the best thirty teams go forth. Party is at the mansion tomorrow night," he shouted, and the stands shook with their stomps. As much as Superior wanted the mates to fear him, he also wanted them to like him. Wanted mates to join the Guard. Be on his team. Sev wanted to scoff at his tone. Reminded him of a college student inviting others to his dorm. That thought was disgraceful. He clamped his eyes shut.

Superior of all. Superior for all time.

Superior waved his hand, and Sev signaled to the Guard at the line. The Guard raised his Lightning Zap and released it into the sky. Blue electricity shot out thirty yards in the air before evaporating. The sound was unlike any other. Like a bolt of electricity striking beside him. And like that, the teams were off.

It wasn't hard to find Team Wrath in the mix. Mason had a neon blue helmet on with a dark blue visor. And Maia had the opposite to match. They stayed side by side and kicked other team members off their bikes as they tried to pass.

Sev's creatures were meticulous and conniving. One rider in dark red sliced off the arm of a Seekler he'd made a couple years back. Seeklers were popular last year in Graves Valley. Cyra Covington put them in her third race. They would come out of the ground and pounce on their prey like jumping spiders. Wrapping their seven legs around and pulling them underground to feast. Their teeth were like a wood chipper. Their new and improved tongues were like a tube. Once it entered your vein, it sucked you dry.

A rider in hot pink went around once before they fell into the hole of acid fog. They melted slowly into the earth beneath as the crowd stood to watch. The next rider tried to kick off another and failed when they grabbed their foot and pulled them off their bike. Another rider pushed them into the dark river beside the track. They drowned in the thick liquid Sev created. It was meant to pull you under like a magnet. No escape from drowning.

Team Knuckles took the lead when their captain, Bullet, shoved a rider off their bike into a pit of spears. His metal fist rose up, and the crowd cheered for him. He lost his hand two years ago during the Championship. A creature severed it clean off at the wrist. Bullet crossed the finish line in second because of it. The screams that left him still rang in Sev's ears. He tried to attack the rider that beat him. The Guard intervened. That day changed him. He became a ruthless menace. Constantly boxing on and off the track. Fighting his teammates bare-knuckled, with his metal hand behind his back.

The captain had short, light hair almost to his scalp with dark eyes. Stubble covered his chin, upper lip, and jawline. He was stocky with bulky legs and shoulders. Girls in the stands always swooned for him. A deep voice and hardly spoke unless spoken to. Never seemed to get in trouble unless another mate started it first. Or so his team says.

Sev remembered designing the metal hand for him the day after the race. He never came for any readjustment or updates. Assumed the rider figured out how to adjust it himself.

A small smile played on Superior's lips. He waved an attendant over to fill his glass of wine. The blue liquid sloshed, and a drop fell to Sev's shiny boot. When they locked eyes, he growled. She stumbled back. Superior pat his shoulder in approval.

"Keep them in order, Seventeen. No room for failure in the Valley."

"Yes, sir. Agreed," Sev said and looked around the stands again for any potential threat.

A few groups around them were concealing weapons. That wasn't uncommon in the Valley. Other than guns, weapons were allowed. Use of one was prohibited unless used for self-defense. If you hurt another mate with a weapon, Superior added to your dues, or it was immediate execution.

Sev noticed knives in several sheaths and Stick Tasers he created years ago were popular with the young mates. He designed a taser to be more powerful in a lighter object. His first model was smaller than a ruler. The new ones were the size of a pencil. Sleek and thin. Bright yellow. Easy to spot in the arena of dark colors.

Sev focused back on the race. Wrath was now in the lead. A member from Knuckles was right behind the man in blue. He threw blades at the rider behind him in yellow until he got him in the chest. The rider from Knuckles raised his left fist in the air. Covered in a black riding glove. His right hand was bare. Strange, Sev thought. Shouldn't a glove be worn on your dominant hand?

The last two riders in pink met their fate with his scorpion. One got stung and hit the wall. Cracked their skull. The second rider tried to swerve from it but scraped the bike on the track and ended up rolling off right into the scorpion's path. It ate the bike in two chomps. The metal crunched and groaned as his body went down its throat like butter.

Sev needed this race to work in his favor. No way Mason would survive his scorpion. The stinger would do the trick for sure. Some riders met their fate as they maneuvered the track. Others faltered, and a couple went above and beyond. Maia was one of them. Impressive. Mason was right behind her, though. Sev didn't add that to his calculations. He forgot human free will and the amount of training Mason put into being a rider. Sev let out a low sigh.

This would not do. He had to fall here. Sev would not stand for this. His life had a path. No time for distracting forbidden thoughts.

Mason approached the scorpion, and Sev straightened in his seat. He sped up, and the stinger hit the dirt twice in its attempt before getting a direct hit in Mason's shoulder. Sev's lip twitched. He knew he could count on his creation. Mason hit on his gas harder. Blood spilled from the gash.

Dread coursed through Sev. Three hours. Mason would have three hours before his body would shut down. The venom would kill him. He'd never see those amber eyes again. Never see that smirk. Hear his sultry voice.

He imagined Mason's lifeless body on the track. Sev's breath halted. Frozen in his throat, his eyes started to bulge out of his skull. He couldn't blink. Not yet.

Sev's fist tightened, and Lynch tapped his boot with his own. He unclenched and blinked just before Superior smiled at the pair.

"Glorious when fate works for you, hm?"

"Yes, sir," Sev responded in his normal tone. Still, his eyes glued to Mason.

He crossed the finish line, and Maia ran to him. She screamed at their team for help. One of the brothers ran to the parking lot. Mason smiled at his sister as he threw his helmet to the remaining brother. Maia laughed at something he said. They knew his fate. Mason seemed to have accepted it fast.

Sev couldn't.

Wouldn't.

Mason had looked at the art in the library. Smiled at him. Laughed. He was the opposite of Sev. He felt lighter around him. His rich voice when he thanked him. The carefulness of his touch when he grabbed his arm. The softness of his eyes when he looked at his ticker. Sev had never experienced anything like it. Like him. He couldn't let him go now.

The race ended shortly after, and the crowd cheered for the thirty teams that would go forward. Superior stood, and Sev heard it before he saw it. The buzz in the air.

Sev dove in front of Superior and took the arrow in his shoulder. Shoved into Superior from the hit. Superior shouted at Sev until he saw the bare shaft sticking out of him.

"Attack," he ordered, but Sev was already gone.

He locked eyes with the assailant. The mate tried to run. Fool. The crowd shoved him toward the arena when they saw Sev coming. He went over the wall and flailed all the way down. Sev pushed through and jumped, landing on his feet. He pulled the arrow from his skin and charged the mate with the bow on his back.

Fear coursed through the man's features. Wide eyes. Trembling breath. All Sev could see was red. He shoved the arrow through the man's eye and punctured it through the back of his skull. The mates around them screamed in horror. Sev ordered the closest Guard to clean up the mess.

"Nobody defeats Seventeen," Superior called out.

Six Guard crowded Superior as the mates rallied for him, but Sev's focus was elsewhere.

Maia tried to pull Mason out to the parking lot. He was looking directly at Sev. He'd watched him kill that man and didn't seem disgusted.

Sev turned away and went through the Guard passage to the medic area. It was for Guard, so only the best of the best were allowed in. He ordered the few inside to leave him. Once he was alone, he ripped his uniform shirt off and bandaged himself. He wouldn't dare let an attendant patch him up.

Grabbing three needles, he headed out. Two he slipped in his pocket, and one he jabbed into his shoulder. Elastaderm would've been better. This would do for now. He threw the empty tube on the ground and jogged to catch up to Wrath. He stayed underground to get to them quicker.

As he suspected, they were bickering in the lot. He climbed up the ladder and burst through the fake sewer cover. Maia yelped. With one side of his lip turned up, Mason shook his head at him. Sweat coated his pale face. There was a green tint to him.

"Man, what the hell? You live in the sewer, too?" Maia wiped her face. Her clothes were covered in dirt. Her face streaked from crying.

"Wait two hours, in the left shoulder." Sev shoved the glass tube into her palm and wrapped her fingers around it. She stared at him. Then he turned to Mason and lifted his shirt. He stabbed him in the stomach with the last syringe, and Mason screamed as Sev plunged the medicine into his body. "Don't let him fall asleep until after that second shot," he told Maia. He slid the empty needle into his pocket, and Mason grabbed his arm. His grip was weak, so it didn't take much for Sev to release him. Once Maia administered the second shot, he should be alright. He needed the Elastaderm substitute first to mend him. Then the antibiotics.

His eyes were almost black from the venom. Mason opened his mouth to speak, but no words came out. Sev didn't understand his own actions, so there was no chance he could piece together what Mason was about to say. He'd made it just in time.

Maia was frozen beside her brother. Her expression bordered on anger and confusion and hope. She nodded to Sev, and he turned on his heel.

Superior walked out as Sev held his position at the entrance. Lynch stepped in line beside him, and they led the way to the car.

"Found the medic, Dragon?"

"Patched and ready, sir." Sev nodded and led the way back to the car. He locked eyes with Maia, who watched them enter the vehicle alongside Superior.

four

Twenty-seven riders lost their lives on the track during the first race. In the past, Sev would have added the new tally in his tablet. All the lives he was responsible for. He stopped after it reached 500. Sev didn't believe in heaven or hell. As he studied the tallies, he figured wherever he ended up would be the worst one.

The day after the race, Superior called Sev to the library. The one room he'd been avoiding for a week. An attendant by the window made Sev do a double take. Picturing Maia with Mason when she found the maze. *Count on it, baby bro. We'll go through it.* The room was over-stocked with books and plaques hung on the wall of all Superior's victories, yet it felt empty without the Wrath twins.

Sev announced himself and stood properly awaiting his mission. Superior waved the attendants out, and Sev relaxed his shoulders. A pin was in Superior's fingers. He had forgotten.

"Your heroism will never be forgotten, my Dragon." Superior placed it on Sev's lapel next to the other three. "Four times, you've beaten death in my place, and it has not gone unnoticed."

Sev nodded once in appreciation.

His fourth save. At least it wasn't a bullet this time. Back then, it was easier for mates to grab a Guard revolver and turn it against them. That was the main reason Sev modified them. Made them unable to shoot more than once without a reload. Only able to pull the trigger with a fingerprint scan. The death rate decreased instantly. It became easier to kill with a blade than a gun. And mates were reluctant to learn how to wield a sword, let alone carry one around.

Plus, Sev had mastered fencing by then. He no longer trusted a revolver over his sword.

When the pin was secured on his uniform, Superior ordered Sev to finish his last two creations. He locked himself in for three days. The only interaction he got was when he closed his eyes. Every night, Mason died by a different creature Sev had created. He became desperate for a night of darkness where he didn't see the rider plead for him.

A Seekler dragged Mason on the ground as he clawed the dirt and tried to escape its grasp. Crying and screaming for Sev to help. Nothing ever saved him. Every outcome was the same. Mason died a horrible, awful death, and it was Sev's fault. Like every other rider who lost their life in the arena.

Sev sat up fast in bed, covered in sweat. His ticker beeped louder. He reached for the purple glow coming from his nightstand, gasping for air. The pain seeped into his lungs. He rubbed his leg as the medicine worked its way through his body. He flopped down on the sheets and rubbed his chest. Stared at the ceiling for a minute before he got ready.

His door opened, and he didn't have to look to know Lynch was there. He sighed and finished clasping his top button.

"You care for him."

Sev whirled around. Heart pounded in his chest. A rock formed in his throat.

Lynch smiled at him. "I've known you since you were eight years old. Never knew you were gay." Lynch shrugged. "Not judging. Just thinking, how terrible it is for you." He turned to look at Sev's newest invention in the corner before he added. "Hope he didn't die."

Gay? Sev had never thought about it before. Thinking back to all the women the Guard would point out. They were attractive, sure. Compared to the shirtless Guard training on the field though? No comparison.

"He didn't," Sev whispered.

He couldn't sit back and let him die. Those thoughts he pushed down. He didn't have time to decipher what it meant. It was wrong. Wouldn't make that mistake again. Mason needed to die. It was the only way.

"I hoped you went to his aid." Lynch picked up one of his smaller inventions and placed it back down when Sev glared. Glad he didn't press the release button. He'd smell sulfur for weeks.

"Why? It was the most reckless I've ever been. I wanted him to die. He *needs* to die."

"No." Lynch shook his head. "No. He needs to win."

Sev stared at him. Dumbfounded. What was he suggesting?

"Help him win. He'll leave town. Forever. You'll never see him again. I'm assuming that's your concern. You can't handle the butterflies in your stomach." Lynch rolled his eyes at him.

Sev grabbed his wrist for comfort. Felt the ticker with his fingertips. What the hell was he on about? "Butterflies?"

"When your heart beats faster, and your breath hitches in your throat. Your stomach clenches when he's near. When you look at him, I can see it all over your face. You've got it bad. It only took two minutes." He sighed. "True love."

Suddenly, Sev had his throat in his hands and squeezed until he was blue. Lynch clawed at his arms as he choked. Finally, he kicked Sev in the leg, and he eased off.

"Sev!" he wheezed. "You've lost it!"

"Shut up!" Sev spun around, and his lungs were on fire. Eyes heavy. "Silence!"

His chest felt tight. His breath came out in quick spurts. He'd taken his meds already, though. Sev placed his palm on his chest. His lungs were not getting enough oxygen. Did he need his oxygen mask?

"Stop. Breathe. Two, three, out, two, three. Come on. Sit." Lynch lowered him to the ground gently and sat next to him as he calmed. Lynch took deep breaths with him as his cheeks returned to their normal cream color. "I won't say it again, but you need to face it. You're letting it destroy you. You must fight it. Fight for him."

"No," Sev snarled. It was forbidden. Every word Lynch was saying to him. Every situation Sev played in his head. Every possible outcome between them. It all ended in death.

"Fight Superior's ways. Allow yourself to help him. Rig a creature or two," Lynch suggested. "You can't watch him die. I saw you. You know I saw you."

Sev tried to calm himself. His vision got clearer as he breathed. Mason died every time Sev shut his eyes. Over and over, with every creature Sev could think of. Every creature he'd ever created took Mason's life. In different ways. Mason's lifeless body slumped to the dirt of the arena. Bile burned in Sev's esophagus as he swallowed it down.

Lynch was right. Sev wouldn't be able to kill him. Wasn't strong enough to watch him die. Sev was screwed.

"I know," Sev whispered. Opened his eyes.

"So, what happened when you got that Lightning Zap?" Lynch winked. Sev growled. Hated his games. "Alright, fine. You gonna see him again?"

"No." Sev slammed his fist into the wall beside him. Two knuckles spotted crimson. "Forbidden. Understand?"

"No. I do not." Lynch shook his head. His cap loosened on his head, and he fixed it back down. "Now, come on. Or we'll be late. Superior has a mission for us before the party."

Superior sent them across town to pick up extra Guard for the event. Once Lynch and Sev made it back, they took the underground passage to avoid the guests around the mansion. These tunnels were home to Sev. He knew his way around. Every crevice and every door. Most of the doors led to storage closets or other secret tunnels. And some needed his thumbprint to open. They increased their pace to arrive on time.

They appeared beside Superior as if they'd been present the entire time. He waved to allow Lynch to wander the grounds.

"My Dragon was never one for parties, I do believe. Maybe tonight will be different. Any girl catch your eye? I could send one to your room if you like," Superior offered.

"No, sir. You are correct. Not one for parties," Sev murmured and kept scanning the crowd for his team. They were not his team. Team Wrath. Stop searching.

Superior grinned at him. "In that case, don't leave my side tonight. I heard whispers of another attack. Every year, someone tries." A soft laugh came from him. He wanted mates to try. Each time he defeated one, it was another notch on his belt. More mates would fear him.

Sev nodded. He was always prepared. Tonight would be no different. Other than his wandering eyes and thoughts of sweat dripping from a bronze bicep. He sucked in a breath when he found him. Mason was in a suit. Black with a deep green tie. Maia was fixing his collar, and Sev could practically hear his groan. He was alive.

"Seems those twins are worth more than I thought, hm?" Superior motioned down to them. Mason glistened in the twinkling lights. His dark hair flowed over his ear like normal, with a touch more product to make it stay.

"Sir?"

As he spoke, Mason caught his eye and smiled. Maia looked up and waved. Sev didn't react. She dropped her hand, and Mason brought his attention to the brothers hollering beside them.

"They seem to like you." Superior turned to him.

Sev locked his jaw. Quickest route to the Underworld was to get Superior's attention. "They like to play games. As you know, I'm not a player."

"Maybe you should be," he said. "I've changed my mind. Go fetch Lynch."

"Sir." He bowed out and headed into the crowd.

Sev took the steps and knew it was a mistake when he reached the foyer. His head started to spin. He ducked into the kitchen to sit. Shrimp were being peeled, and the salt in the air stung his nostrils. Which wasn't helping. Attendants stared until he glared at them. His lungs began to fill, and he stood slowly. The stars left his sight, and the disease crept back into its crevice once more.

He looked down at his wrist: 8:57. Nine hours until his next shot. Sev sighed as he forced himself to walk out the front door. Superior wouldn't wait much longer.

Lynch stood on the sidelines as riders drank too much and danced inside and on the lawn. They were loud and rambunctious. Two things Sev did not particularly enjoy.

"Superior summoned you."

Lynch gave a genuine smile. Sev didn't understand. He followed Lynch up to the balcony. Took his time going up the steps. Lynch eyed him in silence. They walked out together, and Superior ordered Lynch to keep guard. Instead of him? He was Second.

"Go join that team. Be a player. Figure out what they want. And report back tonight. I don't want to see you again until the party's over." Superior waved to an attendant to fill his empty glass.

"Sir." Sev bowed to him. Hated games. Especially Superior's. What would he report later?

Lynch smiled at him as he walked by. Sev sneered. This was dangerous. His Third should understand that.

It was easy to find Wrath by the fountain a couple yards from the main entry. The two brothers erupted with laughter when Sev approached. Mason smiled ear to ear. A man stood next to Maia as she turned and placed her hand on her hip.

"It worked!" The guy laughed beside her and brought his mouth to her temple. His dark lips caressed her neck, and he tried to pull her away. She didn't budge. Sev recognized the mate from the night he retrieved the Lightning Zap.

"Jameson, quit it," she said to him as he tried again to pull her.

Teams laughed in groups around fires. Drinking from tall glasses in formal wear. Sev could point out the select teams high on Corzantine. A hallucinogenic that had a calming effect on the mind. Usually, the mate would sit still while moving their eyes around them. Their imaginations would take control. The bad side to the drug was it was highly addictive.

The race parties at the mansion were the only times mates dressed up. No other reason to celebrate in the Valley. The wind brought the smell of burning wood towards them. Reminded Sev of the other night he straddled Mason in the grass. Which angered him. Didn't they understand their lives were at stake?

"What are you doing?" Sev snarled at Mason.

"I told you I wanted you to walk me through the maze," he said. "Lynch said the best way to get you down here was to convince the king you were needed. Maia came up with the plan. It worked like a charm, huh?"

Sev was anything but amused. "He wants information. Your lives in his palm is fun to him."

"Yeah, yeah." Mason shrugged it off.

Nothing Sev said was getting through his thick skull. Fools. Superior would have their heads. Sev looked around at the other teams. Most in matching colors of their team jackets. One group nearby had glitter gold jackets and bright white pants. It hurt to look at them.

Sev turned his attention to Maia when she pointed at him. "Hurt him, I kill you."

"You could try," Sev said. Imagined her holding a sword to him and wanted to laugh.

Maia smiled at him.

"I don't like this," the eldest of the brothers commented. His blond hair was slicked back and tucked behind his ears. A scar on the top of his right hand was shaped like a snake up half his wrist. The deep pink shade made it easy to spot.

"I like that smile on my brother's face, Patrick, so deal with it. Seventeen is sticking around whether you like it or not." This time, when the man beside her pulled her toward the doors, she let him.

Sev hated the words coming out of her mouth, yet that feeling was back. That sick feeling Lynch told him about. The one where his stomach did a somersault, and he wanted to stab himself in the chest for it to go away. The brothers left them next, and Mason turned to face him.

"So, how are you?" Mason asked.

Sev's lip twitched, and his brow dropped.

Mason smiled at him. "How was your day?"

He wasn't sure how to proceed. "I brought Guard to the mansion."

"I didn't ask what you did. I asked how it was." Mason crossed his arms in front of him.

A mate screamed and Sev searched quickly to find the source. Flames covered a rider's arm. Another mate pat him on the ground. They cheered when the rider jumped up and held up his fists in triumph. Just a drunk standing too close to the fire.

Mason coughed into his fist and brought Sev's focus back to his question.

"Why?" Sev didn't understand why anyone would ask him that.

"I get the feeling you don't get asked very often." Mason started to lead them to the back of the mansion, toward the maze. It was a slower pace than he was used to. He could actually breathe at this speed.

"Never," Sev answered honestly. He couldn't remember the last time someone had asked him a personal question. Lynch had only begun his bullshit after he met Mason.

"So?" Mason nudged him with his elbow.

"Boring," Sev responded.

Mason laughed. "Because you didn't get the chance to slit anyone's throat?"

"Something like that, yes." Sev didn't know how to hold a conversation like this. A strange part of him hoped it didn't show. The awkward silences between their sentences proved him to be an amateur. He sighed at his social skills. How could he perform for Superior if he couldn't even speak to the sole person the mission was focused on?

"You wanted to kill me the other day. How come you didn't?" Mason asked. His question was bold. Up front.

"Superior didn't give that order. You're in the race. He would've puni—" He stopped talking. His throat went dry. Those were secrets.

"I figured," Mason said. "Then why give me the cure yesterday? That was definitely not allowed."

Mason had cleaned up for the party. He wondered if Maia forced him to come or if he came of his own accord. His face was freshly shaved. He didn't smell of grease. More clean linen. Had a dash of makeup on one cheek. Glitter in a line to match his twin. Yet it didn't look bad on him.

"I don't know what you're talking about," Sev said and started to walk ahead of him.

"Whoa, where are you going?" Mason grabbed his hand. Sev yanked it back. Warmth spread over his skin where he'd touched him. He looked down at it to make sure he hadn't set it on fire.

"Maze," he said and led the way.

Mason ran to catch up to him. "You walk fast."

"Required."

"How do your lungs handle that?" he asked.

"How'd you know what I was taking?" Sev spun toward him at the entrance of the maze. Not a single rider was around them now. Most knew the stories of the green walls in front of them. Knew to keep their distance.

Mason smiled at him. "I know someone who took it."

"Proceed." Sev took a step inside the maze. Mason followed him. Once they made the first turn, he stopped.

"Your eyes are purple because of the drug. People don't get close enough to you to notice, I imagine." He grinned at him. "It messes with your mood. Makes you rage instead of processing anger like the rest of us. It's probably why you have a hard time empathizing. Or feeling any sort of emotion more than an ounce at a time. But I think if I convince you to take the alternative..." He leaned in closer to him and boxed him into the floral wall. His eyes bore into his. Sev held his breath. "I could show you what I'm feeling."

Sev never thought about how frequently he felt angry. It was just how he was. Wasn't it? Or was it only since he entered Ashbury Valley?

Superior started dosing him with Prophilac when he was a child. What would it be like to take something else? Whatever it was, it was forbidden. Going against Superior.

"Don't you want to know what I'm feeling?" Mason asked. His fingers brushed Sev's shoulder.

"No," Sev said. *Maybe.*

Yes.

Mason smiled at him and backed up. "Tell you what, I get us to the center without your help, and I will give you a sample of the alternative drug. By the way, it's a pill. And you don't have any side effects. Other than keeping the disease from entering your lungs, of course. Oh, and," he reached for Sev's wrist and raised it between them, "you can gain strength. It won't restrain you from any physical activity."

Sev ripped his arm away from him. He was sure Mason had other physical activities in mind when he said that, but at this moment, all Sev could picture was the wind in his hair.

"I could run?" he asked.

He looked straight ahead at Mason's green tie. Reminded him of the lush grass behind the mansion that he trained on all those years ago. Now, he trained Guard on the course he created. Tonight, he could picture himself running instead of heaving on the sidelines halfway through.

Sev had never experienced running before. Sure a few sprints when he had to. To attack. But, as Mason put it, that was when he was raging. He wasn't worried about his lungs in those moments.

"You fantasize about that?" Mason asked. Sev gulped. His tongue hit the bottom of his top teeth as he spoke those words, and he wanted to see it again. Sev gripped his fist beside him. He clamped his eyes tight and tried not to imagine Mason leaning over him again. His body so close. Sev cleared his mind and opened his eyes again.

"Okay," Sev said.

"If I get us to the center by myself, you'll try the other drug?" he confirmed.

It was unlikely they'd reach the center. On the chance they did, if he took the drug and it didn't work, he wouldn't lose anything. If it worked, he'd be able to breathe. Run. And if it killed him, at least he could die knowing he tried something new.

"Yes."

"Shake on it." Mason held out his hand.

"No." Sev didn't want to touch him again. It forced those forbidden thoughts.

"So I'm just supposed to trust your word?" Mason smirked at him. Sev rolled his shoulders to prepare himself.

"Deal." Sev grabbed his hand, and Mason squeezed back.

When Sev tried to let go, Mason pulled. He leaned down and pressed their foreheads together. His breath hit Sev's mouth as he whispered. "Deal."

five

Mason walked ahead of him two paces. Trailed his fingers along the wall. His hair in the slight breeze had Sev's eyes locked on his bare neck. The teams shouting turned to a low hum of static beyond the hedges of the maze.

Could he really feel more if he took a different medication? Was that possible? He wondered what would happen if he stopped taking his shot every day. He tested that theory years ago. Twenty-five hours was the max. He hadn't been past that in years. Too risky.

Those years were rough on Sev. Always resulted in blacking out. Fainting. Then he started testing his body instead of his lungs. How long could he run? How far? Too many times Lynch had to haul him back to the lab or grab the oxygen mask.

Mason made a wrong turn, and Sev waited for him at the curve. He crossed his arms in front of his chest, and Mason bit his lip.

"You and Lynch close?" Mason asked as he righted himself on the path.

"No. However, he is the only person I speak to."

"No friends inside the castle?" Mason asked.

Sev chuckled. Mason stopped, and Sev almost ran into his back. He turned, and his smile was wide. "You laughed," Mason pointed out.

"I do that occasionally," he said.

Mason turned back to the maze with his smile still present. They took a couple turns and Sev waited patiently at the end of another wrong one. As they went deeper, the only smell he could decipher were the walls of greenery around them. The smoke from the mansion blocked from entering the maze. He preferred to be in here.

"How long have you been in the Valley?" Sev asked.

"Oh, you think it's your turn to ask questions?" He raised an eyebrow at him.

"Is it not?"

"No," Mason mocked his tone. Sev smiled at his back. "We've been here eight months now. It's way different than Graves Valley. That's for sure."

"What makes you say that?" Sev asked.

Mason paused. He bit his lip before opening his mouth again. "My friend was there while we were in the Cove. We write letters."

"Even now? Guard don't intercept your mail?"

The mate with the gun told him that. That was true?

"We have a friend in Greenford." He smirked.

Greenford was the largest mailroom in the Valley. Sev held in his smile. Mason trusted him enough to not turn him in. Secrets shared within the floral walls. What else would he share with him here?

"Most mates join the races after a full year. You didn't want to wait?" Sev realized as they went around another turn, he'd used the term 'mates.' Would Mason be offended by that? Judging by his facial expression and tone, he was not. It was darker now. They were deeper in the maze. Almost to the middle. The moon was barely a crescent, so it didn't help light their way.

"I had never been on a bike. It took me a couple months to be comfortable. Once I did, you couldn't get me off of it. Of course, it took me

the longest." He released a heavy sigh. "Maia's always been stronger than me
."

"It's not about strength."

"Well, I'm sure whatever it is about, she's better at it than me." The way Mason spoke made it seem like it was deeply rooted. He didn't understand the statement, though. Everything he'd seen of Mason so far was impressive. Compared himself to his sister in ways that didn't matter to Sev.

"Hm," Sev said. Mason loosened his tie and undid his top two buttons. Revealed more skin. Toned and beautiful. Sev would never be able to do that. His uniform was a part of him.

Mason smirked when he noticed where Sev's focus had turned to. "Is this going to push you into a fit?"

He ignored his question and kept pace with him. "You're a better fighter than she is." They walked shoulder to shoulder as Mason made the next few correct turns.

"How do you figure that?"

"I watched you race, remember? She hesitates. It's her weakness," Sev explained.

"And mine?" he asked. His voice wavered. As if he didn't really want to hear.

"Your focus. You should have predicted the scorpion attack." The machine attacked over and over in his mind. Every moment after he was stabbed was critical. Couldn't believe how careless he had been. Not paying enough attention. Foolish. Could have died.

Should have died.

"I'm sure you're right. Had a lot on my mind." Mason shrugged as they entered the middle of the maze.

It was a circle carved out of the large hedges with a small bench in the very center. White flowers lined the walls while the top was covered in a beige terrace. Vines and blossoms hung down and brushed the top of Mason's head. Tiny solar lights lit up the top of the terrace like stars.

"Alright, pay up." Mason held out his hand toward Sev, and a small yellow pill sat in his palm.

Sev stared at it wide-eyed. Right now? "You brought it with you? I can't take this. Superior will notice."

Sev began to sweat. The cool air didn't help. Searched for a way out. Only to find there wasn't an escape.

"He hasn't looked at your eyes in years," Mason said. "And if you ever had to inject yourself in front of him, it won't kill you. Might make you rage a bit and give you a killer headache. If you take this now, you should feel the effects immediately."

He couldn't believe his ears. This couldn't be a coincidence. The person he happens to be spending time with happens to know everything about his condition and medications.

Impossible.

"Maia." He paused. "She was taking the shot for years before this. Life changer." Mason let out a sigh of relief. A full grin on his face.

"She has Pulmonary Respiratis?" Sev gasped.

He hadn't known a single person with the same disease since the Medicine Trials. They only had enough of the drug for one child. Which is how Superior collected them all to fight to the death for it. Sev was the lucky winner. Superior says anyway.

Sev had so many questions. Too many to sort through. First being how she was a rider. How long was she on Prophilac? How long ago was this pill created? How many had she taken?

"Yes," Mason answered.

Uncertainty washed over him as he stared at the small, round yellow pill. If the effects were immediate, wouldn't the risks be worth it? He could *run* out of here.

Sev held his hand out to him. Instead, Mason held up the pill with his thumb and forefinger. Sev hesitated as he dropped his hands to his sides. Slowly opened his mouth. Mason pressed the pill to his tongue, and Sev swallowed.

Mason gnawed on his lower lip. Peered around the maze. The stars above them. The flowers. "I'm honestly shocked," he said.

"The worst thing it'll do is kill me. And there's worse than death," Sev responded.

Mason sat on the bench, and Sev joined him. His hands on his knees as he looked at the white flowers that surrounded them. Mason couldn't keep his eyes away from the night sky. Eventually, he turned to face Sev. Swung his leg over the bench and leaned his elbows on his thighs.

"What will you tell your Almighty about tonight?" Mason asked.

Sev copied his movements and faced him on the bench. Needed to watch his reaction. If he lied, would he have a tell? "What do you want me to tell him? That we took a stroll in the maze, and you somehow knew the exact way to go?"

"I memorized it from the window." Mason smiled at him. "I'm good at puzzles," he whispered.

"Must be why you're obsessed with me," Sev murmured.

"Huh, you are capable of being funny." Mason laughed. The sound echoed off the soft walls around them. Sev took a moment to take in the sky the rider was engrossed with. The way Mason's hair flowed. His jawline so profound with his clean shave.

"Why did you bring me here if you already knew the way? You said you needed someone to take you through it. You lied."

"I did, yes." He raised his fingers to Sev's temple and brushed his hair away from his eye. Sev didn't move. He needed him to pull away. "I wanted your company."

"Why?" Sev grabbed Mason's wrist tight. He forced his hand away from him. Sev's eyes didn't leave Mason's.

"Because I like you," Mason said. Sev stiffened. "I know you feel it, too. Just not all the way. Maybe in an hour or two."

"No. This, whatever you think is there, is nothing. Understand? You will win the race. And you will leave Ashbury Valley."

"You want me to leave?" Mason pressed his lips together tight. Letting that sink in. "It's a choice, though, isn't it?" He poked the bear. Didn't know that Sev wasn't a game player.

"You *will* leave," Sev growled at him. "The faster you're gone, the better."

"Then why not just let me die?" he asked. "If you don't want to see what the hell is pulling us together, then why torture me?" His eyes were darker, his jaw tight. Mason gripped his fist in his lap.

"Maybe I want to watch you suffer," Sev spat back at him.

Mason straightened his back and towered over him. "I don't believe that. Not for one second," he said and then whispered. "You don't fool m e."

Sev wished it were true. Wished he could kill the rider like every other mate he's harmed in the last two decades. Would make his life easier. Next best thing was for him to get out.

"I don't want to play your childish games. Stop messing with Superior. He'll have your head. And Maia's while he's at it. Win the damn race and leave." Sev stood up. It was too fast. He grabbed his head and sank to the dirt. Pain shot through his skull like a bullet.

"Sev? Sev!" Mason was at his side. "Hey, cool it." He guided him to sit up and helped him slow his breathing. Sev couldn't see anything. Everything kept getting darker. He clamped his eyes shut so it would stop spinning.

Sev tried to talk. Nothing came out right. His tongue felt two sizes too big.

"Can you hear me? Just take deep breaths. It takes a minute. I'm right here. Keep your eyes shut," he whispered and kept his chest to Sev's back. Their asses in the dirt. His arm around him with a palm on his chest. Rising with each inhale. "I got you."

Sev listened to his voice and saw his eyes staring back at him in the library. His bright white smile. Mason bickering with his sister. His smirk on the camera playback. Sev leaned into him and let this stranger hold him. In the middle of the maze, he felt found.

six

Sev opened his eyes to crisp green walls. Creamy velvet flowers. Clean air. Sev could smell cedarwood and some sort of mint. He faintly remembered that scent. Never this strong. He tensed when he realized arms were around him.

Sev rolled out of the hold and got up quickly to face his opponent.

"It's okay, you're good." Mason held up his hands and stood in front of him.

His eyes were brighter than he recalled. His tie was greener than before. Forest green less moss. Mason was calm. Steady.

"What did you do?" Sev looked around and then back to Mason. His world had shifted.

"The pill, it makes you see clearer. You'll be able to sense more now. Prophilac blocks you from experiencing certain things. You're adjusting to it. It'll mellow out. Just stay calm. Take deep breaths." Mason's tone was neutral as he kept his distance. "Do you remember where we are?"

"Of course."

"My name?"

"Mason," Sev said.

Mason took a step closer. "Say it again." Sev felt a familiar flutter and took a step back.

"No." Blood pooled on his cheeks. He reached up to feel the warmth there, and Mason smiled down at him.

"See," he whispered. "You can feel it, too."

"No." Sev headed for the exit. He made three turns before he stopped. He wasn't out of breath yet. Had the pill really worked? Could he really run? Sev walked faster and faster, and nothing. Sev didn't feel any different. He stopped when Mason caught up to him.

"Hey, quit running away from me," Mason said. Sev smiled at him. He couldn't help it. Mason looked him up and down. "You alright?"

Sev put his hand on his chest. His lungs filled and emptied twice before he responded. "I can breathe."

Mason let out a quick breath, more like a laugh. "Yeah, it works fast."

A scream echoed through the party, and Sev winced. Too loud for his ears. Another shout. He spun around. Trying to pinpoint the direction. Mason trailed behind. Sev rounded the side of the mansion and reached the front yard.

Three teams attacked each other by the fire pits. Sev didn't hesitate. He slammed his palm into one nose to break it instantly before he jabbed his blade into another's throat. Blood rushed out of him. Everyone stopped. The group parted. Sev panted behind the man with the blade in his jugular. There was no burning sensation in his chest. Only adrenaline.

"Leave. Now," Sev ordered in a booming voice. "Party is over."

Groups left in droves. Riders ran from the dead body like they'd never seen one before. This was Ashbury Valley. Guard killed on the streets daily, and the races became more brutal every year. So did Sev.

Graves Valley was half the population of Ashbury Valley. Sev couldn't imagine how small it must feel to live there. He liked being able to get on his bike and head in one direction for an hour before being able to see the Guard wall. Maybe he'd be able to take a ride next month. When all this nonsense was done. The Championship. When Mason was out of his life and off his mind for good.

Sev peered up to see Superior nod. He bowed to him. Mason stared at him across the grass. Sev wanted to know what he thought of his attack on a fellow rider. But now, they were being watched.

Maia grabbed Mason and pulled him out of there. Practically tripping over herself to get him away. Sev entered the mansion and headed to Superior. Sev knew what he wanted.

Lynch and two Guard were excused the moment Sev walked out on the balcony. He stood beside Superior until he was ordered to sit across from him. His back to the yard of riders fleeing.

Superior wore his infamous red uniform, and his thinning hair was slicked back. His mustache damp from the wine he'd been slurping all night.

"Spill." Superior grinned.

He had thought of a story, but hope was long gone. It wouldn't work. Superior would kill Mason. Well, he would try. At that moment, Sev realized he'd stand in front of Mason if Superior tried to hurt him. He wasn't sure if that was because of the pill he'd just taken or his actual thoughts and emotions on the rider. Either way, if Sev could prevent Mason's death, he would. Even if Sev died in his place. Strange. He just met the rider. Didn't know him. Yet he wanted him to survive.

"They want to get close to you. Use you to get more fans. More fame. They think it'll help them win the race. If they get me on their side, it'll get you on their side. Using me as bait to get popularity," Sev spoke in his normal, clear tone.

Superior liked every word that came out of his mouth. Fed into his ego. "Well, we might just make good on that. What do you say, my Dragon?"

"Sir?"

"Let's get them some more fame. And get rid of that team from earlier. Now." He waved his hand, and Sev bowed.

He jumped from the balcony and rolled into a crouch before he stood. Most mates didn't notice him as he passed by. Like a ghost floating beside them. He caught up to the rider with blood pouring down his face. The blade met the back of his spine before a word could be spoken. Groups started to scream as the rider bled out in the grass.

The team was all in green, so it was easy to spot them. He reached for the nearest rider and snapped his neck before going for the next one. Dead. Five men in thirty-four seconds. Sev closed his eyes and listened to the riders run from him like scared mice. Blood splattered all over his uniform and face. He gripped his fists as he felt a wave of regret form.

That was new. It'd never been like this before. Sure, he used to write the number in his tablet and feel some sort of way about the lives he took. Full regret over mates he'd never even met? Not once. They were criminals. Pests.

But they were all Mason, weren't they?

Superior didn't accept hesitation. So Sev would never. His orders were followed through to the end.

Lynch met him under the balcony and pulled him into the secret passageway. He handed him a cloth, and Sev wiped his face.

"Thanks," Sev whispered.

Lynch froze. Two minutes, and he'd already messed up. "You've never said that before."

Sev tried to play it off. "Sure I have." He stepped, and Lynch grabbed him. He turned his flashlight on right in his eyes.

"You took it," Lynch said, turning the light off.

Sev pushed him away. His back collided with the wall. Lynch laughed.

"Maia told me. You'll be alright in a few days. But you should work on your acting for Superior. He'll cut your dick off before Mason can suc—"

"Shut up!" he screamed at him and took off running. Needed to be alone.

The next four days he spent in the lab. Needed a fresh look on the pill and his disease. Research videos and lessons from when he was a child were saved on his computer. When he was done with those, he did a generic search. How long had this disease been around? How many people died before they found the cure? No results.

Medicine Trials. Twenty-four thousand videos and photos appeared.

Most were of Superior with his hand on Sev's shoulder. He was eight and covered in dirt and grime from the dragon he'd blown up. An attendant gave him a shot in his leg. Lynch held his hand as he squirmed. Sev didn't remember any of that.

Sev took a break and rested his eyes. They still stung. Bright lights were the worst. He tried to sleep it off. Didn't help much.

Lynch informed Superior that Sev had fallen ill. That bought them a few hours. Until Superior sent in a doctor. Sev explained he didn't want any medication. Just needed rest. The man was persistent until Sev pressed a blade to his temple. He backed off quick.

When Sev was a teenager, he would help doctors during surgeries to gain more knowledge in the medical field. Superior needed his Dragon to be well-versed in all subjects. He even helped with a spine replacement. A metal rod into a boy not much younger than him at the time.

When Sev wasn't in bed, he worked on his next invention. It was all he knew. His machines. His creatures. Lynch came to bother him about eating a hundred times before Sev folded and took a bowl of soup from him. Broccoli was the only taste he could decipher in it.

For a man he'd known almost his entire life, he really didn't know much about Lynch. He'd just always been there. Lynch had witnessed him kill the dragon. Healed his wounds when Superior allowed him. Helped him gain confidence on the training field. Sev had surpassed Lynch by the time he was fifteen. He had transformed into a machine himself. Just like Superior wanted.

"Lynch," Sev said as he took another spoonful.

Lynch sat in the chair across from his bed in the dark room. A quiet hum in the background from all the equipment in the lab. His extra swords hung on the wall in a locked clear glass case.

"How did you enter the Valley?" Sev asked.

"Hm." Lynch smiled at him. His fingers tapped his thighs before he began. "Long time ago, I watched the Guard take my younger brother over to Graves Valley. My Sammy. Drove me mad. Near to insanity." His fingers dug into the sides of his leg, and he glared at the wall above Sev's head. "And then a miracle happened." His eyes lit up, his hands eased on his knees. "His wife had a baby a few months later. She didn't know she was pregnant when they took Sammy. She lived in the Cove near me. Back then, you could send letters. We would send one almost every week. Until she was killed. The Guard took the baby." Tears wet his eyes as he sniffled. "I haven't seen that child since he was three years old."

"What happened?" Sev asked, sitting up further. Couldn't believe he'd known Lynch for so long and didn't know any of this. Looking at him now, he could see it behind his eyes. All the pain he kept wrapped tight.

"I tried to fight. I don't know what I thought. Maybe I'd go with him. Take care of him with my brother." He shook his head. "Then they sent my nephew to Graves and me to Ashbury." Lynch tapped the bowl in Sev's lap to tell him to keep eating. He took another bite.

"So, you don't even know if the kid is alive?" he asked around his mouthful.

Lynch gave a smirk. "There's perks to being Superior's Third, buddy," he said.

Sev gasped. "What did you do?"

"I sent the kid a letter." He shrugged.

Someone else was sending letters past Superior? Was it the same method? "Did he respond?"

"I told him not to. Too much risk. Later that year, someone let me know. He got my message." Lynch wiped his hands on his legs and eased out a soft sigh.

"So, he's alive?" Sev was fascinated. He never knew any of this.

"Oh yes." Lynch smiled. "I hoped he was. And he's more of a man than I could ever be. Strong. Resilient."

Sev stared at him. Shocked. He broke rules. Defied the system. Superior. And he was still here.

"And your brother?" Sev asked.

He shook his head somberly. No response necessary.

"Eat. We'll talk in the morning," Lynch said and patted Sev's leg before he whispered. "I'm glad you took the pill. You're becoming human again."

Sev was beginning to agree.

Six days since Sev had seen Mason, and he could feel the effect. Longing for his eyes to be on his. His scent to be around him. His towering frame above him. Sev found himself having to try harder to concentrate on his inventions. He kept going back to the feeling of Mason's fingers pushing

Sev's hair out of his eyes. Never in his life had he allowed such distraction. Disgraceful.

A week before the second race, Sev showered and began to get dressed. His pants and shoes were on, and he tightened the wrap on his thigh that held his blades. His leg was no longer sore from the injections. He rubbed the spot in memory.

He tightened the blades on his leg again when his door creaked. Sev let out a sigh and leaned over his desk by the wall.

Those footsteps weren't Lynch's.

Sev grabbed a blade and pivoted. Recognized the build before letting it fly. Mason stood with his hands raised. His eyes fixated on Sev's bare chest. His scars on display. It was too late to cover them. Especially his back. He'd seen too much.

"How the hell did you get in here?" He pointed the blade at him from across the room.

Mason raised his hands slowly. "Lynch."

"Fucking dumbass piece of shit fuck," Sev whispered to himself and grabbed his uniform shirt. He started at the bottom, and Mason took over after the second button. Sev allowed him, considering his hands were shaking. Mason finished the top button and slid his hands up to his shoulders to rest there. "What are you doing here?"

"He did this to you?" Mason asked as his eyes traveled down his chest.

"When deserved," Sev said.

"You don't actually believe that, do you?" His head tilted toward him. Sev held his breath.

Sev didn't know how to respond. He did believe that. It was wired into his core. You mess up, you were punished. It was the way of their world.

Mason's long-sleeved button-up shirt clung to his chest. He looked nicer than he normally did. Not as nice as the party. He hoped to see him in a suit again.

No. He needed to go away. He needed to leave. This was forbidden.

"Why did you kill them?" Mason asked and brushed his fingertips down Sev's chest.

Sev gulped and took a step from him before he replied. "Orders."

"Did you enjoy it?" he asked.

Sev's pulse raced when the riders screamed. Their eyes bulged out as he replayed the scene. "No."

"That's all I needed," Mason said. He turned to leave when Sev grabbed his hand.

"Wait." Sev slowly raised his hand to Mason's head and slid his fingers through his hair. Sev stopped halfway back and yanked hard.

Mason yelped as he revealed six strands in his fist.

"Thanks," Sev murmured.

"The hell is that for?" He rubbed his head and scrunched his nose.

Sev walked over to lab two and scanned his eye to gain access. Mason followed him inside and gasped at the creations that weren't covered or underneath the floor.

"Sev." He stopped to gape at all of them. "I didn't know."

Sev had never shown his creatures to anyone before. It wasn't necessarily a secret that he made them, but it wasn't general knowledge. Superior made it so. Sev didn't care anymore. He wanted to show him. Wanted to know what Mason thought.

Sev pulled out the keyboard next to the six-pawed tiger. He pressed a few buttons and a compartment opened on the underside of the tiger's stomach. Inserted the hairs into a small box before placing it inside. The computer dinged when the compartment closed. Sev walked in front of the tiger and stopped to cut his palm with his short blade.

"What are you doing?" Mason grabbed his hand to look at the damage. His blood spilled at their feet. Sev felt the heat going to his cheeks again and stepped away.

"Here." Sev pointed at the floor several paces away from the red drops. He handed the blade to Mason, but he handed it right back. Mason held his palm out. Sev didn't hesitate. He sliced into his skin, just not as deep. His blood dripped to the tile, and they walked back to the computer.

Sev tried to reach above the cabinets to grab the black tin that sat on the edge. He groaned on his tiptoes. Mason chuckled behind him, placed his hands on Sev's hips, and pushed him aside. He grabbed the tin and handed it over with ease.

"Thanks," he said, and Mason nodded.

He opened the tin of Elastaderm and pulled Mason's hand into his. Rubbed the ointment on his cut, and it healed instantly. Mason's eyes went wide.

Sev was used to seeing the ointment's magic. Superior had to cover his body with it multiple times a week from all the duels he'd get himself into. He turned back to the computer and pressed a few buttons, and the tiger growled.

"Holy shit." Mason jolted. He watched as it attacked the spot of Sev's blood on the ground. Not Mason's. "Did you do that?"

Sev didn't respond. This was more than forbidden. This was insanity.

Mason grabbed Sev's hand and spread the ointment on his cut for him. His hand healed like Mason's had. He sealed the tin and put it back on top of the cabinet. His shirt raised as he reached and Sev noticed his bare skin. It was so fast, less than a second, and yet his cheeks heated. Sev hoped to forget it soon.

"You really want me to win. So I'll leave?" Mason asked. His words came out thick. Sev glued his eyes to Mason's. Needed him to believe.

"Yes," Sev lied.

Sev realized he didn't want the rider to go. He must. Or he would be killed one way or another. The silence hung in the room like fog. Hard to see past it. Mason looked around the lab and his eyes landed on Sev's computer. The password box blinked in the corner of the screen. Waiting for the correct key.

"Why did you come tonight?" Sev asked.

"I didn't feel great leaving you like I did," Mason said.

"You had to." Sev remembered the look in his eyes when he left the party. Right before he massacred an entire team.

"I'm not under the Emperor's rule like you are." Mason put his hands in his pockets and started to walk around the room. He looked at each object and creature with interest. His eyes wandered every inch of them. "Show me your favorite."

He searched and went over to the far-right corner. He pressed a button, and a cage lifted from the floor. Mason jumped back from the creature. It had eight eyes and long, spiky legs sticking out. Matted fur from being in the tar it survived in.

"Beautiful," Mason exhaled.

Sev stared at him. Beautiful? "You're strange."

Mason laughed. "So they say. Let's see another."

Sev showed him several more before Lynch found them. They were adjusting a sphinx wing together when he cleared his throat.

"Lynch, hey." Mason smiled at him. He returned the gesture. Sev glared at him from across the room. Mason didn't smile at Sev like that.

"Glad I found you like this and not the alternative."

"Lynch." Sev clenched his jaw.

"I hear ya. Anyways, let's go. Maia will slit my throat if I let Superior find you in here."

"See you next week," Mason said. Sev pursed his lips. He expected him to leave with Lynch and realize his insanity of coming here, but Mason stopped and turned back to him. "Pretty eyes, by the way."

And then he was gone.

Sev stood there alone as his second in command took his man home. His friend? His risk. At least he was his. But he wasn't.

Sev threw his tablet at the wall. It had an indestructible case for this reason. He sat down on the tile and held his head between his hands. Gripped his hair between his fingers.

What was he thinking? Putting a barrier on the tiger. He'd get caught. At least Mason would live. He would win. He had to. So he could be f ree.

Sev would deal with the pain of his absence. As long as he was gone and not dead. He could imagine him having a good life outside. Not in here where he could watch him be with someone. He nearly lit Lynch on fire for smiling at him. He can't imagine what he'd do if it had been Mason with that skinny man at their garage instead of Maia.

seven

His ticker beeped, and Sev threw another dose of purple liquid down the toilet. Tomorrow was the race, and he finally felt ready. Seven days straight in his lab. Working and coming up with new designs for his tiger and fixing his other creations that riders had destroyed in the first race.

Each time Guard brought in a new creature that had been messed up, anger washed over him. It was getting easier to calm down. Bright lights were still bothersome. Loud noises, too. Maybe he'd ask Lynch about that. Would he know?

The morning of the race, a small bag of yellow pills sat on his desk with a handwritten note underneath.

to keep them green, one pill every seven days

It had been almost twenty years since he'd seen his natural eye color. The deep shade still felt foreign to him. His senses had calmed a bit, yet he desperately wanted to see Mason. Another week without him, and his heart raced in his chest. Lynch smiled at him in the doorway as he got ready.

Toothpick in his teeth. "Buddy, you're glowing."

Sev glared at him as he passed by. Even Lynch and his damn toothpick wouldn't be able to ruin his day. He was ready. Confident. And it had nothing to do with the fact that he was going to see the twins today. Not at all.

Sev rode with Superior to the event. Thirty teams competed today. The track would be harsher. What kept him collected was the fact that Mason would get past the feline. Hopefully without anyone noticing.

Today, the mates would be impressed with the arena. Sev designed the atmosphere this time. Fog at their feet in the stands to match the ground of the arena. Smoke pits filled with Memory Bombs. Once the motion detector clocked a rider, it would gas you with the drug. You forgot everything, even your own name, instantly. It lasted ten minutes. Long enough for a rider to lose the Championship. Once they came out of the pit, it took a couple hours for the grogginess to go away. Other ones Sev modified to last longer, and others just put you to sleep for half an hour. Superior used these for personal battles before Sev tweaked them enough to incorporate them into his creatures.

Since Ashbury Valley made most of the medicines for several Valleys, Superior could get his hands on new ones or doses to be tested. Sev himself had been a guinea pig when he was a teenager.

Superior tried to make him stronger and faster. More like his machines than a man. Seemed he got what he wished for.

The crowd was rowdy today as they filled the stands. Groups hollered at each other across the arena and held signs with different teams on them. That's when one caught his eye. A group of six men across the way. Each holding handmade signs with bold lettering of various sayings. Then he realized it was a team that had lost the Championship last year.

TRACK IS RIGGED

ONLY THE FAMOUS TEAMS WIN

Superior gnawed his upper lip with a scowl. "Dragon," he started. Then let out a grunt of frustration. "Never mind."

He stood and addressed them specifically. Sev prepared for war. Smacked Lynch on the shoulder and aimed his gaze at the men in purple across the track from them.

"Gentlemen, you've come to the wrong event to piss me off. If you wish to die, by all means, raise those signs high for all to see. But hear me, this is not true. Each of the creatures on the track are handmade by my very own, Seventeen. In fact, if you'd like a demonstration, he'd be happy to oblige. Wouldn't you, my Dragon?"

"Sir." He bowed his head and jumped over the rail into the dirt of the track. Sev heaved a sigh. Superior just made everyone aware of his inventions. He was the creator of all the death machines on the track. No doubt he would be a target from now on. Sev waited for a Guard to bring him a bike and scoffed at it. Bulky and hovered a few inches off the ground. He looked up at Superior and shook his head once at him. Sev found Team Wrath and made a beeline for Maia.

"Your bike," he said.

"Asshole," she whispered, and he smirked. Riders parted the way as he punched the gas. He barreled through the forest of Parklings, trees that had branches of steel. Twigs shot small spikes into your tires and legs. He dodged every strike.

Sev surprisingly enjoyed Maia's bike but preferred his own. Hers didn't have as many buttons and accessories. Maybe he could add some for her...

A Crimple he'd made a decade ago came running toward him. The crowd screamed as he rammed his fist into its torso, knowing that was its weak spot. He escaped the fire pits and screaming fog. Fireballs launched at him from every angle and he swerved to miss those.

The track itself was like all the others: gravel and with lots of curves and jumps. Other Valley's changed the weather and foliage. Ashbury didn't waste time on such nonsense. They switched out some of the Parklings and moved them around. For the most part, the differences were in the creatures Sev created every year. Each race became more challenging than the previous. More to defeat. More to succumb.

The tiger swiped and snapped at him as he rode over the jump nearby. His familiar metal friend snarled as he got away. Sev stopped next to Maia again and fixed his wind-blown hair using his fingers as a comb. He completed a full lap around the track for them all to witness. Maia smiled as he hopped off.

"Alright, you might still be an asshole. But damn, you're a good rider."

Sev nodded to thank her and locked eyes with Mason. Those amber orbs twisted the knife in his gut. Don't look at him, he told himself twice before he turned back to Superior.

"If Seventeen can be targeted, anyone can. Don't spread your bullshit here in my Valley. At my event. Dismissed. Guard." Superior snapped his fingers, and they escorted the group out of the arena. One shouted, and Superior let it slide. Sev jumped up the wall and joined Lynch again.

"Great show, Dragon. Quick thinking with the bike."

"Thought you might approve, sir," he said.

Sev knew Superior almost as well as he knew himself. One thing Superior loved was a good show. Especially ones that made mates seem foolish while simultaneously making Superior look spectacular. Sev knew his performance was flawless, but at what cost?

Superior smiled as he waved his hand, and the Guard walked out. In front of the first row of Chaos bikes, they shot the Zap in the air. Riders charged the front, and Mason stayed to the side. Teams were vicious this year. Side-swiping each other with blades to slice another rider's arm. The number of tires popped was making Sev's ears ring. His senses were still sensitive to certain things. Every time a fireball went by, it made him squint.

Two members of Team Knuckles appeared beside Maia. One on each side. Their deep red leather stood out. Bullet swung his metal hand at her handlebar and missed by a couple inches. Maia swerved into the rider on the other side. She recovered fast and drifted around Bullet before she stomped on the gas.

A rider tried to fire a shot at a Parkling that wouldn't let up and caught fire to three of them. Sev sighed in annoyance. That would be a day's worth of work to fix.

Maia went around the track twice before joining Mason's side. A creature Sev was very fond of crawled up the wall of the arena. The Ogle, he called it. The body was the size of a large dog. Legs like a spider. Large wings covered its back. Ten eyes grouped together in the center of its face. The head swiveled around so it could see the target before pouncing. Sev counted down in his head before it leaped. Landed on Maia and knocked her off her bike.

Mason launched himself into the creature. The Ogle thrashed as Mason cut its thin wings. It tossed Maia away.

He opened his helmet to shout, "Get back on! Go!"

She clambered on and wiped herself off as she went over the next jump. Mason punched the Ogle in the head before he stabbed one of its eyes. He jumped back into the Championship, leaving the screeching creature for the next set of riders.

Once the twins were side-by-side again, they stayed that way. When the tiger swiped, it appeared to be attacking both of them.

Sev thanked the stars as they crossed the finish line with little injuries. Other than Mason's hand. He shouldn't have punched the metal creature bare-knuckled. However, Sev had done worse himself, so he couldn't speak on that.

Wrath finished in sixth place. Bullet had finished in third putting his team in the top five again. Superior smiled at the team in red. He certainly liked the way they fought on the track.

Once it was over, Superior spoke with a group of Guard before allowing Sev to lead him to the car. He was about to open the door when a shout caught his attention. Six large men in red with black gloves on their left hands.

Team Knuckles surrounded a group in blue. Shit.

Bullet had his human fist at Maia's gut while two other members held Mason back. Maia yelled at Bullet. Called him names. Mason thrashed in the rider's arms as he tried to save his sister. His eyes bulged out of his head as he screamed at Bullet. Sev had never experienced love before. Watching it was something else entirely.

Sev released his Nin Spin before he could even blink. It cut the side of the rider's neck and flew right back into his hand. He caught it and got in the car beside Superior. He knew it had worked but couldn't turn to witness. That stung worse than seeing Mason in pain over his sister about to be beaten.

What was wrong with him? Maybe the meds really did change him. Only two pills so far. What would happen after his third dose? A full-blown meltdown played in his head. Others inside the mansion would fall to their knees in grief or misery, but he'd never experienced that. A rush of emotion so powerful it brought you closer to hell. His thoughts carried him to the day he'd say goodbye to Mason forever. And he thought maybe, just maybe, he'd be brought to his knees the same w ay.

Lynch drove them back to the mansion, and Superior sent them on a mission while everyone was still calming down from the race. Simple intel this time. Which was fine with Sev. But boring.

They arrived at the abandoned building Superior ordered them to. A group of Guard chatted as they took their helmets off and rested. Three of them stayed up watching the entrances. Laughter filled the empty spaces between them. Others slept by the fire they had made in a trash can. It smelled of musty paper, probably an old newspaper factory from the looks around them. Large machines and tall ceilings. Before Superior allowed electronics inside the walls, the newspaper was the only source the mates had around the Valley.

Lynch's focus stayed on the Guard. He took his hat off and flattened his hair before fixing it back on his head. "Scares you, doesn't it? Having feelings and being able to run around without keeling over."

He was reluctant to talk to Lynch. Lynch seemed to trust him though. Why shouldn't it go both ways?

"I'm not sure what I feel," Sev answered honestly. "It's been so long since I've experienced any of these emotions. Well, that's not true. I experience all of them, just through a sheet of glass. Does that make sense?"

"Actually, yes." He chuckled quietly. "I watch you sometimes. To see how you react to things. Normally, it's just a twitch. A tightness to your grip, a lift of your lip, sometimes even a wet eye. You've been trained well. So, you know what that means? You can unlearn it. I have hope for you." Lynch clapped him on the shoulder lightly. "Superior might have gotten under your skin, but he does not own you. He might order you, but it is your choice to obey. Understand?"

"But, if I—"

"No. It is your *choice* to obey." Lynch's eyes bore into his. They'd never really had a conversation like this. Normally, they were quiet on missions. Was this another result of being off Prophilac? "There are consequences to actions. But I'm talking about you choosing your future. You keep thinking that getting rid of that boy is going to help you. It ain't." Lynch shook his head before turning back to the group of Guard.

"How can you say that? Of course it will help. He'll be gone. My life will go back to how it's always been." Sev would be able to breathe easily again. No worries of races or teams or mates. No thoughts of saving someone from being beaten in the parking lot. He could go back to normal. No more concentration issues or daydreams. Sev thrived on order and structure. This was anything but.

"If you think that, you're a moron." Lynch scoffed.

Sev's rage started to rise until Lynch looked back at him.

"You're on that new shit. Nothing will ever be the same again. You think you won't miss him every second he's gone? Think you won't regret sending him away?" He shook his head at him.

"You don't know a damn thing," Sev said. Lynch tried to ask him questions, but he didn't give any response. They needed to focus on their mission.

The Guard started talking louder as their conversation became more heated. Lynch and Sev sat up, ready to run, just in case. This was an intel mission only. Even if the men killed each other, they were not to be seen.

"Graves is coming. They heard Superior wants their land. If you heard someone was coming for our Valley, you'd do the same thing. Prepare an army and fight. Even try to get the upper hand. Get them when they least expect it."

The men were too far to get a good look at them, but Sev could hear the older, deep voice of the first man. And the younger voice from the second. Barely out of puberty.

"You think Superior Matthews is any match against Superior Ashbury?" The young Guard laughed and slapped his leg hard. "You're an idiot if you think that kid could beat our Superior. He's a savage. A true warrior."

"But he hasn't made his move yet. Why?"

"What are you saying?"

"You think he's getting too old?" the third Guard asked. He stood and stretched as he paced around them. His long hair wrapped in a blue bandana.

"That's exactly what I think. We might be losing this war, boys. I'm just saying prepare yourselves. Get your dues in order." The Guard stood and peeled his jacket off and then his shirt. A hawk covered his back in brown and yellow ink. Sev could easily see from their hideout.

"I think you're nuts to think Ashbury is losing anything in the next decade. You were there the night of the raid on Treasure Valley," the younger Guard said.

"That doesn't count. His father had just passed," Hawk Tattoo said.

"If you ask me, Superior is even worse than his father." Blue Bandana shook his head at the floor. "Seems to never have a plan of attack. Just goes based on his gut. You can't lead an army like that. You need a roadmap of where you're taking the group. A goal."

"Oh, he has a goal," the young Guard sighed. "Death. Destruction. And power."

Hawk Tattoo nodded. "He wants all of the Valleys. That's for sure. Wants to be king of the world. I hope Matthews comes and knocks his head clean off."

"From what I've heard, he's even worse than any Superior I've ever read about," Blue Bandana said. The three men became quiet again.

Sev and Lynch stayed another hour before heading back to the mansion. Lynch checked his watch and looked down at Sev's ticker. They both knew he couldn't take it off. Superior would know. He couldn't find out, or else it would be his head. And Mason's.

They relayed some of the information to Superior. Told him to prepare for a surprise attack. Superior took the news well. As if he expected that.

If Superior Matthews really was planning an attack, what would that mean? Would Superior Ashbury be ready? Sev wasn't sure Superior had enough trusted Guard to fight alongside him. What if Matthews brought an army with him? Sev knew he'd be fighting. But the details mattered. Would he be beside all the Guard in the first group to attack?

When Lynch separated from him after their talk with Superior, Sev went back to the drawing board for a new creature for the third race. At least he had ten days to design it. Two days to build it. One to test. Then show time. He designed something entirely from scratch and was halfway through his thoughts when Lynch fetched him.

"Another mission from Superior. Come on." Lynch waved, and Sev grabbed his uniform coat. He walked beside him down to the secret passageway. Dark and always clear of any mates. He'd only ever seen one attendant in the passageway, and he didn't think it counted, considering she was dead.

"Are you going to tell me what the mission is?" he asked.

Lynch shook his head. "You're going to lose it. Deep breaths."

"What?" Sev placed his hand on the top blade strapped to his thigh. Searched the hall for an immediate threat. Wasn't expecting the threat to be Lynch himself.

Lynch shoved him into an open storage closet. The door slammed in his face, and the lock clicked.

Inside was dim. Only one light bulb hung in the center. Two shelves were on either side of him, and the floor was made of dirt and dust. The brick walls around him made it cool. He didn't mind the tight space. It was the locked door that had him trapped.

He teleported back to the basement and the red chair. The hours of torture Superior made him sit through in the dark. Smoke filled the room while pain soaked him from his head to his toes. He couldn't go back there. Not right now.

"Lynch!" Sev pounded his fist on the door so hard the walls shook. He didn't want to think of the past. Not now. He pounded again and again. Drops of blood formed on the side of his pinkie and wrist from hitting harder.

"Hey," Mason said from behind him.

Sev gasped and turned with wide eyes. "What the hell." His back slumped to the door.

"I know." He held his hands up. He was in a dark T-shirt and jeans. Mason's eyes filled with uncertainty.

"Let me out of here. Right now," Sev seethed. His panic started to bubble.

"Lynch will be back when the mission is done to let us out."

Sev glared at him. He couldn't trap him in a closet whenever he wanted to. Sev had duties to fulfill. Missions to complete.

"Why'd you do it?" Mason asked. He swayed. Brought his hand to his mouth before dropping it again.

"What?" His anger flowed to his bones. Couldn't think straight. His arms shook from the adrenaline. Why did Lynch lock him in here? Were they working against him? Going to kill him? It didn't seem that way. Mason looked rattled with nerves, not ready to maim.

"We left the arena when Knuckles approached Maia. Just started talking shit. Normal rider bullshit. Then, one called her some names. She flipped. Started to scream. The captain got between them before his teammate could hit her. Said he wanted to do the honors. I tried to stop them. They held me back. He hit her once before he froze. Blood just started coming out of him. The side of his neck." Mason stopped and looked up from the floor to Sev's eyes. "And I knew. I knew it was you. I don't know how you did it. You didn't kill him. You could have. Definitely could have."

"I wasn't even there. How could it have been me?" He tried to steady his breathing. It wasn't helping. He was still trapped inside.

Mason scoffed. "Don't try to deny it. I know it was you."

Sev rolled his eyes. "I threw my Nin Spin as we were getting in the car," he admitted, and Mason stared at him. He didn't understand how Mason allowed him this privilege all the time. He couldn't handle his scrutiny this long. The way his hair hung over his ear and barely grazed his shoulder. His muscles squeezing out of his sleeves. Stubble covered his jaw, and Sev wondered how often he shaved. Sev tried to keep his mind off the fact that they were both stuck in the tight room.

Mason took a step toward him, and Sev braced as if he were going to strike. Mason put his hands flat on the door on either side of Sev's head. The air was thick. Only an inch of space between their chests.

"I won't hurt you. You must know that by now." His voice was smooth. Gentle.

"Then back up," Sev said.

"No. I've waited long enough." Mason grabbed his face with both hands. Then smashed his lips to Sev's.

Sev pushed him away and clamped his eyes shut. His heart beat out of his chest. Mason's mouth was so soft. Forbidden. Superior would kill Mason. His blood would be on Sev's hands.

He needed to get out of there.

His breath came out in short hard pants. Nails dug into his palms. Spots formed from squeezing his eyes shut so tight.

"Sev, it's okay," Mason whispered.

He shook his head. Forbidden. Absolutely forbidden. Mason would be killed for this.

Sev opened his eyes and glared at him. "Don't ever do that again," he shouted. "Get me out of here. Now!"

Mason looked broken. Shoulders slumped. And his face paled. Sev stepped to the side, and Mason kicked the handle twice. It popped off and hit the ground with a pang. Sev pushed it open and fled. He ran out of the passageway and onto the road. He hopped on his bike and found his old solo training spot in the woods.

He knew he was fleeing. Running from the rider. His own thoughts. Was he supposed to allow this behavior? And have Superior kill Mason?

Sev collapsed in the dirt and vomited. Tears ran down his cheeks, and he didn't understand. He was furious. More emotions waved in and out. He wasn't used to this. Twenty years of feeling through a thick curtain. Walking in a fog. When Mason's mouth was on his...it was like diving into a deep fire pit naked.

His entire body shook as he tried to stand. He got to the creek and washed his mouth out. Arms convulsed as he splashed cool water on his face and neck. Superior would hunt Mason down. What was he doing?

eight

Lynch waited outside his door in the morning. Sev didn't speak. He would be the best Second Superior had ever seen. Go back to normal. Before Mason entered the mansion. Before he almost died. Before Sev rigged the race in his favor. Before he...kissed him in the storage closet.

"You're mad at me. I get it. I ain't sorry."

Sev glared at him from the left as they walked shoulder to shoulder. "You want us to get killed. Mason to be murdered."

This wasn't Sev's purpose or mission. Lynch should be trying to contact his nephew. Not attempting to set him up with a team captain.

Lynch let out a quick sigh. Spoke clear. Locked his eyes on Sev. "No. I want you to live. I want you to experience life. Love."

Sev tried to pound his fist into his stomach. Lynch blocked him.

"See. That. Anytime I even mutter the word, you freak out. Why is that? Scared? Scared he doesn't feel the same? Scared he'll actually leave when he wins? What!" he yelled at Sev. Pushed on his shoulders. Sev huffed and growled at Lynch like an animal. "C'mon! Spit it out!"

"You're wrong. I want him gone." He sneered. His voice a whisper in the empty halls. "Gone," he repeated louder, and they walked into the dining room to greet Superior.

"Ah, my Dragon," Superior said at the head of the long table. His grin gleamed in front of his guests. The clattering of plates halted as the attendants looked up at them in the doorway. They were clearing the table from breakfast.

Lynch and Sev froze.

Seven heads turned toward them from the long table. Riders in gear. Three in purple. One orange. Maia and Mason on one side of Superior in blue. And on the other side of Superior was a rider in deep red. Bullet.

Sev bowed his head as usual. "Sir."

"Sir." Lynch followed suit.

Sev stood behind Superior. Lynch stayed in position by the entry. An attendant held the door for five Guard to leave the room. Sev kept his eyes away from the twins.

"Back to business. Graves Valley is coming. We must prepare. Sev and Lynch will be taking you to train. They've trained every Guard for me the last fifteen or so years. I trust they'll train the seven of you better."

Superior was creating a small army. Seemed he wanted another pin for his uniform, after all. It had been years since he'd gotten the last one.

"Sir?" Lynch questioned.

Sev scowled at him.

"Just an inquiry."

Sev released his shortest blade, and it entered Lynch's cheek to the hilt. The rider in orange screamed before Lynch did. He pulled it out fast, and blood trickled from the cut. Deserved his punishment. Superior's Third knew better. Bullet chuckled from his seat across from Maia.

"You sonofabitch." Lynch pointed the tip at Sev.

"Interrupt Superior again," Sev spat.

An attendant ran to Lynch with a tin of Elastaderm to repair him. He wiped the blade clean on his pants and threw it back at him. Sev didn't move. Mason flinched as it glided right past Sev's head and stuck in the wall behind him. Two riders in purple yelped. One had an eye patch over his eye, while the other had long dark hair in a braid down his back.

This was about more than Lynch questioning Superior. And now they both knew it. Lynch glared at him from the entrance. Both knew who the better fighter was. Lynch should know by now not to mess with Superior's Dragon.

"Your aim needs work," Sev murmured. Lynch rubbed the blood from his face on his gray sleeve, and Sev turned back to Superior. Nodded once to proceed.

"Now that's settled," Superior spoke to the group, "you'll be my front line. You will not hesitate. You will maim, kill, and remain standing."

"Sir?" the rider in orange asked. He averted his eyes from Sev and trained them on Superior. He was short with dark skin and a thick gold hoop through the bottom of his nose. It hung over his lip and shined in the light. "Why would they attack us? Aren't they just like us?"

"Nobody is like us, Jorge. The mentality of a rider is something to be reckoned with," Superior said. "Dragon, get the hand press."

Sev went to the far corner and approached the locked cabinet. His hand pressed to the scanner, and it popped open. He grabbed his strength test and turned back to Superior.

"Each of you will follow after him. Right here. Right now." Superior stood and allowed Sev to sit in his seat. They all watched as he placed the contraption in front of him on the table.

The square had fifteen spikes sticking straight up from it. Quarter of an inch high. Maia let out an exhale as Sev placed his palm on the top. Blood oozed down the spikes as he pressed harder. When he looked up, Mason was wide-eyed. He wondered if Mason was experiencing what he'd felt during the first race. That gut clench when he witnessed Mason being injured. Sev brought his focus back to the test as Mason exploded.

"Okay, we get it! He doesn't need to do it the whole way." Mason's voice came out broken and shaky. As if it was the first thing he'd said all day. "Next."

Superior chuckled. "Rider, you must care for my Dragon."

"I do." He didn't hesitate in his response. "I am human. I don't like to watch *anyone* in pain."

"You'll have to get over that. Might as well be today. My Dragon has trained his entire life for these tasks. For war. And look how frail he is," Superior responded and shook his head at him.

"Pain is temporary," Sev said to them all. His eyes landed on Mason as his fingers reached the table.

"Unnecessary torture," Mason whispered.

Superior sighed. "Unnecessary?"

Bullet crossed his arms in front of his chest. He scoffed at Mason. "You're being childish."

"I meant for him." Mason ignored him and turned to Superior. "I get that you want all of us to prove we are good enough. I understand your fucked up ways, even if I don't agree. I can still comply even if I don't agree. What I will not comply with is Seventeen sitting here going through this demonstration when we do not need one," Mason snapped, and Maia stood to put herself between them if necessary. Sev got there first with his words.

"It is my duty. The prize I received from defeating that dragon was my place beside Superior. If I must sacrifice my blood, feel pain, or even die by his hands or someone else's, that is my duty to fulfill. It is not your place to question Superior. You're up." He slid the spikes to Mason. An attendant came and quickly cleaned the machine before spraying a sterilizer. Mason pulled it closer.

Without breaking eye contact with Sev, Mason placed his palm on top of the spikes. He pressed hard as the spikes entered. His fingers reached the table in seconds. Mason hardly flinched. Sev would've been impressed if he wasn't so enraged.

An attendant came with the tin, and Mason fixed his hand like new. Sev kept his bloody hand out of sight from the other riders.

Maia was next. She went slower than Sev, though not by much. Everyone else struggled more as it was passed around the table. Even Bullet. Everyone had used their dominant hand, but seeing as his was a machine, he had to use his left. He locked eyes with Maia as he reached the table. A harsh look in his eye. Always competing with her. She'd done it faster. Sev took the Elastaderm last and fixed his palm with Superior's approval.

nine

Superior ordered Lynch and Sev to guide the group of riders out to the training course. Sev tried to use it once a year to test the limit of his lungs. Last time, he only got about halfway before needing a break.

As they walked to the course in the distance, Sev chanced a look at Mason. Dark circles formed under his eyes. His posture was more caved in than usual. Maia stared at the ground as they walked. About a mile of trees and fallen branches were between the mansion and the course. The riders in purple were helping each other climb under a fallen branch when Bullet grunted at them and pushed the entire log out of the way to clear a path.

One of them patted his back. Bullet shrugged his hand off of him.

"Nice work, bubba." The man had a slight drawl to his voice. He had flaming red hair and a long, trimmed beard. Bullet stood to the side and let the entire group go before him. He stood at the back, taking in their surroundings.

Maia pulled her head up and rolled her shoulders. She quickened her pace to catch up to Sev.

"You're an asshole, you know that?"

"Oh?" Sev figured Mason would talk to his sister. Wasn't expecting her to confront him about it. And not like this. She only knew his side of the story though.

"He likes you, and for whatever reason, you don't like him back. Whatever. Then why play with him?"

"No." Sev shook his head at her. He peered at the group. Mason hadn't noticed Maia talking to him yet. His eyes glued to his shoes. Sev lowered his voice. "He needs to win. He needs to get out of here. The sooner, the better. Understand?" he snapped at her.

A moment of silent confusion played on her face. "You want us to win? Why?"

"So I will never have to see him again," he said softly. The orange rider, Jorge, walked closer, and they stopped their conversation. Maia looked back at Sev. Her eyes didn't match her anger from before. Sadness settled in as her face softened. She believed him.

Bullet clipped her shoulder as he walked past, and she grunted. She glared at his back. He was nearly a foot taller than her and all muscle. His metal hand on clear display as he wiggled his fingers at his side. A reminder of the damage he could do with it. Sev kept his comments to himself about the light bruise on Maia's side he could see when she raised her left arm. Sev was surprised Maia wasn't more injured. He'd seen what a fist could do. Only a light-yellow spot was left behind. However, pride filled him when he caught a glimpse of the scratch on Bullet's neck.

"First, you will each go through the course at a slower pace. Get a feel for it. Then we'll test you on speed the second time through. Yuri, you're up first," Lynch instructed.

The man with the graying braid readied himself and took off like a rocket. He slipped in mud before the first hurdle and got up fast. His purple jacket was now covered in dark brown splotches.

The course was made to test agility as well as strength. Most wouldn't have an issue. But Sev did every time. It was hard to leap and slide and jump without a working pair of lungs.

"Idiot," Maia mumbled, and Sev chuckled at the comment. She wore her usual attire, shorts and a tank top under her dark blue jacket. Her chunky black boots were covered in leaves and mud from the walk over. Her hair was in a neat bun on top of her head. "So, to be clear," she looked behind her to make sure there was space between them and the group, "you like my brother, you're just protecting him? From Superior?"

"And myself. Nothing could ever..." Sev stopped talking. Not that anyone was nearer.

Maia nodded. "I see." She crossed her arms in front of her chest. "Man." She whistled. "What a year."

Sev waited for her to expand on that. She didn't. Mason came to stand on the opposite side of her. He expected they would need space until Wrath won the Championship.

A fresh grass scent filled the course from the attendants who cleaned up the area for them to use today. Superior said he would use this group as protection from Graves Valley. Was it possible Superior Ashbury had done something to provoke Superior Matthews? Or maybe Superior Matthews really was as vicious as the news spewed to the mates. He was creating an army. That was certain. Sev would have to keep his guard up and his ears clear.

Sasha, the red-haired rider, cheered for his teammate. Freckles coated his nose and cheeks. When he stroked his beard, he plucked a leaf from it. His other teammate, Locke, was the one with the eyepatch. He kept his focus on Yuri as he came across the last obstacle.

"When's the last time you did this?" Maia asked Sev, pulling his attention back to her.

"Four months ago. I test myself. See how far I can get before I lose my breath."

Maia smiled at him. "The little yellow guys are wonderful, aren't they? I'll never forget that first time I ran a mile. I just held my chest and cried."

"You cried?" Sev asked. Maia seemed tough. Ready to throw a punch or stand up for herself at any point. Something Sev rarely got a chance to do. Envy spread through him. He wished he could say whatever he wanted. Throw punches at who he wanted, not who Superior ordered him to.

"You didn't?"

Sev shook his head. "Not about that."

"Why'd you cry then?" Maia asked, raising her brow at him. She had a knowing grin. Sev grunted at her in response. "Yeah, I figured. So, now's your time to shine, Dragon Bitch."

"Don't call him that," Mason said. He didn't take his eyes off Yuri in the course.

It was the first he'd spoken since he joined them. Sev would have forgotten he was there if it wasn't for his scent wafting around them. Cedarwood and mint. Since taking that pill, he could place the exact scent he yearned for when he wasn't near.

Lynch stood beside Sev and hit his shoulder with his hand. "C'mon. You're up."

"No," Sev told him.

"Why not?" Maia asked. "Scared you'll fail?"

"Right." Mason rolled his eyes. "Remember him going around the track? I don't think he's capable of failing anything."

Sev looked at the dirt in front of him. The way Mason spoke about him as if he was capable of anything. His heart swelled before he replaced it with steel.

"I've seen him fail more times than anybody else," Lynch supplied.

Locke fixed the patch over his eye and Sev caught a glimpse of a glass one in the socket. Sasha stood beside him and pointed at the obstacle course. Giving each other tips to get through it faster on the next go. Sev couldn't help but remember the first years out there. Every slip. Fall. Injury. All the times he'd have to limp back to the mansion to fix himself.

"True," Sev said. Remembering what they were talking about.

Honest shock came across Mason's face.

"Difference is, he always gets back up." Lynch smiled at Mason.

"Like when you pulled that arrow out of your shoulder, that was wicked," Locke yelled out from behind them.

"Or in there with the palm thing, that was crazy!" Jorge added.

"Mason did the same thing, in fact, faster than me. That proves nothing," Sev said. The riders all stepped closer to look at him. Their eyes scanned him up and down. Mates never understood how Superior's Second was so scrawny. It didn't make sense. They didn't realize someone deadly could look so harmless.

"I'm a fucking wimp, Sev, I did that in there to prove a point," Mason said.

"It was impressive," Sev said. Mason looked away fast. His face pinkened.

"Normally, he pukes at the sight of blood." Maia chuckled.

Yuri did the course when Sev said no. He was almost to the end when he slid in the mud. Balanced himself before falling completely. The group watched as they chatted on the sidelines.

"That only happened once. And that was because I could see your bone sticking out of your arm. It was disgusting." Mason gagged, and everyone laughed, even Bullet. Sev understood it. Only because of how many times he'd inflicted that.

"Yuri's done. You're up." Lynch pushed Sev to the start.

Sev sighed. Ran his fingers through his hair.

"Nobody here will speak of this to Superior, understand?" Lynch said.

Maia glared at Bullet. He surprised her with a nod of agreement. Everyone else followed.

Sev walked to the start line, and Lynch held up a thumb to tell him he was ready to press the timer. Mason stood in front of Sev, and he pulled back.

"What are you wearing?" Mason asked.

Sev scrunched his nose. "What?"

Mason laughed. "I mean, under your uniform. It's harder to run with this thick shirt on. Are you wearing anything under it?"

"T-shirt." He shrugged.

"Let loose," Mason said and held his hand out to him. His raven hair blew in the slight breeze. Sev gripped his top button and paused. Would he be able to pull this off? Run in front of this group and not have Superior find out? Could he trust these mates not to talk? Even Bullet? He looked over at him briefly. He was busy glaring at Yuri. The real question was, if Superior did find out, would this moment be worth it? He started unbuttoning fast.

"Ow-oww!" Maia hollered, and the group laughed.

Sev felt all their eyes on his bare skin. His visible scars from his years beside Superior. Answering every call. Taking every hit. Every bullet. He handed his shirt to Mason.

Sev tucked his black T-shirt into his pants and faced the course. Focus, he whispered to himself.

"Run." Mason winked at him.

Mason stood back with Lynch and Maia. Bullet and Jorge stood beside the three in purple. Intrigued to watch him fail. Lynch motioned for Sev to take a deep breath. He nodded and then copied him.

Sev cleared his mind and then sprinted. He got to the first jump and flew over it. Landed on his right foot, fell into a roll, and stood back up to run faster. Forced himself up the rock wall before sliding down the other side. The material he created made it impossible to climb back up. The pile of mud at the bottom slowed him as he dragged himself to the large holographic tires on the other side. If you touched the edges, it sent an electric shock through you. Sev went through those with ease. He had always been a good jumper. He had to reach high for the handles above to guide him to the next section. His hand couldn't get a good grip, so he didn't land gracefully.

On the other side, the rope course started. Swinging from one to the next, Sev got through that in seconds before he reached the tower. Slats of wood in a triangle were set up to climb. The wood boards were mostly rotted, so the third one he touched broke off in his palm. A splinter stuck from his hand, and he pulled it out fast when he got to the top. Blood pooled under his skin and he kept going. Stopping wasn't an option. His lungs hadn't even begun to sting yet. He jumped down and headed to the next area.

Holographic fireballs flung at him, and he dodged them all. He spun at the last one and slipped. A chuckle slipped out of him as he stood and climbed up the last wall. It was similar to the first one but slippery. The texture was smoother. He got to the bottom and ran as fast as his legs would take him toward the finish.

Lynch stopped the clock and smiled at him. Sev slid in front of Lynch and held out his hand to steady himself.

"So?" Maia asked.

"I could breathe the whole time," he whispered. "How exhilarating."

"Bet you can't beat me," Mason said with a grin. They were almost back to their normal back and forth. "What was his time?"

"Three minutes, twenty-three seconds," Yuri groaned. "Basically, half my time."

"Ready," Mason said and tossed Sev his shirt.

Even over the mud, Sev could smell Mason on the fabric. A wood scent. Maybe pine? Sev shoved his arms through even though he was filthy. He buttoned it up hoping to trap the scent inside. Imagining other ways to transfer his smell. Mason on top of him. In his room. His bed. He stood beside Lynch and tried to slow his racing mind.

Mason grinned when he started the course. Too confident.

Three minutes, forty-nine seconds.

Sev couldn't help his smile as Mason crossed the finish line. Maia was up next. She flew through the first half and fell three times in a row at the end. She did it in almost four and a half. Bullet's downfall was the tires. He got stung twice in a row before he plowed through them like a bull. The veins protruded from his neck as he fought the pain. Lynch said his time didn't count. It was longer than Maia's, anyway. Steam was coming out of his ears when he heard four minutes and fifty-six seconds.

Everyone else was over the five-minute mark. Maia couldn't stop smiling at her brother. She looked proud.

"Tomorrow, we'll focus on speed. Meet here at seven," Lynch instructed.

The group headed back to their bikes. Jorge tapped Locke on the shoulder and ran to race through the trees. Like children. Yuri yelled after them something in a different language. Sev assumed he was calling them immature. It's what he would've said anyway. Maia and Mason slowed their steps to walk with Lynch and Sev. The twigs and leaves crunched under their boots. Maia balanced on a tree root before Mason pushed her off. She flipped him off before their steps were in sync again. Maia rolled her eyes at her brother when he let out a long yawn.

"Tired?" Lynch chuckled at Mason.

Maia sighed when she responded. "He didn't sleep last night. He was working on his bike like a maniac."

The twins had a silent conversation as they glared at each other. Mason pulled his fingers through his hair to comb it to the side.

"What are you doing to it?" Lynch asked. "If I'm allowed that knowledge."

"I was adding a fireball shield to the front and sides. I couldn't configure the measurements to match the inside." He paused and squeezed the bridge of his nose. "Never mind. It's too hard to explain."

Sev stepped in. "You have to maximize your space on the inside of the bike to match the outer components of the shield. If it folds in or expands as it slides, you'll have to work that into your configuration. If you multiply—" Lynch covered Sev's mouth with his hand, and Sev elbowed him in the gut.

"Sorry, I thought I was going to fall asleep over there. You two can talk geometry some other time." Lynch laughed, and Sev sneered at him.

Maia pat Lynch's arm with her elbow. He smiled at her with a nod. Sev thought that was odd. Did they know each other well enough for that? Or was that just Maia's personality?

Mason smiled at Sev. "You could always help me put it together."

"We live at the garage," Maia said. "Stop by anytime you can escape."

"You live there?" Sev asked.

Mason chuckled. "Cheaper than paying rent. Mates got dues to pay, you know."

Sev thought back to the night he showed up. When he tackled Mason. When he'd smiled up at him. The group of guys that were there. The blond brothers and the bald Black man Maia had her tongue attached to, Jameson.

"Who all lives there with you?" Sev asked.

"Just us. Reid has a house on the outskirts, near Taisley's Bar," Mason answered.

Lynch reached into his front pocket and pulled out a toothpick. Sev kept his mouth shut, though his habit irritated him. Itched at his insides. He wanted to snatch it out of his mouth and stab it through his throat. The toothpick was a symbol of rebellion. Sev was always taught to conform. Stand in line. Keep your mouth shut. And Lynch teetered on that line when he had that damn pick between his lips.

"Is that far?" Lynch asked.

Was it not common knowledge? "Twenty-three minutes if you're on a bike," Sev said.

Maia rolled her eyes. "God, not you, too."

Sev furrowed his brow.

"Mason does that shit too?" Lynch asked.

"He has a photographic memory. Freak of nature," Maia replied. She and Lynch walked faster to get ahead of them to join Jorge, who was showing off his bike to the other riders. It left Mason to walk beside Sev.

"That's how you did the maze," Sev said, linking his fingers behind his back.

"Yes." Mason chuckled. "It's a neat trick sometimes. Although, usually, it just gets me into trouble."

"Hm," Sev said. "I believe that."

Mason smiled again at him.

"You look…" Sev wasn't sure why he was about to tell him. He'd never felt worried before. He feared his glass shield between him and the world was shattering.

"You can say it. I look like shit. I'm aware. Maia won't shut up about it." Mason's shoulders slumped. He looked up at the trees as they walked. The branches above them kept the sun from their eyes. "She doesn't know everything, just so you know."

"What do you mean?" Sev asked.

"About us. Well, the lack of us. I didn't tell her. Well, that you…we—"
He shook his head. His hair fell in his eyes and he swept it over his ear
back to normal again.

"Understood," Sev said. He placed his hands behind his back again.
Taking position as he should on the mansion grounds.

"I don't want you to think I tell people. It's dangerous. I'm aware
of that. I know the risk. I know you could be killed for anything and
everything we've ever…I just like you, Sev. And I understand I fucked
up. I shouldn't have kissed you. I'm sorry."

Sev was not expecting that. Most things he could work out. Prepare
for. This stung. He regretted the kiss. That thing that forced life into his
soul. The thing that made him cry for the first time in years. Like running
a mile did for Maia. Running became her life source. Like Mason became
his.

He hadn't really understood that until now. Sev stopped walking.
Mason didn't realize it for a handful of steps. He turned back to him.
Cheeks flushed.

"Why did you do it?" Sev asked.

Mason opened his mouth but closed it. He looked over his shoulder
at the group getting on their bikes and heading down the drive. Lynch
and Maia stood by the pair of blue bikes the twins had brought. Maia
giggled at something Lynch said.

Mason shrugged. "I told you, I like you."

"That doesn't mean you…do that."

"You protected my sister. You've protected me several times. You push
my buttons. You infuriate me. Suffocate me and then set me free. I can't
stand you, and yet I crave you." He chuckled at himself. "This would be
the outcome of my first real crush. Typical Mason bullshit. Falling for a
guy he can't have." He bit his lip. His words came out faster the more he
spoke. "But you have a plan, right? I'll win the race, and we'll never see

each other again, right? Just like you want. Can't fucking wait." His eyes said the opposite. His Adam's apple bobbed as he swallowed.

Sev took a moment to settle his breathing and nerves. His stomach clenched under his uniform.

"You speak as if we're both riders on the same path to victory. You know where I stand. I've never said otherwise. So, you will leave." He gulped at the words and his impossible thoughts. "And you will live a life worth dying for. A life I can only dream of. And I will stay right here. With a Zap on my hip and my blade in someone's throat."

Sev turned to Maia as she waved at her brother to get moving. But he stayed still. His eyes back on Sev's. His voice dropped low. Words meant only for him.

"If you could leave, would you?" Mason studied Sev's face. He didn't respond. "In that life worth dying for, the one you dream of, am I beside you?" Mason asked.

Maia yelled out to him. He didn't look away from Sev. Waited for his answer. But Sev couldn't tell him that. Couldn't tell him the truth. It would give him hope.

"Do you dream of me?" Mason whispered. His eyes so bright until Lynch patted him on the shoulder. Mason jumped.

"See you two tomorrow," Lynch said. He pulled Sev away from him and headed into the mansion. They took their usual route and entered the passageway. Lynch shut the door and lit his flashlight.

"Looked like you needed a save," Lynch said.

Sev felt frozen. What was he doing? This was a damn joke. This was all forbidden. Everything in his life. Absurd. His mouth was dry. He began to sink.

"Whoa, hey." Lynch grabbed him and hauled him into the closest locked lab. He scanned his thumb and locked them in the room. He flipped the light on, and Sev slid to the ground. Wrapped his arms around his legs and put his forehead on his knees. Tears hit his thighs as he allowed himself to cry. "Shit, Sev."

"What the hell is going on? What am I doing?" Sev whispered. Lynch rubbed his hand on his shoulder. The man he'd known more than half his life, yet he'd never called him a friend. He was, though, right? He was always there. He must be a friend.

"I think you're finally breaking." He smiled at him. "And I'm so excited, I could burst." Lynch laughed. Sev glared at him. Raising his head to do so. "Let him in," Lynch whispered.

"No. He needs to go."

Sev dreamed of Mason almost every night. Would never confess that. Mason needed to leave the Valley. Needed to leave Sev alone. Everything would go back to normal the second Mason left.

"I agree with you there. He does."

He agreed? Finally. Sev wiped his face. A sigh of relief escaped him.

"But so do you, buddy," Lynch said and patted his cheek with his palm.

Sev leave Ashbury Valley? He really was mental. Lynch knew what that would mean. Knew what Superior would do. And what that would mean for himself. Sev would be the object of Superior's rage.

"Are you insane? I can't leave Superior."

"You could." Lynch nodded. "If you got out."

"Only way out is the race," Sev reminded him.

"No. Two ways out. Pay your dues."

Now that was funny. Pay off his dues? "All I've ever done is rack them up. I've never worked. I don't have money."

"Law doesn't say you have to pay for it yourself."

"Who the hell would pay for me to get out of here? My dues are double, if not triple, what any other mate's is."

Just because Sev was Superior's Second didn't mean he wasn't adding his kills to his dues. Every few years, Sev would check his amount. It only ever went up.

"Hm, maybe that boy you won't allow yourself to fall in love with? He's going to be rich soon. He's about to win the race, no?" Lynch winked at him. Sev felt his stomach flip. He really was mental.

"Superior wouldn't allow that."

"That's out of his hands. He's got no control over that, you and I both know," Lynch said. "Now, c'mon. Let's go."

Sev stood and fixed his uniform before remembering he was covered in dirt, so it didn't matter anyway.

"Lynch?" Sev said.

"Yeah?" He opened the door for them to walk back out to the hall.

Thanks for being my friend, he thought. He couldn't say that out loud. Lynch nodded as if that's exactly what came out of his mouth.

ten

S ev stayed up late and configured plans for a fireball shield to come out of a ChaosMotors bike. He folded it up and crammed it behind his least-used blade. Nobody would think to check there. He knew Superior would see something in his pocket. He was a stickler for uniform.

Superior finished his breakfast as Lynch and Sev entered the dining room.

"Perfect timing. Dragon, you'll be taking the riders on your mission today," Superior said. He took a sip of his wine and dabbed his mouth with a cloth napkin.

"Where are we taking them?" Sev asked.

"Greenford." Superior paused to smirk at him. "Find the traitor. One of the mates is slipping letters past the Guard. This cannot continue."

Sev stiffened. Did Superior know about Mason?

"How did you find out about it?" Lynch asked.

"Rumors. The usual." He let out a tired sigh. "Find them, kill them, and report back."

"Sir," Lynch said, and they both bowed before two attendants opened the door. They walked out and headed toward the training field.

"You can't." Sev stopped. "Lynch," he tried again, "we can't allow them to stop." He couldn't believe he was botching their mission. Their orders. "The letters. They must keep coming and going."

Lynch nodded. Gave him a smile as he patted him on the back.

They reached the group, and Maia stood out the most. The only female rider. But she stood tall amongst them. Bullet was beside her. Arms over his chest and his lips tight.

Mason had his back to Sev, which was perfect for him to slide the paper into his pocket. He hadn't even felt him do it. Sev bit his lip to contain his smile.

"Morning, change of plans. Mission." Lynch informed everyone of the details, and Mason didn't react. Maia raised a brow to her brother. When he didn't acknowledge her, she turned back to Lynch.

"Grab a partner and hop on a bike," Lynch said.

"We have to ride bitch?" Bullet grumbled.

"A mission is secret. Confidential. The fewer bikes, the better. One person talks, you're done. So, get on and shut your mouths," Sev said.

Maia got on the back of Yuri's bike, and the others left fast. Lynch got on his own bike and winked at Sev as he whipped by. Sev looked at Mason, and he smiled at him.

"Yours or mine, baby?" He chuckled.

Sev rolled his eyes. He pressed his thumb on a black button secured to the closest tree trunk, and the concrete folded next to them. His black bike raised from the ground, and he swung his leg over. Mason got on and wrapped his arm around his torso. Sev never had to ride doubles before. He accelerated like he shot out of a cannon. Mason gripped him tighter.

He passed the others before the first turn. Mason laughed in Sev's ear. His hands stayed on his stomach and hip, and his brain put every fantasy to work.

Fantasy Mason rubbed Sev's stomach under his shirt. Kissed the side of his neck. Ran his hand up and down his thigh.

Sev felt his pants get a little tighter and hit the gas harder.

"You were meant to be a rider, Sev," Mason said. That wasn't what he heard. *Ride me, Sev. Ride me.*

Sev shook his head and stopped the bike at the entrance of Greenford. Mason got off and stared at him. Sev didn't want to move. Not yet. He wanted to live in the fantasy world where Mason touched him, and he allowed it.

"You alright?" Mason asked.

His voice snapped him out of it. Forbidden. Superior would kill Mason. Sev stood and turned toward him. The others were a few minutes behind.

"You need to be more aware," Sev snapped.

"Excuse me?" He looked around them at the invisible threat.

"I put a piece of paper in your pocket earlier. You didn't feel it. That's a problem. Means someone could slip you a poison or steal off you, and you wouldn't even know."

He looked confused until he started to search his pants and found the paper in his back pocket. Mason unfolded it. Instead of being angry or understanding what Sev had been saying, he grinned. His eyes lit up.

"Is this for my bike?"

"I told you I knew what to do," Sev said. "You just need to configure the measurements."

Mason's smile got wider as he folded it back up and slipped it into his front pocket. Sev walked the perimeter of the entrance three times before Mason looked around the side of the building. A sigh escaped his lips.

"I'll figure it out," Sev told him. "We'll pin it on someone else."

"What?" Mason's chest tightened as he crossed his arms in front of him. His T-shirt didn't hide his upper arms. Sev glanced at them twice before recollecting himself.

"You told me. Inside the maze, remember? You spoke of your letters. I'm not an imbecile."

"You remember that?" Mason tilted his head.

"I remember every moment with you," Sev said. He messed up. The words were out there. His cheeks went red. Mason held his hand up when he tried to explain.

"Can't ever say what you really mean. Can't ever give me an inch of hope, right? That's what you do. I get it. I'm leaving, you're staying. Every day on repeat with you. But it's the words you don't say, Sev. That's what keeps me so fucking enamored with you."

He choked on his inhale. "Enamored," Sev whispered to himself. He hadn't meant to repeat it out loud.

"Yeah," Mason said. "See, I'm not ashamed of my feelings for you. I don't give a shit that it's wrong. I still like you. And you keep doing this." He tapped his front pocket. "Keep surprising me. It's infuriating. You don't need to put your neck out for me. But I know you will, no matter what I say. Right?"

"Yes." No reason to deny it. Even if he couldn't act on his thoughts or feelings. It didn't change anything. "If I didn't, you wouldn't be able to talk to your friend. You wouldn't get another letter in here."

"Why do you care?" Mason asked.

Sev was silent. He had that effect on him. Made him speechless. He was never a man of many words until Mason came along. Messed up his entire life. His entire path. It wasn't a path anymore. It was an empty parking lot. No arrows. He was lost. And he didn't want to be found. Unless it was in the center of that maze.

"Because...I care." Sev swallowed the lump in his throat. "About you."

Mason laughed. He put his hands on the back of his head. He slowly spun in a circle and looked up at the clear sky. His hands dropped back to his sides, and he laughed again. "Sev, you can't even tell someone you care about them without looking like you're going to throw up. Don't you think that's a bit fucked up?" he asked. "What do you live for?"

"Superior," he said without thinking. Wrong question to ask. That red chair came back into his mind, and he bit his tongue. He held onto the ticker around his wrist as he looked away from him.

Mason pursed his lips. The other bikes came up the road and found them in the street by the building. The conversation would have to wait.

Sev led the group into the building's basement and separated them into two. He took Mason and Sasha. His dark eyes were trained to hunt. Always searching the woods at the course. It was worse here. Maybe he didn't like to be indoors.

The long hall they were in separated the mailrooms. The walls on either side were lined with six windows. One window per room. Guard could oversee the twenty-five mates as they worked all day. Every letter being opened and read. Anything suspicious would be handed to a Guard. Who would take it to Superior Ashbury personally.

The rooms were small. Only enough room for the tables and the tubs of mail. The Guard stood and watched every mate all day. It was hard for Sev to imagine Mason's friend getting the letters past them at all. It seemed impossible. Unless they knew a Guard personally. That didn't seem likely.

Maia took Yuri and Jorge into a secondary hallway. Lynch brought Bullet and Locke with him. Sev looked down at the mates sorting and reading the mail. They scouted each room, and it didn't take Sev long to figure out which one it was. Sev ordered Sasha to join Lynch.

Mason looked at one man longer than the others. Recognized him. Short auburn hair with a tattoo of a spider on his neck. Mason slowly slid the glass window open so they could hear.

Sev started to evaluate the rest of them. The mates all stood in horizontal rows in front of a long, narrow table. Roughly half of the room was over the age of sixty-five. Gray hair and frail bodies. Then of that group, six of them were sitting in chairs instead of standing like the rest. Of those six, four of them shouted at their peers.

He focused on the four he singled out. Tried to listen to their conversations. First one complained about his lunch. Second whined about his dues. Third yelled at the man across from him to shower because he smelled like shit.

Then there was the fourth. Sev's ears perked at the topic.

"Nah, that guy is a machine. You can't compete with Superior's right-hand man. Remember the day of the Medicine Trials?" the man asked.

The woman across from him shook her head. Too young. Maybe thirty.

Sev gripped his fist beside Mason.

"I'll never forget the look on that kid's face. Pure horror. The arena filled with all those dying kids. Yet he was the one who survived. I remember those little screams. The ones they killed. Poor bastards. Each and every one of them deserved to die. Fucking rats. Superior spends millions on medicine for incurable diseases to send to the Cove instead of putting more food on our tables."

Sev gasped when Mason put his hand in his. Mason's eyes never left that old man. He'd heard that, too? Had he been searching the same way Sev had been? A replacement to take the fall.

"How did the kid do it?" the woman asked. Her jaw slacked. Movements had slowed. Too enveloped in the story.

"Kill the dragon you mean?" The old man laughed. "By accident. He crawled up into its belly and pulled some wires. He shut it down. It threw him out of its mouth before it exploded. Took him less than two minutes. It's how he won the Trial. Superior went nuts."

"So that skeleton-looking guy that's always up Superior's ass, that was the dragon kid?" the woman asked.

"The very one. Whole thing is a mess if you ask me. Should've killed himself while he still had the chance." He laughed.

The man was laughing at the fact that Sev had lived? All the other kids died. Died because of him. So he could survive. So he could receive the cure.

The woman snickered right along with him. "I can't even imagine. Last time I saw that kid, he had a spike through his palm and was still beating some poor soul." She shook her head. "Superior really messed him up good."

Sev glanced down at his free hand where the scar had been. He remembered that spike. A mate had fought another with a blade and sliced his arm clean off. Superior had ordered his death immediately. Not before he'd gotten Sev in the hand, though. He'd died a second later. Sev pulled the spike out himself. Punishment was forced on him later. Superior didn't like his Dragon making mistakes. And a spike through his palm was a mistake in his eyes.

"Got that right. He killed all those kids just to suck Superior's dick." He chortled.

Sev hadn't felt Mason pull the Nin Spin from his belt until it was too late.

It went right between the old man's eyes and out the back of his skull before it came back. Sev reached up to catch it. The woman screamed as blood coated her face.

"Superior what?" Mason called down to the workers. They responded immediately.

"Superior of all! Superior for all time!" The chant continued as Sev wiped the blood off on his pants and placed it back on his belt.

It was smart. The mates would assume they'd killed him for his slander of Superior, and eventually, Sev assumed, Mason would tell his acquaintance it was to save him.

Guard pulled the old man's body to the side of the wall. Blood slowly dripped down his face and onto his lap. Guard would leave him there until the end of the day. A message to the mates working.

Sev gathered everyone and led them back to the street. Shocked that Mason had killed the mate before he could. Why had he done that? He didn't understand his actions. Could never predict his next move. It was dangerous.

"Get back to the mansion. Superior will be waiting," Sev barked his orders at the group, and they fled. Maia raised her brow at her brother before she chuckled to herself and got on the back of Yuri's bike.

"Why did you do that?" Sev asked when the others had left.

"You chose him before I did," Mason snapped. "What do you mean?" Sev raised his voice back at him. "I was going to do it."

"I'm perfectly capable of killing. Just like you." He rolled his eyes. "We're just not all robots. That woman in there, she was talking about something I've seen you do. Continuing on when you have an arrow in your shoulder. Do you even feel pain? Or do you hide that, too? You're so far up Superior's ass you don't even see anything but him, do you?" Mason shoved him, and Sev tripped back.

He braced himself in the dirt and lowered his chin. Glowered at Mason. Anger ran through his body like usual, only this time, it didn't stay.

Sev unclenched his jaw. Undid his fists and took a deep breath. His shoes slid over the pavement as he headed toward his bike.

"Hey," Mason said softly and grabbed his arm. Sev turned to him, and he let go. "I'm sorry. I don't mean to be a dick. You were forced into this. I know that. It's just frustrating...No. It's sad. It makes me want to rip

Superior's eyes out. When I saw your back that day, all those marks on you." He shook his head. "I can't imagine going through anything you've been through. The mind games on top of that were probably worse than any physical pain he put you through."

That red chair. The strap with a tiny spike that dug into his wrist to hold him down. He was too young and clever for handcuffs. He kept getting out of them. Superior learned fast. Unfortunately.

Sev didn't know what to say. They stared at each other for a long moment before Mason opened his mouth again.

"I'm trying to understand you," he said on an exhale.

Sev didn't respond. Mason eventually straddled the bike and waited for Sev to get on behind him. He glared at Mason. Get on the back of the bike?

"Come on, Dragon boy." Mason laughed.

"Don't call me that. You can call me whatever the hell you want, except that," Sev said. He gave in. Swung his leg behind Mason and wrapped his arm around him. Put his cheek on his back and felt Mason relax. Instead of moving, he put his hand on top of Sev's. Sev felt heat travel through him.

"Lynch calls you buddy sometimes," he said.

Mason tensed when Sev let out a laugh. It was rare he made that sound.

"That's what you want to call me?" Sev asked.

"No," Mason whispered.

Mason patted his hand to signal to hold tight, and he did. Mason passed Maia and the purple rider, and she flipped them off.

They pulled into the mansion, and Lynch and all the riders were talking by the course starting line. Mason waited for Sev to get off before he stood beside him. Sev had to look up to talk to him. But he didn't mind.

Mason licked his lips and Sev stared. Wondered how he got in the Valley. What had he done to get arrested by the Guard? This time, he didn't bite his tongue.

"How'd you end up here?" Sev asked.

Mason smirked. "Come see me at the garage, and I'll tell you."

"Mason, you know I can't."

Maia arrived and parked next to Sev. Yuri ran to his teammates to chat about the mission. Jorge ran the course with Bullet as they waited for everyone.

"Then you'll never know." He gave a lazy shrug and joined the group by the course. Sev joined Maia as she walked past.

"Why'd he do it instead of you?" Maia asked.

Sev studied her. How did she know Sev hadn't been the one to throw the Nin Spin?

"Between the eyes. It's his signature move," Maia said. "I'm assuming you don't swap death stories."

"So, he's killed before?" he asked her softly.

She laughed loudly. The entire group turned to the pair of them. "Man, you're funny."

Lynch cleared his throat, and they all turned their attention to him. He instructed them to have another go on the course once the two made it back to the start line.

"The ones who don't beat their time will be dismissed. Understood?" Lynch asked. Everyone agreed.

Mason beat his time by thirteen seconds. He really pushed himself. Threw himself at the finish line and rolled into his landing. Maia chuckled at him as he stood. He panted as he walked over to Lynch to get his new time.

"You're the best in the group, dummy. Chill out, man," Maia told him.

"Had to beat my own time, not yours, dummy." The twins bickered back and forth.

Bullet beat his time by six seconds. The lowest in improvement. Lynch suggested he take up running in his spare time. He grumbled to himself about it for five minutes until he calmed down.

Sev joined the group beside the course, and an attendant brought over a bucket of short-throwing knives for them. Ten targets were set up in a row a few yards away from a white sprayed line in the grass. Sev began his lesson in throwing techniques, aim, and stance.

Maia was the best thrower by far. Her knife hit the bullseye every time. Lynch was wildly impressed. Bullet had the most trouble. The knife slipped and made a metal-slicing sound from his fingers. Before he could bend over and pick it up, Maia had it. She hesitated before grabbing his left hand and putting the handle there. She took a step away from him and demonstrated how she threw with her non-dominant hand. Hitting the bullseye yet again.

She waited patiently as Bullet gripped tight with his left, and before he released, she stopped him. Put her hand around his.

"Gentle, big guy. Not too tight," she said.

He growled at her. Loosened up. And when he let it fly, it hit the middle. A little to the right, inside the red target. His mouth dropped open, and she hit his arm playfully. When she joined her brother again, he raised a brow, and she scrunched her nose. The silent conversation began again. Sev was getting used to those.

Mason tried again and again and kept missing the target entirely. Another knife in the grass.

"You'll get there, Mase. You're just not used to these knives," Maia said as he kept throwing too high. Unless it was a perfect shot, you might as well not shoot at all.

"You're taller. Remember that. Your sight will be different from all others. You have to compensate for that in your throw. Along with the wind and weight of the blade and handle." Sev balanced the tip of the knife on his pointer finger, and Mason watched him in awe. He flung the blade in the air, spun around, caught it, threw it right past his ear, and hit the target's bullseye.

The group cheered. Maia bowed to Sev dramatically.

"Man, Dragon Bitch got skills. Now, show me how you did that." Maia pointed the knife at him.

The following half hour, Sev tried to teach her how to spin without losing sight of the target. That was the hardest part. Mason kept to the side and threw dozens of knives at the other board. Attendants collected them and brought them back for him to throw again. Each time they'd flinch as others threw without a second thought to the women around them in brown.

Once Mason got the hang of his throw, he couldn't stop getting bullseyes. Maia smiled at him and slapped his back. That was when the twins began their game. Best two out of three.

Mason hit the bullseye, then Maia, then Mason, until Maia threw her last one right at the target and sliced the handle of his knife in half with hers. Sev laughed at Mason's astonishment.

Lynch chuckled and clapped for the twins. He looked at his watch and dismissed all the riders for the night.

"I've seen some shit, but never that." Jorge applauded as he headed toward the mansion.

"Later Jorge!" Maia called after him and waved. "Show me again?" she asked and held out a knife to Sev. Bullet stayed to watch. Sev noticed the space Mason kept between him and the captain. Their eyes locked every few moments only to turn away with anger.

Sev hadn't really paid any attention to Team Wrath's jacket. Ash fell from their shoulders down the entire back. A fireball was in the middle with a sword sticking out of it. Wrath was in black lettering on the side going up. On the front was just the name. No image. He wondered about that. Most teams were self-centered. Needed their logo in every spot they could fit it. Now that he thought about it, their logo wasn't on their bikes either.

Superior walked out of the mansion and headed for the targets. Sev took his stance with his hands behind his back. His fingers gripped his ticker. Superior took his spot beside Lynch. Mason looked at Sev as he held his position.

"Well, let's see, Dragon!" Superior yelled, and he bowed as he took the knife. The twins backed up and gave him room as he did his little spin trick again.

"You ever hit a real moving target before?" Superior asked Maia.

"A few," she said.

Superior waved and nobody moved. Mason's jaw clenched. "Dragon, run, well, as far as your lungs will let you, that is." Superior chuckled.

Bullet opened his mouth to speak when Mason stepped forward. "I'll run instead. She can hit me."

Superior raised his hand to stop him. His red uniform a few shades brighter than Bullet's. A ring on his index had a stone the same color. Sev shuddered when he looked at the pins on his uniform. He had already moved them around to make space for a new one.

"He can actually run," Lynch added.

Superior put his hand down and nodded. He smirked at Mason. "Alright. Let's see if your sister will show mercy on you."

"Doubtful," Mason murmured. Sev bit his tongue so he wouldn't smile at that. He knew Mason had just taken a bullet for him. Aware

Maia was about to throw knives at her brother. Yet he couldn't help feeling...giddy.

He had never felt this before. Not sure how to accept it. His feelings for Mason. Forbidden, yet impossible to ignore. His chest ached. Yearned for the rider.

Mason took a deep breath and started to sprint. Maia hit him in the shoulder, and he grunted. Immediately pulled it out, threw it at the target, and hit the bullseye. Superior laughed and made them do it again.

He loved a show.

This time Mason turned at the last second and caught her blade and threw it back at her. It entered her forearm all the way to the hilt. She yelped from the surprise and pain, and he ran to her. He yanked it out, and the attendant handed him the tin of ointment. Mason healed her, and Superior leaned to his ear.

"That is why I chose you."

Sev recalled Superior specifically asking for Mason and not Maia. But knowing everything he did of the girl now, how was she not a valuable asset to his army? Wouldn't you want both of them?

Sev stood beside the attendant as Superior waved them to leave. His hand was already around the tin. Mason didn't react. His eyes told Sev he knew it was coming. Blood came down his back and seeped through the fabric of his shirt.

Mason stopped Maia from throwing a fit with a curt nod. She bit her tongue as her eyes blazed. Bullet took a step back from the group like he usually did. Kept on the edge. Observing. His eyes met Sev's before darting back to Superior.

"See you all tomorrow," Superior said. Once he entered the mansion, Sev got behind Mason. He hesitated before he gently grabbed Mason's shoulder. He slid his hand up the back of his shirt and rubbed the Elastaderm over his stab wound. Sev shoved the tin into Mason's front pocket. Sev was already following Superior inside when Mason turned to face him with a fixed wound.

eleven

When Sev's ticker beeped, he tossed the Prophilac into the empty trash can. He dressed for the day in his required uniform. Stopped at the mirror to check his pins and run a lint roller over his front. In the corner of his eye, he saw the purple tube. He swiped it from the can and tapped it twice on his temple.

He brought the dose to his lab and carefully dripped some onto a slide. Pushed it into the computer and started the diagnostic. He'd come back to check it later. It would take hours. Maybe even days. Sev would change the lab entrance code. If Superior tried to enter, he would blame it on faulty wiring. Superior hardly came down here anyway.

An attendant stopped him on his way to Lynch's room. First, she gave him a note to meet Superior on the balcony. Then she handed him an apple so he could eat as he walked. At least it was red today. Green was his least favorite. He handed the silent woman the core right before stepping out to greet Superior. He was standing with his hands on the ledge, looking out at the garden. A plate of fruit and a delicate berry sauce sat beside him. The table was covered with white linen and fluttered silently in the wind. Superior grinned when he turned to face his Dragon.

"Mission today."

"Sir." Sev went into position.

"We need more members in my army." Superior stood straight and ran his palm down his chest to flatten his uniform. "You must have loads of questions. In all due time, things will be revealed. Until then, don't trust Guard. Keep your wits about you."

Sev didn't respond. He knew there was no point. And he would be punished for speaking out of turn.

"I need you to keep an eye on that twin. Mason. See, Dragon, he's my," Superior hummed as he scratched the side of his mustache with the nail of his thumb, "star. My general. The leader. Understood?"

"Yes, sir."

Superior chuckled menacingly. Sev kept his eyes on him. "You think I'm a fool for not choosing his other half?"

"I had wondered," Sev said. Then quickly added, "Sir."

"Maia is clearly a force to be reckoned with. But the boy..." He paused and looked around the table before biting into an orange slice. "Has a heart. And that is something you cannot learn. Maia is too hard already. Mason can be clay in our hands."

Maia cut to the chase. Didn't have an issue harming others. Innocent or otherwise. She was ruthless. Methodical. Cunning. The first time Sev had seen Mason, he had looked around the library at the art on the ceiling and the books on the walls. Wouldn't hurt someone unless they had thrown the first punch. Or he was protecting someone he cared about.

"You want to mold him." Sev was beginning to understand.

"I want to break him," Superior corrected.

Sev got to the center of town before he noticed a car following him. He parked his bike and hopped off, ready to fight, when the car turned down another street. Paranoid. He needed to focus on the mission for Superior. He only had another hour to return.

Superior asked for intel on a team he wanted to recruit. They hung out in town by the fountain. It was one of Superior's gifts to himself when he first overtook the Valley. The fountain stood twenty feet high, and the circular base was roughly fifty feet wide. Full body sculpture of himself holding his sword straight up in the air. The white marble shined in the sun until nightfall when solar lights lit the base of the fountain. Water sprayed up around his boots and shot out toward the edge of the fountain. A remarkable piece that Superior cherished.

Sev saw the sky-blue leather jackets in the distance when a group in brown caught his attention. One held a baseball bat while another swung a metal baton over his shoulder. Two riders came from the ChaosMotors shop on the corner holding hammers and joined them.

When one pointed at Sev, his instinct kicked into overdrive. He began to count. Six on his right, four on his left, seven coming up from behind. About thirty-five possible riders in the square and roughly sixty witnesses. He couldn't turn back to his bike. Wouldn't make it. He'd have to try on foot. Trees led to private property on the other side of the fountain.

A rider in brown shouted, and all the mates rushed him.

Sev dashed toward the team in light blue. He pushed one aside and vaulted into the middle of the shallow fountain. Shoved a mate into another to create a blockade. The water slowed him as he ran to get to the opposite side. His boots filled to the brim. He leaped over the edge and slipped before he got his bearings.

A screwdriver went past his ear, and he skirted a wrench. Men from the shop started handing out their tools. A pair of pliers whizzed by, and he went up the hill as the mob chased after him.

He headed for the trees. Knew that was his best option. He skidded and turned in the opposite direction of the mansion. The mates would think he'd go home. A group of twenty shouted and ran in three directions. Their numbers were decreasing, which meant his chances were better. Sev launched himself up and grabbed onto a low branch. Pulled his body up and kept going until he couldn't reach anymore. He waited a couple minutes and caught his breath up in the branches.

Four riders in yellow ran past before he jumped down. He hadn't seen the fifth rider hanging back. He threw a metal spike at Sev, and it grazed his arm. Blood dripped from the scratch, but at least it didn't stick. Sev turned to the man and threw his entire weight into the punch before slamming his elbow up into his nose. He dropped. Sev felt the bruise form on his skin instantly.

His team heard the commotion and came running. The other rider in brown came at him hard from the opposite direction. Swinging his fists but not fast enough. Sev dodged every blow.

"You created every creature that killed us!" the man shouted at him. "Traitor! Killer!"

Sev grabbed his wrist and spun him around to shove him at the yellow team. He fell to the ground, and the others tripped over him.

Sev took off and came to a chain link fence. Barbed wire strung on the top, and the group stopped in their tracks as they watched him climb. He grabbed the wire carefully. It stung as the razors split his palms open.

He jumped down on the other side when an alarm blared. The riders ran for it.

"You're a dead man walking!" they shouted at him.

"Dead!"

Sev took a few steps away from the fence when he heard a gun cock behind him. He turned to see Patrick in his dark blue leather jacket. The older brother from Team Wrath. His face painted with a smile. His jacket pulled up to reveal the mark on his hand and wrist.

"Seventeen, isn't it?" Patrick said.

Sev eyed the gun. Early model. One of the first he'd modified. A rifle but smaller. You could easily use it with one hand. Lighter too. Only worked on Guard fingerprints of course, but somehow, Sev knew he'd figured out how to override that feature.

His palms throbbed as the blood dripped onto the grass from his wounds.

"Didn't see the fence?" he asked. The barrel still aimed at his head.

"I was being chased," Sev said. His chest was on fire from running. His lungs weren't used to this kind of strain. He tried his best to use his normal tone. Stay calm. Like his scar, the rider could attack like a viper.

Patrick took a step toward Sev and looked at his arm. "One of them got you?"

"Your fence did worse damage." Sev revealed his mangled palms.

"Gonna bleed out?" The corner of his mouth twitched up.

"Don't think so."

"Shame."

"Could pull the trigger." Sev shrugged.

"Could." Patrick sighed. "Won't." He stowed the gun in the back of his pants.

"Why's that?" Sev asked. The grass tickled the sides of his ankles. Grown out all around them. The tips of each one were brown and pointed. Like little daggers prickling his skin.

"For whatever reason, my friends seem to think you're one of the good guys." He shook his head and motioned for Sev to follow. He didn't move. "Unless you'd rather climb back over, I got a gate." He walked toward a wooden shack hidden behind a body of wide trees. A few yards away, he didn't see it from the other side of the fence. Clever.

Sev trailed behind him. His eyes scanned the property. "What's with the fence?"

"Keeps the big cats out. Pops has a farm out there." He pointed over the shack, and Sev squinted to see corn and another crop too far out to decipher. "Sometimes we get mates trying to steal too."

"Is that why you have a gun?" he asked.

"No." Patrick spun to face him again, stopping in his tracks. He squinted at him. One eye twitched. Lips a straight thin line. "I have this gun to kill any mate who tries me. So, one step out of line, and you're done. Got it?"

"Understood," Sev said. What he didn't understand was why he hadn't killed him already. Or why he was out here behind that fence.

Sev could easily take the gun from this man, but there was no point. Energy wasted instead of recovering from the run. He was still shocked he was able to do that.

Patrick opened the door to the shack and let Sev inside. He stopped a foot in to see a loveseat, a fridge, a TV, and a bathroom in the corner. A small kitchen was littered with dirty dishes.

"Wasn't expecting company," Patrick said and led him to the bathroom. He grabbed a small hand towel and wet it under the faucet. He handed it to Sev as he rolled his sleeve up to reveal the scratch on his arm. Patrick's eyes widened at his past scars. Sev tried not to notice the man's pity.

"Not a man of many words, eh?"

"No, sir," Sev said. He began to treat his cuts. He'd be able to use Elastaderm when he got back to the mansion. He washed his hands in the sink and wrapped them in strips of fabric Patrick handed him. Then he wrapped his arm and covered it back up with his uniform shirt.

"How long you been in the Valley?"

"Medicine Trials."

"You know," he started. It was the tone he used that had the hairs on the back of Sev's neck stand. "I remember that day. Those years leading up to it. All those kids."

Sev kept his eyes trained on him. Stayed silent. Waited for the rider to continue.

The rider waved his hand as if to say, 'never mind'. He sighed and pulled his gun out to place it on the end table. Patrick threw an empty cup into the sink and sat down on the sofa. He motioned for Sev to sit at the table a foot away. A solitary chair was pushed in. The shack had wooden floors that creaked with every step, cobwebs in the corners, and a ripped dark green rug in the very center of the room.

"This cure they created could only save one. And they didn't try to save any more. Why not two? Three? Odd, don't you think?"

"Sir?" Sev said.

"I'm saying, you ever think about how you got there?"

How he got to the Valley? Lynch spoke to his parents. Made a deal. His parents dropped him off. End of story. He had Pulmonary Respiratis. Like every other kid that entered the trials.

"I have Pulm—"

"No," he interrupted. "I mean before. Who brought you to the Trials?"

"My parents," he said.

He thought back to the day. It was hazy. Sev could see them dropping him at the checkpoint.

"No parents were allowed. Who brought you to the Valley? Think."

Sev shook his head. His dad waved to him from the other side of the gate. His mother smiled through her tears. "My parents. They said goodbye at the gate."

"No. Think! Seventeen think!"

Sev jumped at the sudden change in his tone.

A wave of flashbacks came to him. Lynch knocking on the door. His blond waves free in the wind without a cap on. His pearly white teeth shined as he spoke to his parents. Convinced them of a deal of a lifetime. Convinced them to let Sev go with Lynch to the new Valley. Ashbury

Valley. Superior had just won the war. Became leader two short years prior.

He remembered Lynch handing his parents an envelope on the front stoop as Sev screamed and cried in the back of the car. Lynch drove away from the small house they lived in. Gray shutters and a yellow door. The memory got fuzzy when Lynch gave him a puff of oxygen on the way to the Valley.

"Lynch." Sev looked down at his hands in his lap. Fiddled with the fabric that was turning red with drops of his blood.

"There you go. Now it's coming back," Patrick said with a sly smile.

Sev kept quiet. He looked around the shack again. This time with new eyes. All his senses. There weren't any photos around. A stale scent in the air. Mold and dust. Did he actually live here?

Patrick chuckled, and Sev's eyes went back to him. "I don't live here full time. Not anymore." He stood and walked over to a closet in the corner. He opened the door, and Sev bolted up. A Guard uniform hung on a hanger.

Superior had warned him not to trust any Guard. There had to be a reason he wanted to replace them. Wanted to create a new army. Was this why? Because the Guard could leave when they wanted?

"Weren't you curious how I had that gun?" He raised a brow.

Sev eyed the man again. Had to be in his late forties, maybe early fifties. Dirty blond hair in a ponytail at the nape of his neck. Light blue eyes and a crooked smile. And he used to be Guard? How did he get out? Was he out?

"I, too, had to pick a child from Sunset Cove," he said. "But hear me, that child wasn't sick when I brought him to the Valley."

"You brought a child to Ashbury who didn't have the disease? Why?"

"You're not listening." The man sighed. Closed his eyes as he did. "Nobody had the disease. It wasn't in their system yet."

Sev was about to explode on this rider until his brain started to run in circles. He'd been sick for years before Lynch picked him up. Years of coughing and spitting up blood and not being able to breathe.

Right?

Years of lightheaded, dizzy spells and black spots and tunnel vision.

Right?

Sev sat back down at the table. His body tried to allow his brain to catch up. Most of those memories were foggy. But when he thought of his house in the Cove, it wasn't. No fog. Clear as midday.

What was real and what was fake? He tried to process all the information. The memories. Superior had him strapped in that red chair for hours and hours when he first got to Ashbury Valley. There was a haze over all the memories they spoke of in that room. Walking to a swingset, no haze. Parents waving goodbye, haze.

What did he force him to believe?

"You said, yet," Sev whispered.

"Now you're listening." Patrick smiled at him. "I think Superior put it in you. He gave you a shot when you arrived. Or maybe after you won. You remember that?"

Sev nodded. Vividly. Right after he won. No haze. When he tried to remember shots before the trial, there was a heavy fog.

"I think he injected that poisonous shit right into your lungs."

"What about the trial? Like you said, why just one? Why not fifty of us?"

Patrick rolled his shoulders back and took a deep breath before responding. The air in the shack became thicker as Sev waited. "Superior only needed one right-hand man. He wanted to create you."

Like clay in his hands.

"No. He wanted to break me."

When Sev left Patrick's shack, he checked his wrist. Six hours and forty-three minutes. Superior would punish him for his tardiness. Might as well try to find the light blue team so his mission wasn't botched entirely. Maybe Superior wouldn't punish him as badly if he came back with good news.

The team still sat around the fountain in the square. Sev quickly approached, and the captain looked to his teammates before the six of them stood, anticipating a fight. Each had black riding gloves covering their hands.

"I'm not here to brawl," Sev said and kept his hands at his sides. Visible.

The captain took a step toward him and puffed his chest. Easily six foot and more than 250 pounds. The other members braced themselves. Three of them took their jackets off and placed them on the table they were standing near.

"What do you want?" the captain spoke first.

On his lapel was a golden trident. Sev understood the blue shade of the jacket now. Team Neptune. Roman god of the sea.

"Superior would like a meeting. With all of you."

A rider cracked his knuckles, and another took a glove off before bringing his fingers to his mouth. A loud whistle sounded, and Sev winced. His ears still sensitive.

A seventh rider came around the corner in a light blue hoodie. No jacket. Maybe he wasn't a rider after all. He looked too young on second glance.

"Fetch us our blades, apprentice," the captain said to the boy.

"Sure thing, Knox."

Sev waited for the boy to come back. The mates in the square started to circle the team to observe. The young man handed Sev a blade. He took a step back and held it in his hand, learning the weight and testing its swing.

"Beat me, and we'll go to this meeting. Lose, and you'll have to outrun us next time we see you. Deal?"

Sev couldn't help but hear that last word in Mason's voice inside the maze. He nodded and held his hand out to Knox.

"Deal," Sev said.

Knox put his gloved hand in Sev's. The leather was soft, but when he squeezed, the rider winced. Was the glove covering an injury? He took a step back, and the duel began.

The circle expanded and moved as they did. Neptune gasped as Sev jabbed at their captain. He ducked and rolled to the side as Knox attempted to spear him in the gut.

This game was fun for Sev. He enjoyed the chase and the opportunity to fight with a weapon he was comfortable with. A master with, if he was being honest. He would let the captain have his few minutes before destroying him in front of the entire square.

Knox smiled as he took every swipe and stab. With no success. Each time Sev would block or dodge, Knox would get more angry. Until Sev blocked him for the last time and made sure to lock eyes as he grinned at him. Knox flinched, and Sev went hard. In three moves, Sev knocked the sword from his grasp, spun him, and pressed his chest to Knox's back. Then Sev's blade was at his throat.

Sev spoke into his opponent's ear, "Meet Superior tomorrow morning. Nine sharp. At the mansion."

The mates yelled and screamed that Sev cheated until Knox raised his hand. Sev gave the young apprentice the blade he'd used, and the man dipped in a slight bow.

"There was no foul play here. Seventeen defeated me fair and square."

Sev nodded to him with appreciation. The captain saved him from another chase. He kept his eyes on the other mates as he raced back to his bike. Most still wanted him dead.

Sev entered the mansion and found Superior in the dining room. He was holding a map in his hands and folded it up when Sev walked into the room. Whatever it was, he didn't want Sev to see it.

"Neptune will be here at nine in the morning, sir."

"I gave you an hour, Dragon."

Superior didn't waste time. Sev prepared himself on the ride back to the mansion. He knew what he was in for. He slid his ticker off his wrist and slid it into his front pocket. His eyes dropped to the floor.

"Why must you defy me? You make me do this." His nostrils flared as he shut his eyes with disappointment. "My father taught me everything I know. Taught me to be strong. How to fight. How to take a hit. How to control your emotions. My mother was terrible at this. Which ended in her death. I'm sure you've heard the story. I was young when she defied my father. He had enough. Rightfully so. Ungrateful. He also taught me how to be prompt."

Sev stayed silent as he waited for his order.

"Basement, Dragon. Now."

"Sir," Sev said. His voice cracked. Tears started to fill. He wouldn't dare let them fall. Not in front of Superior. He led the way down the stairs. How would he feel in the chair now? With all his senses intact. Would he try to mess with more memories? Or would it just be pain? He preferred the latter.

Sev unlocked the room inside his nightmares.

Dark wooden walls. And one red metal chair in the center. Bolted to the floor. The armrests had to be redone soon. Worn and rusted from all the years of him sitting and struggling. He settled into the only chair he'd ever be able to call his throne.

The chair kept him still with a metal bar over his lap, and a spike, a quarter of an inch tall, entered his wrist beneath his ticker. Superior would never allow mates to see the damage he caused his Dragon. A small pool of blood formed on the rest and dripped to the floor. Superior tightened the straps that went around each armrest. Held him to the chair like a statue.

"Why are you in that chair, Dragon?" Superior started.

"Late."

"Why were you late?" Superior grabbed the familiar helmet from the far wall. Three metal spokes on the inside poked his temples and the back of his neck when placed correctly. A chill ran down his back when Superior fixed it on his head.

"Mates attacked me."

Superior froze. He spun to eye him. "What do you mean, Dragon? What did you do?"

"Now they know I invented the creatures on the track. They are angry, Superior."

Superior grinned. A genuine one. The skin under his eyes puffed up. Pure glee. "Ah, yes. I forgot about revealing that little piece of information. How exciting. You'll be the talk of the Valley." Superior pressed a few buttons on the side of the helmet. It began to hum. The spike entered Sev's wrist a bit more, and he stayed still. Trained to experience this level of pain without reaction. Sev focused on Superior's elbow. The red sleeve scrunched in rigid folds until he straightened his arm again.

Sev closed his eyes and accepted what he deserved. He knew the rules. He broke them. The punishment would be over soon enough. The spike never killed him before, it wouldn't today either. Sev knew he wouldn't die as long as he stayed calm. His thoughts began to wander. Those amber eyes stared into him from across the library, in the maze, at the Championship, in the closet. Those lips on his. Some words replayed over and over in his mind. *I crave you. Enamored with you.* He wouldn't allow his mind to think of anything else.

Superior clapped in front of his face, and Sev opened his eyes. He stood with his hands clasped behind his back in position. His blood-red uniform crisp. His black pants tucked into his boots. So shiny he could practically see his own reflection in the toe.

"Where did you go, Dragon?"

"The Trials, sir." Sev thought fast. It was the first thing to come to mind. Patrick had him thinking since their conversation earlier. All of the memories he'd have to sort through. He'd have to write them out to decipher the real versus fake ones.

Superior circled the chair twice before Sev spoke again. "Sometimes, I think back on the day of the mission. Plan out different ways I could've done better against the others."

They went back and forth for another half an hour before Superior released him. His wrist felt raw as he hooked his ticker back around to cover the new wound.

twelve

The next day, Sev walked down to the training field early. It wasn't until he got closer that he heard grunting. He stayed in the shadows of the branches to see who was running on the course.

Sev spied from the trees as Bullet crossed the finish and checked his watch. He sat down and hung his head. He slammed his metal fist into the dirt. Bullet took a few breaths as he readied himself at the start line. He glanced at his watch and took off running. This time, he only tripped on one tire. Everything else, he did without fail. Climbed up the wall and slid down. Dodged every fireball. Sev met him at the finish line when he checked his watch again.

He was practicing on the course without anyone's knowledge. Bullet panted as he put his hands on his head and paced around the area. Sev took his position beside him and peered at the clock.

"Not much better than your original time."

If Bullet could shoot lasers out of his eyes, he would. "I don't run." He panted as he tried to slow his breathing.

"I can tell."

Bullet opened his mouth to retort when the twins came out of the opening in the trees. Bullet grunted as he took slow, deep breaths.

"What's going on?" Mason asked when he reached Sev.

Sev thought that was an odd question.

"You think I'm trying to steal your man?" Bullet laughed.

Mason stiffened. Sev kept his position with a racing heart.

Sev had known Bullet was observant, but how had he known there was something between them? There wasn't even anything there.

"Bullet," Maia started. "That's not funny."

"Don't worry. I won't tell your secrets." Bullet winked at Mason. "He's not my flavor anyway."

Mason scoffed. "I find real comfort in that."

"He won't tell," Maia said.

Bullet eyed her and crossed his arms over his chest. His metal hand on top. Sev noticed his eye twitch.

"Why are you siding with the captain who beat you just the other day?" Mason snapped at his sister.

"I'm not siding with him. And he didn't *beat* me. He hit me because I called him names. I hit him first." Maia tried to push her brother away from Bullet. He didn't budge. Sev could see him twist his heel into the dirt. He was planted.

Mason sneered at Bullet. Sev put his hand on his knife, ready to diffuse the situation.

"I'm not allowed to defend myself?" Bullet asked.

"You're not allowed to hurt my sister," Mason snapped. "You have a metal hand, asshole."

"And you have a heart." Bullet poked Mason's chest. Sev tilted his head at that. He remembered Superior saying that.

Mason stumbled over his words. Didn't know how to respond to that.

"Never mind," Bullet said and grabbed his jacket before heading for the trees.

"Where are you going? Training is about to begin!" Maia called after him.

The tension rose around them. Would Bullet tell others? Maia didn't seem to think he would. Mason never trusted the captain. Sev wasn't sure what to think. He could use the information to get ahead of others in the army. Closer to Superior.

Mason and Maia lost themselves in another silent conversation. As Sev went to walk away from them, Team Neptune came from the path in the trees. Mason put his hand on his knife. Bullet was behind them with Jorge. Bullet nodded to the twins as if they hadn't just seen him moments ago.

Lynch came with the rest of the riders, and they each took turns on the course. Knox came up to Sev and pat him on the back. Mason watched as Knox held his hand out to Sev.

"Nice duel, Seventeen. Maybe one day we'll have a rematch."

Sev gripped tighter than he did before the fight to gauge his reaction. He didn't wince like before. His hand was harder, too.

"Yes, and maybe you'll be good enough to call it a fair fight," Sev said. Mason smiled as he turned away from them.

Knox chuckled and shook his head before heading to the course. He took his shirt off, and Bullet grumbled next to Sev.

Jorge raised a brow at him.

"Showoff," Yuri provided.

"If you ask me, he doesn't have anything to show off," Maia mumbled, and Bullet was the first to laugh. Mason crossed his arms in front of his chest before looking over at Sev. He rolled his eyes at his sister.

Sev looked out at the course. Knox had gone through half of it. Sweat dripped down his chest, and Sev agreed with Maia. Nothing great about him. He was an average rider, fighter, and runner. Which made him question Superior. Again. Why this group?

After each rider went through the course, Bullet was up. Sev met him at the line.

"What?" Bullet snapped at him.

"Don't concentrate on anyone but you. Approach it like you do a race. Nothing else in front of you but that finish line. I can see your focus wander as you watch us all. You're better than these riders. Prove it."

Bullet stared at him for a minute. Sev thought he would have something to say. Bullet turned to the line and closed his eyes. He took a deep breath and mumbled to himself before he opened his eyes and spoke clearly.

"You remind me of my sister, Seventeen."

Sev wasn't sure how to take that. Bullet took his jacket off and had a plain dark T-shirt on. Sev had only seen his bare arms a handful of times. They were defined and full. But he much preferred Mason's.

"It's a good thing," he added. And suddenly took off.

Four minutes and twenty-one seconds. Bullet smiled at Sev.

"Quite an improvement, Bullet," Superior said from the back of the group. Nobody had noticed him join. Lynch and two attendants flanked him.

"Yes, sir. Still room for more," Bullet said, taking his position beside Sev.

Superior smiled at him. "Might go faster if you took your shirt off like the rest of the men."

"I'm fine with it on. Thank you for the suggestion, sir."

Sev handed the jacket out to Bullet. Before he could grab it, Superior stopped him. An attendant came and took the jacket instead.

A few of the riders shared glances. Nobody dared say no to Superior.

"Lynch, do I make suggestions?" Superior asked.

"No, sir." Lynch locked eyes with Bullet. Pleading with him to follow his orders.

Bullet gripped his fists, and Sev took a step away from the rider. Instead of glaring at Superior, he kept his eyes down. He pulled his shirt over his head and threw it to Sev. He caught it easily. Bullet was broad-chested with sculpted abs and a toned stomach. He wasn't sure why he would be shy to strip in front of the group.

"Run it again," Superior said with a grin.

All the riders watched in silence.

"Fuck," Bullet said to himself.

Once he turned around, a gasp left a few mates. A metal rod ran down his spine. No. The rod *was* his spine. Sev turned to Superior with wide eyes. He remembered. No haze. That was real.

One night, he was in the middle of creating a monster for a race when Superior burst inside with a small boy strapped to a table. A spine injury. Superior ordered him to replace part of it. Superior had three doctors inside with him, and they created it together to save his life. Had clearly been in some sort of accident. Burns covered his entire body. As if he'd been hit with a Zap.

Sev always thought the boy had died. He'd never heard anything about him again. Why would Superior keep it secret until now?

Bullet ran faster than he ever had. Sev assumed it was the anger coursing through him. He jumped the tires without a single mishap this time. Bullet crossed the line and sat down in the grass as he settled down.

"Four minutes thirteen seconds," Lynch said.

"Thank you for your suggestion, Superior," Bullet said from the ground.

Maia sat down next to him and crossed her legs in front of her. Her shorts showed off her dark legs, and she had taken her jacket off. Mason sat down next to his sister with a groan.

Superior paced in front of them. An attendant brought him water. He sipped it twice before handing it back to her.

"I now have a bigger army. And while you sit there and say you all need improvements, you are correct. Some need more than others. Bullet, realize your strength is why you're here."

"You mean his metal parts," Maia said in a snide tone.

Superior chuckled. "Tomato, tomahto. Why do you think you're here, girl?"

"Her stamina," one rider in light blue joked, and the rest of his team laughed.

"I'm only here because Mason wouldn't come without me. You don't want me here at all," Maia said. "I'm not an idiot. You didn't want a woman in your army."

Superior raised a thick eyebrow. Gripped his hands behind his back. Eyed her from head to toe. "You're the clandestine soldier, child. The unexpected," Superior explained.

The group was quiet a minute as his words sunk in. Maia didn't even have a comeback like she normally did.

"A woman isn't that uncommon to be a fighter," another light blue rider said.

Superior turned to the group, and Sev knew the signs. Superior brought a blade to the man's throat and slit it in front of everyone. Knox ran to his teammate.

"You psycho!" another light blue screamed, and Superior went for his chest. He slumped to the ground. Knox took a step back in horror. Two of his teammates lay dead in front of them.

Superior put his blade away and slid his palm over his hair to tame the wild. He turned back to the group and pointed at Bullet.

"Stand," he said.

Bullet followed his order that time.

"Duel," he said. Motioned for an attendant to bring Knox a sword. And then Bullet.

All of the riders sat down to watch. Knox took deep breaths as two of his friends were killed, and the other three watched from the sidelines.

An attendant handed Sev Bullet's jacket. He held it tight with the captain's shirt.

"First hit wins; don't kill him," Superior said to Bullet.

He gripped his sword tight before loosening. Maia put her hand to her chest. Wide-eyed. Mason seemed bored.

Bullet swung the sword a few times beside him before he grinned at Knox.

"You think you're better than me, big guy?" Knox said.

"You're too cocky," Bullet said and waited patiently for him to attack first. Knox tried again and again as Bullet dodged and spun. Sev couldn't help the deja vu. Bullet flipped over his blade and chuckled when Knox gasped. Their swords clashed and clanged before Bullet swerved and pressed the tip to Knox's chest.

"Point," Superior said with a smile.

Bullet took a few steps from him, and Knox yelled at his bare back.

"So, what? You're half robot, and that's how you're better than all of us?"

Bullet rolled his eyes. "I'm not a robot."

"Then why all the secrecy?" Knox yelled and swung his sword at him. Bullet blocked the blow and maneuvered closer, their swords between them scraped together. The metal-on-metal sound made Sev's teeth clench.

"He didn't want mates to know who pieced him back together. Couldn't stand who saved him all those years ago." Superior laughed, and Bullet pushed Knox to his ass. Again, poking his chest.

"Seventeen put me together like one of his fucking creatures." Bullet crouched down to be on Knox's level. "He's the one who made my hand when they cut it off, too. Think I want everyone to think I'm like him?"

Mason looked over at Sev. He kept his eyes on the fight. Not right now. He'd talk to him later about it. And the memories. And the disease. And Superior. All of it. Not right now.

"You're not like him," Knox said and stood back up fast to try attacking him again. "You're worse."

Bullet laughed as he tripped him. Knox landed on his back and yowled in pain as Bullet tapped his chest for the third time.

"Maybe you'll learn to stay away from me then," Bullet said and threw his sword to the ground.

Knox grunted as he sprung up and tried to blitz attack him. Bullet grabbed the blade with his metal hand and snapped it in half. He pulled the handle from him and threw it. Knox snarled at him and Bullet interrupted before he spoke actual words.

"You need to learn to control your anger. It'll be your downfall," Bullet said. "Your teammates just died. And you lost a fight. Be glad I didn't kill you."

"Spoken like a true warrior. Thank you for the lesson, Bullet. Knox, you're dismissed. Head out with your team. Come back tomorrow," Superior ordered.

Superior was never kind. There must be another plan in place.

Neptune all headed to the trees as Knox shouted about his fight with Bullet. Sev tossed Bullet his shirt, and he pulled it on before Superior had another order for them to follow.

Superior had each rider duel another for the rest of the day. One-on-one fighting as Sev pointed out their wrongs. While Lynch gave them preferable techniques to use.

Superior left them to train and Lynch had everyone trade partners again. Bullet faced Jorge. Their blades met in the middle before Jorge spoke.

Jorge chuckled and said, "You know, I remember you. Only kid walking alone at night back and forth from the bakery."

"Bakery? Were you a fat kid, Bullet?" Yuri laughed as he fought Mason beside them. His braid swung back and forth across his back as he moved.

"I worked there, asshat," Bullet snapped.

Maia charged again at Locke. He sidestepped before losing again to her.

"You're good at this," Locke said out of breath. "I need practice. Again."

She smiled as they took their starting pose. All around, the weapons clashed with every swing.

"Not all of us had parents to take care of us," Bullet added as he hit the rider's blade again. "I baked bread all night so they could sell it in the morning. Paid me under the table. I could eat one loaf a night. I slept in their storage closet for years until I could afford a place of my own."

"You weren't born here?" Yuri asked him.

"I was eight when I got to the Valley," he said.

Everyone stopped fighting, lowered their swords, and faced him. Sev continued to circle the group. The riders stared at Bullet in disbelief. It didn't come as a surprise to Sev. Lots came to the Valley as children. Even himself.

Bullet rolled his eyes. "Oh, now everyone gets sappy on me?"

"No stopping!" Lynch yelled out. "Start over! Beginning stance."

Lynch switched up the pairs and put Maia with Bullet.

"I'm not fighting her," Bullet snapped.

"Why not?" She glared. "Didn't have a problem with your fist. Now that it's not real, you're out?"

"I'm not fighting her," he repeated. Not meeting her eyes, he dropped his sword. Maia moved to stand in front of him.

"Because I'm a girl?" she asked with a scowl. Straightened her back.

"No." Bullet scoffed.

Sev grabbed a sword from an attendant and nodded to Bullet. He picked his sword up and stood in his ready stance.

"This will be fun," Sev said.

Maia took a step back and watched as they dueled each other. Ten minutes went by, and still no point had been made. They both dodged and spun and flipped over each other and went around all the other riders. Bullet laughed when Sev tried for his throat. Sev pushed him into the dirt, and Bullet rolled out of his reach. Sev tripped and flung over him before they were back at the starting point.

"Seems we're a good match, Seventeen. I don't think your boy is going to like that," Bullet whispered to him.

Sev glanced at Mason, who seemed to have smoke coming out of his ears. Was he jealous? Mason moved faster. With more intention. Swung harder. On the third strike, he broke his partner's blade. They stood in silence, staring at each other before an attendant came with new weapons.

Sev slid closer to Bullet and whispered back. "I don't think you want everyone to know how you feel about his sister."

"You don't know what you're talking about," Bullet said through gritted teeth. He faltered. Sev brought his blade up to his cheek.

"Point," he said.

"Bitch," Bullet mumbled.

"That speech you made earlier about anger, that's your own weakness. You let others get in your head too easily. Put up another wall before entering another duel. Maybe put up a few and duel that girl."

thirteen

By dawn, Superior had set up a room for dueling inside the mansion. Mats on the floor and no furniture except a chair for Superior in the corner. Swords decorated the walls, and targets were along one wall to practice with throwing knives.

None of Team Neptune showed up.

Superior paired the first four riders before pairing Lynch with one and leaving the twins to duel Seventeen. Of course.

Sev fought the twins one at a time before he fought them as a team. Each strike they messed up, he would stop and instruct their mistake.

"Again," Sev spoke.

Mason and Maia both took turns attacking. Sev escaped every hit.

"Tell me how I keep beating you," Sev said.

"Because you're a robot, man," Maia groaned. Hard for her to accept defeat. Her eyes gave her away. Glowering anytime he got a win.

Sev knew mates called him a robot. He didn't blame them. Sometimes he felt like one. Superior's little machine.

"Because you're working separately instead of together," he corrected.

Mason stopped and locked eyes with Maia. Smirked at each other. The game had finally begun. The riders stopped to watch the three of them instead of learning the next fighting stance from Lynch.

Maia swiped as Mason jumped. Sev lunged as Mason ducked. Maia tumbled as Sev vaulted over her. Mason dove as he landed and straddled

Sev, finally pinning him to the floor. Sev bit the inside of his cheek. Mason's body on top of his.

Mason winked at him, and Sev felt his entire body heat up. This was nothing like dueling Knox or Bullet. He felt lighter. And flushed.

"Good," Sev mumbled as he pushed him off, and they dueled again. Took more breaks between fights than the other pairs. They were being careful not to exert too much energy in front of Superior. Lynch regained the group's attention and went on to teach them another trick.

Superior stopped everyone and switched partners to watch them duel others. He raised his hand again and ordered the riders to sit in front of him on the floor.

"Locke and Jorge."

Everyone watched as they fought hard until Locke pressed his tip to Jorge's stomach. After each pair dueled, Lynch gave pointers to the entire group to learn. Mason dueled Sasha and won quickly. Next, he paired Sasha with Yuri. Sasha won with a point to the jugular. Superior sat up straight when he called Maia and Bullet.

Maia smiled and practically ran to the center of the mat.

"Why do you want to duel me so bad?" he asked as he prepared his stance.

"You're a good fighter. Only way to get better is to fight others who are better than you," she said.

Bullet stayed quiet. Sev walked the perimeter of the room to see the fight from all angles. Bullet looked at him, and Sev nodded before they began. Each dodge and block, calculated in his brain.

"Stop," Sev said.

"Seventeen," he groaned.

Sev motioned for him. He hung his head before he walked over to the corner of the room with him.

"You're not fighting her. You're playing. Fight," Sev whispered.

"What if I hit her?"

"She can take care of herself, isn't that what you said? Treat her like you do everyone else. Now," Sev said and pushed him back to the mat. Bullet rolled his eyes and readied himself in front of Maia again. Her long black hair pulled into a ponytail. Her jacket hugged her arms. Protected her, too. And she wore shorts. Like every other day.

"Needed a pep talk before fighting the girl." Locke chuckled, and Jorge laughed.

"Fuck," Bullet whispered.

The riders wouldn't look away from the two in the center of the room. Superior gleamed with pleasure at the scene. He loved causing tension. And loved to see blood spill.

"Don't listen to them. Just fight. Block everything else out except the sword in your hand," Maia said.

"That's what I'm afraid of," Bullet said softly.

Maia raised her weapon. He locked his dark eyes on hers. "You don't want to hurt me?"

"Are we going to fight or just chat?" He sneered.

Maia lunged first, and he blocked. Then he swiped. He spun around her and tapped her stomach.

"Point," Superior said. "Again."

Bullet groaned loud. Veins popped out from the side of his neck.

"Why?" Maia asked, raising her sword again. He didn't answer.

This time, he moved first, and she blocked him several times before he got another point. Then another. Another. Superior wouldn't let them stop.

"You ever gonna tell me?" Maia asked on their sixth duel.

"You ever gonna beat me?" Bullet asked.

She glared at him. Eyes darkened.

"There she is, the real you." He smirked.

"That's my anger. You must think that's the real me because it's the only emotion you provoke."

"Now, we both know that's a lie." He flashed her a wicked grin as he got another point. This time brushing his sword over her cheek. Soft enough to not leave a scratch.

They started another duel when she chuckled. "Is that what it is?" she asked as they scraped their weapons together. "You have a crush on me?"

Bullet glowered. Clenched his teeth. "You don't know what you're talking about, Maia."

"Oh, that's it, isn't it?" A small smile crept over her face. "Why you don't want to hurt me. Why you can't fight me. Can't handle a little blood."

She went harder, and they spun around each other twice before clashing their weapons one more time. He stepped closer to her. Their swords crossed between them.

"Just run to your little boyfriend and tell him all about the rider on Knuckles. How he wouldn't hurt you," he spoke through his teeth. Hard to hear him over the clashes of metal between them. "Except the one time I did, he was nowhere to be found. Why is that, I wonder?"

"He wasn't at the race," she said, and they clanged their steel again.

The riders exclaimed at the fight and cheered Bullet on. Sev noticed Maia reacting to the riders in the room. The words didn't bother her. She wanted the fight. She was telling the truth earlier.

"Didn't want to watch his pretty little girl ride around in circles?" Bullet said.

"He didn't want to watch me die."

"How cute."

"Jealous?" she asked and rolled on the mat to avoid another blow.

Bullet laughed. "Of that guy? No. Bitch probably can't even hold a sword."

"That's why I dumped him," she said. "Couldn't keep his sword raised." She winked before pressing her sword to Bullet's jugular. He howled in laughter as Superior called the point. Maia smiled at him as Superior finally let them sit.

Eventually, Superior dismissed the rest of the riders and kept the twins. Sev slapped Bullet on the back, and he nodded once to Maia. Mason glared at the rider as he left the room. The Chaos bikes could be heard from the window as they left the mansion.

Lynch pointed out other points of attack they could utilize. Sev forced the twins to duel each other before giving more tips. Then he joined in again. The twins against him was a fun workout. Not a real challenge, though. Not yet.

Lynch chuckled when Maia tripped and fell onto her knees. She flipped him off as she spun around, and Mason helped her get a hit on Sev. Her sword stabbed his upper thigh too deep, and blood squirted out of him like a fountain. Mason gagged.

An attendant ran over with a tin of Elastaderm.

"No," Superior told her, and she paled as she stepped backward to her post by the door. She wouldn't move until he ordered her again.

"Superior," Lynch said, but he waved him off.

"We get to use it and he doesn't?" Maia gasped.

Superior nodded. "Because you are somebody. And he is...Dragon?"

"Nothing," Sev supplied. Blood ran down his left leg.

"He's going to bleed out," Mason said. Fear coating his words. His eyes. His hands shook. He dropped his sword to the floor. The clang echoed in the room.

"Dragon." Superior waited for his response.

Sev looked up at Mason and averted his gaze as he repeated what he should, "I deserve every hit I did not prevent."

"Shut up, Sev," Mason seethed. "This is so fucked up!"

Superior grabbed his sword from his hip. Sev knew what was coming and prepared himself. He took a breath and held it as Superior lunged.

Sev stepped in front of Mason.

Superior's eyes widened as his sword slid into the side of his Dragon.

Maia screamed. Mason gripped Sev's shoulders from behind as Sev slid to the floor. Numb. Sitting like this reminded him of waking up in the middle of the maze. How he wished he was there now.

Lynch ran to his side. Blood coated Sev's teeth. So thick.

"Dragon, what on earth made you do such a thing?" he asked, his tone confused and annoyed. A terrible inconvenience for him.

"He didn't deserve that fate, Superior. I did. I will deal with the consequences of my actions. Thank you for the lesson," Sev spat out in between heavy breaths. Blood dribbled down his chin onto his shirt. Mason's arm wrapped around his front to hold him.

Superior rolled his eyes. "What a mess." He headed to the exit and stopped to tell the attendant to give him the tin. "Everyone out. The lesson is over! Clean up when you're done here, Dragon."

"Sir," he spat out.

Mason grabbed the tin from the girl and lifted Sev's shirt. He lathered his wound from behind him before he reached into the rip of his pants to cover that one, too. "You fucking asshole."

"Mase," Maia hissed.

Lynch ordered one of the attendants to grab the medicine he needed. They always had some on hand for Superior's injuries.

An attendant came back a minute later with two syringes. One to make him sleep and one to heal him. A more intense strain of Elastaderm for serious injuries. Lynch jabbed his thigh twice, and Sev hardly noticed. He would be asleep soon enough. Lynch snapped at the attendants to l eave.

"Why did you do that? He could've killed you. He almost killed you!" Mason rested his forehead on the back of Sev's head, and Maia covered her mouth with her hand. Lynch grabbed Sev's hand from beside him.

"You're nuts, you know that?" Lynch asked him.

Maia pushed Lynch out of the way to kiss Sev's cheek. He tensed, and she laughed at him. "You saved my brother. Thank you. Lynch is right. You're absolutely insane, but thank you."

"You're welcome," Sev choked out. Mason still had his arm around him, and it wasn't until it was quiet that Mason let out a sob. Sev could feel him shake behind him.

"You have to go," Lynch said. "He'll need to rest. He's drifting fast."

Mason nodded and released Sev. Lynch helped him stand, and he wobbled before he smiled. He could feel the blood on his teeth. His mind was fuzzy. Was he dreaming already? He was used to blacking out from testing his limits on the medicine for years.

Must be dreaming. Mason was standing so tall. His hair as dark as a raven. Eyes so bright and shiny. Maia stood beside him, ready to fight, as always. So strong. Lynch was next to him with his cap low on his head. Black spots formed around them.

"Couldn't let the cute one die," Sev said to Lynch. He could see Mason was still there. In his dreams, as usual. Lynch chuckled.

"You're out of it, ain't ya?" Lynch said.

Mason stared at him. Red-eyed and worried as Maia tried pulling him out of the door.

"Am I asleep?" Sev asked. Slowly lifted his fingers towards Mason. He was so close to him. If only he took another step.

"So you do dream of me?" Mason asked.

What a bold thing to say in front of other people. Sev laughed.

"Can't dream of nothing else." Sev sank to the floor again. Lynch let him lay on his back and he put his hand to his forehead. "Lynch, make him go away. I can't look at him anymore. Forbidden, you know?"

"Yeah, I hear ya, buddy," Lynch said.

And the dream went black.

fourteen

Sev woke up in his bed, working a splitting headache. Shirtless and in his boxers. His ticker beeped, and he sat up to grab his shot when he remembered he didn't take it anymore. He counted back the days to the last pill he took. How many had he taken so far? Three? He rubbed his face and stretched before Lynch walked in. That's when it came rushing back.

Can't dream of nothing else.

"Shit." Sev put his head in his hands.

"Coming back, ain't it?"

"I didn't say that out loud. I didn't. I wouldn't say that to him." Sev shook his head over and over. His stomach flipped as the realization settled.

"Oh, you did. And Mason looked just as shocked as you do right now." Lynch laughed. He sat down on the edge of Sev's bed with a toothpick between his fingers. "It'll be fine. You'll just go back to pushing him away like you always do."

Sev didn't want to push him away. He wanted Fantasy Mason and the real one to be one and the same. That wasn't his reality, though. Lynch cleared off the nightstand and made sure everything was presentable to Superior's standards.

"I'm shocked Superior let me live," Sev said quietly, breaking the silence.

"Must have something worse planned for you." Lynch returned the pick to his mouth and rolled it with his tongue.

"Probably." Sev nodded. "He has to get out of here. Lynch, he has to win. Understand? I can't— He can't—" he began to stutter and couldn't complete his thought.

"I know. It's alright," Lynch said. "Rest. I'll wake you in an hour."

Lynch left the room and placed a tin on his nightstand. Sev covered his cuts again. Took his time. His skin stitched itself back together slowly. It took a while for Sev to calm his mind before slipping back into a dreamless sleep.

Lynch was right, of course. Superior had worse plans for him. They met at breakfast and watched him slurp a bowl of soup. He wiped his mustache with a napkin before he glanced up at Sev.

"Interesting that you'd step in front of that rider, Dragon. Very interesting. I'd say damn near suspicious," Superior said. He spoke as if he was telling him the weather. Didn't take his eyes off his meal. "Speak one word to him today, and he'll lose a limb."

Sev knew something was coming. Was not expecting that.

He had witnessed Superior cut limbs off mates in the past. Not one he cared for, though.

Superior followed the nine of them out to the field through the trail in the trees. Seven riders in various colored jackets and his two dogs, Sev and Lynch. Nobody had to ask where Team Neptune was. They all knew.

Sev wouldn't look at Mason. Couldn't face his eyes today. Had to be the day after he'd said that shit to him. Had to be.

When they reached the clearing, targets were set up for archery in ten lanes. Attendants were scattered to retrieve the arrows, and some were set up behind them to assist Superior.

An attendant handed Sev his bow, and another handed him an arrow. He released with a slow breath. Right in the center.

Lynch led the lesson and used Sev to demonstrate. Yuri and Jorge paired up at the end of the line. Yuri shot first, and Jorge stepped up to give him tips. They got better as the day went on. For two riders from opposing teams, they seemed to work well together.

Maia stood with Sasha, and he helped her get comfortable holding a bow. She got fed up with him when she realized he wouldn't help her stance because he refused to touch her arm. She whipped around, and Bullet was behind her, shooting the center over and over.

"So, you are good at something," Maia quipped.

He eyed her, and she walked into his lane to get a better view of his shot. Sev rounded the group one more time before Maia waved him over.

"Dragon Bitch, help a girl out. What did Lynch say about my elbow?" she said and turned to take her stance. Sev looked to the rider in red.

"I think Bullet is more qualified than me for this lesson," Sev said. When Maia turned away, he shot Bullet a grin.

"You motherfucker," Bullet mumbled.

"What?" Maia dropped her arms. Confusion crossed her features. Always competitive. Hated not being great at the task. "Am I doing it wrong?"

"No, no, you're fine." His posture relaxed as he took a breath. "If you want to miss the target."

"Very funny." She rolled her shoulders back.

Bullet hesitated before placing his hand on her elbow and lower back. She raised the bow, and he straightened her back. Then he moved to lower her other arm as she squinted at the target.

"Okay, now release," Bullet said.

She grinned wide at the arrow in the red circle. He rolled his eyes at her.

"Don't get cocky. Do it again."

This time, she didn't need help with her pose but her aim. Four arrows flew before she hit the target again.

Sev walked around the riders again. This time, Locke kept missing the target. Every arrow hit the grass. Once he got to Mason, he knew it was trouble.

"Ignoring me today?" Mason asked, thick with annoyance. He couldn't blame him.

Sev didn't respond. Mason raised his bow and missed his first shot. He reached to grab the next arrow. Sev angled him lower. Trailed his fingers down his blue leather covered forearm before he went to the next rider to assist them. Difference was he told them how to improve. Didn't touch them.

When he looped back around, Mason tried again.

"You really won't talk to me?" Mason chuckled darkly. "Ridiculous."

Sev raised his hand to his arm again, and Mason looked at him from the corner of his eye. Sev refused to look back. He mimicked a deep breath, and Mason understood. Closed one eye and breathed in deep. His jacket whined as he stretched. His least favorite sound. On his exhale, he released the arrow and hit the bullseye. Sev almost smiled.

But he couldn't. Superior watched his every move from the sidelines. And Lynch's.

The rest of the day, Sev was silent. If he couldn't speak to Mason, what was the point of talking at all?

Superior eventually got bored and sent Sev on a solo mission. He'd have to be fast to beat the storm. It was hot, and the wind died. Lightning would be bad tonight. Could see it in the distance.

Sev traveled to the south wall where Superior directed him. On arrival, he quickly realized why. Six Guard floated face down in the river. He pulled them out and flipped them over on the bank. Held his breath when he recognized one. A blue bandana wrapped around his head. The one next to him, Sev remembered his young voice. Barely out of puberty. The next one, he took his uniform shirt off to reveal his back. Had to be thorough. A large hawk covered him.

These were the Guard Sev and Lynch had listened to that night. They spoke of Superior and his plans. Spoke of Matthews coming to attack. Did they know more, and Superior got scared? Did he try to approach them about joining the army, and they refused? What about the other three Guard here? Sev didn't recognize them.

He searched each of them for weapons. Only useable one was a Memory Bomb. Small one, first edition. Sev slid it into his pocket. No reason to keep it out here for a mate to find.

His legs dried fast in the sun as he piled them up. He pulled out his phone and called Guard to clean up the mess. The moon began to rise above him, and a cool breeze nipped at his cheeks. Six dead Guard. All shot in the chest. Same weapon used. A second-generation Guard pistol. Nowhere at the scene unless it was in the water strapped to something heavy. Those models float. That was a specific request from Superior.

He walked the edge of the river, looking for anything. Any scrap of a clue to point him in a direction. Came up blank. Nothing.

"You won't find anything."

Sev turned to find Patrick standing next to the dead bodies. He wore his team jacket and jeans with a T-shirt. His hair pulled back into a low ponytail.

"What makes you say that?" Sev asked him as he walked back toward him. His boot slipped in the mud, and he had to steady himself.

"Guy took the gun with him," Patrick said and pointed toward the trees over his left shoulder. There was a small opening at the crest, and Patrick waved as he began to walk away.

"Why are you out here?" Sev asked and ran to catch up to him.

Patrick smiled at him in response. He pointed up at the darkening sky, and Sev wrinkled his nose. Patrick led them through a small patch of sand, and a bike sat. Black with blue flames. A small, worn logo on the seat was hardly there.

"Were you on a different team before?"

"Pacific." Patrick pulled his shirt down to reveal a tattoo of the team logo on his chest. "It's how I got out of being Guard. A teammate of mine left mine for another. Ended up dying, but his team won the race. Well, I was on his form. I paid my way out of my Guard duty. With Superior Ashbury Senior, of course. But decided to stay in the Valley," he explained with a shrug. "Nothing for me outside these walls."

"You had a choice to leave, and you decided to stay?" Sev couldn't wrap his head around that. Wasn't the Cove a nice place to live?

"If your entire family was here, wouldn't you?" he asked. "I gave most of the money to a friend of mine."

"That's nice of you," Sev said.

Patrick chuckled. "Yeah, I guess. You ready?"

Sev looked up when Patrick did, and they watched a lightning storm come in fast. The older rider grabbed jars from the other side of his bike and handed two to Sev. They didn't have lids. Clear and heavy. Not glass. They seemed to be about half a gallon. Easy to carry.

"Come on, let's see what you got."

Sev headed out to the middle of the sand behind him. Tall, thin metal poles stuck in the ground. Patrick put his jars down and took one of Sev's. When the next lightning struck, Patrick howled to the sky as he ran toward the spot in the sand. There was a small box at the base of the pole. Just beneath a layer of sand, he twisted the jar onto the box where it had grooves and pressed a button. Streaks of white light filled the jar. Patrick pressed another button, and a lid was sealed over the top. He passed the jar to Sev. The light bounced around as he held it in his palm.

Sev stared at the light in his hand. Contained in the jar. His jaw slowly dropped as he looked back up to Patrick.

"Did you just catch lightning?"

"We've been doing it for years. A kid taught me, if you can believe that. No need for a Zap when you got this." Patrick smirked, and Sev smiled back.

Patrick: the Lightning Catcher.

Twenty jars later, he helped carry some back to the bike. He lifted his seat and rested some in the compartment. Then put two in a bag on the side of the seat. The storm had finally passed. No more rain or thunder. A rusted copper scent came from Patrick's bike. Sev wondered how long ago he got it.

Sev looked around them at the trees. How would he begin to track the killer of the Guard? He put his hands behind his back. Sinking into the room in his mind. First, he put up a blank corkboard. With push pins he added photos of all the possible suspects. Then connected locations and evidence with red string.

"Won't get him tonight. You were too late," Patrick said. "Black man, bald, gold rings, you know the guy?"

"Jameson?" Sev asked immediately pausing the board in his mind.

Patrick nodded. "That's the one you're after." He pointed to the clearing in the trees, and Sev thanked him.

He wanted to ask Maia or Mason about it. Wasn't sure they were in on it or not. Killing Guard. What if he couldn't trust them with this? Sev wasn't even sure he could trust Patrick.

Sev got on his bike and headed back to the mansion. He had a bit of time, so he wasn't speeding. Kept his helmet off for this trip. Enjoying the wind through his hair. That's when he noticed a group of riders coming from the direction of town. Instead of passing by, they surrounded him.

He sighed at their attempt. He hit the accelerator and made a quick turn on a dirt path. Some followed. Sev went through the small patch of trees he was familiar with and lost them. No rider was stupid enough to go through that blind. The trees were too close together.

When he returned, Superior's army of riders was long gone. Sev found Lynch in the library with Superior and reported on his intel. The Guard dead in the river. Now he had a suspect, but Superior didn't need to know that. Sev showed Superior the photos of the Guard, and they discussed future missions on the subject. His creations were more important now. Race three was only a week away.

He dismissed Lynch and Sev and went to his room on the third floor.

Sev entered the hallway with Lynch, and he wanted to pull his hair out. His day with Mason was anything but good. He didn't say a single word to him. Left when Superior ordered him to.

"Go to him," Lynch suggested. "He thinks you're ignoring him. I'll cover if something happens."

"Superior would kill all of us."

Lynch shoved him into the wall. "Seventeen! Go! Or *I* will kill you."

fifteen

Sev snuck back out through the tunnels and got on his bike. 42nd
and 283rd. Last time he was there, he tackled Mason to the ground.
The memory of the fire burned his nose. He could picture Mason's smile
under him. Feel Mason's body underneath his.

Sev arrived in seven minutes flat. Parked in the trees to conceal it.
What if Mason wasn't there? Or didn't come home that night? It was
late already, and he didn't see any cars or bikes in the drive on the way
up.

He broke into the closest window and quickly realized he was alone. It
was easy to figure out which room was Mason's. Hardly anything inside.
A small bed with a simple blue comforter. A dresser with three drawers
and a bathroom. The closet doors were open. Clean, crisp shirts hung
and sorted by color. Sev smiled at that. His fingertips grazed the softest
looking one. The garage door creaked open, and Maia laughed.

Sev pulled his jacket off and laid it on the bed beside him. Only a
moment passed before Mason came through his bedroom door and
threw his shirt in the corner. He stepped out of his shoes and grabbed
his pants button when Sev spoke up.

"Might not want to do that."

"Fuck!" Mason jumped and locked eyes with him.

Maia ran in at his outburst. Sev gave a lazy salute, and she laughed and
shook her head.

"Five minutes," Maia said to her brother. Mason nodded and shut the door. He looked back at Sev. His pants unbuttoned. His chest damp with sweat.

"What are you doing here?"

"You said you'd tell me how you got to the Valley if I came," Sev spoke slowly. Watched his every move. His face relaxed. Eyes traveled Sev's body. He never wore anything except his uniform. His bare arms were on display. Suddenly, he missed his long black sleeves.

"We're heading out," Mason said.

"Understood." Sev stood to leave.

"Come with."

Sev's eye twitched. He paused. His mind ran through every conse-quence before landing on how none of it mattered. It would be worth it. "Where?"

Mason smiled. "Two minutes." He grabbed clothes from his dresser and ducked into the bathroom. He cracked the door, and the shower turned on. Clothes hit the floor, and Sev turned away. Didn't want that image of Mason to try and erase. If he ever had the privilege of seeing his body, he didn't want it to be like this.

Sev held his hands behind his back and then let go. His stance wasn't needed here. He was a regular mate tonight. The shelf by the door had novels that piqued his interest. Lots of 'how-to' books and self-defense and the history of weapons. How to fight with only one arm. He picked that one to flip through its pages. It explained in full detail and diagrams how to get out of a hold or handcuffs. Sev imagined it differently. He thought of someone who only had one arm. Or one leg. Not someone without the use of their arm. Boring.

Sev placed the book back, and Mason reentered the room. He had a short-sleeved maroon silk shirt on with black pants and nicer black boots. Sev couldn't help his dropped jaw. Mason chuckled and ran his fingers through his hair to comb it over his ear like usual. The wet strands dropped onto his shoulder. Sev could smell his usual cedarwood now.

Maia knocked on the door and opened it without waiting for a verbal response. Sev squinted at her painted face. Covered in white and bits of black. He wasn't sure if she was supposed to be a ghost or a skeleton. She smiled at him and winked. She wore a tight black dress that stopped above her knees with high heels. And her hair was down. Sev had never seen it that way before. Her face partly hidden by the dark curtain.

Sev slid his hands into his front pockets and felt the Memory Bomb from the river. He didn't think twice. He tossed it to Maia. She caught it and inspected the object for a minute before accepting it. She nodded with approval. Now, Sev wouldn't have to hide it from Superior.

"Hurry up. I'll meet you at the van. I'll do the paint," she said. Mason waited until she was gone before he turned to Sev.

"We'll be back before one," Mason said. He hadn't realized Sev didn't need more convincing.

Sev wanted a moment to soak in what he was about to do. He nodded. Mason's smile radiated as he frantically opened every drawer in his dresser. He threw a pile of shirts on the bed and turned to his closet to add to the pile. He looked back at Sev before shrugging at his pants and shoes.

Sev tried not to think about the river he'd walked through in these pants. At least they were dry. Did he smell? He lifted his arm to his nose when Mason had his back to him. Not bad. Wasn't great either.

Mason went to the bed and held up the first shirt, and Sev shook his head violently. Mason laughed. The next one, Mason didn't even bother showing Sev. A preposterous yellow shade. The next few, he pushed aside. He held up a long black sleeve button down with shiny black roses down one side. Mason nodded. It wasn't as flashy as Mason's. Still just as nice.

Mason placed it down before approaching Sev. Slowly reached for the bottom of his shirt. Sev raised his arms to allow him to take it off. He took a deep breath as Mason looked at his body. Like a caress with his eyes. Sev reached for the button down when Mason got to it first. Put it behind his back. Sev rolled his eyes.

"If you can get it from me." Mason smirked.

Sev glared. He placed his hand on Mason's shoulder and then faked a punch to his gut before spinning him around and grabbing the shirt. Mason was laughing before Sev could start buttoning. Mason helped with the last two and slowly traced his fingers down the front of his chest.

Sev focused straight ahead. Mason's top three buttons were not done. Sev wanted to press his lips to the revealed skin. Assumed it would be smooth and warm. Sev felt his cheeks heat as Mason's fingers fell from him. Sev took a step back.

"It's big, but it looks great on you," Mason assured.

"Are you just saying that because I'm in your shirt?" Sev asked.

"Both. Definitely both." Mason led him out of the garage and to the edge of the property. Maia stood at the front of the van with the back door open.

"We're gonna be late," Maia barked at her twin.

"It's fine. Let's go." Mason sat down behind the wheel and turned his face to Maia. He held his hair back, and she dipped her fingers into a small container. She started covering the top half of his face in white paint and then went over his eyes in black and the sides of his nose. Then did his mouth.

He smiled at Sev when she was done. His white teeth bright against his black lips. Maia pushed Sev into the back seat and slammed the door shut as she got in after him.

"No fights tonight. I'm serious," Maia said. She took the small container and opened it as she turned toward Sev.

Sev bit his lip. "Alright."

"She's talking to me." Mason chuckled.

Maia laughed and pointed at Sev. "I don't care what you do. But this idiot is my responsibility. So, no fights." She glared at her brother.

"Those guys start shit every time," Mason mumbled.

"Don't even. You leave there with bruised knuckles every time."

Maia told Sev to close his mouth and stay still as she wiped the paint over his face. She moved fast, and her fingers were smooth on his skin as she finished.

Mason laughed. "That guy from Crossroads had it coming. He pushed me."

"Sure. And the girl from Taisley's bar? Man, what about the guy from that team...what was it?"

Mason rolled his eyes. "Timber."

"Yeah! Timber. That guy. What about all of those?" She raised a painted brow to him. Mason didn't respond. Sev couldn't stop looking at him from the backseat. Clearly, they had more in common than he thought.

Maia switched hands to do the black over his eyes and mouth and held up a small mirror for Sev to check it out himself. She grabbed a wet wipe from the pocket behind Mason's seat and wiped her hands clean.

"Quit it. You're giving Sev a bad image of me," Mason said.

Sev laughed at the audacity.

Maia stared at him. Clearly shocked he knew how to make that sound.

"Thank you," Sev said quietly. Maia smiled at him. "Why the paint?"

"You'll see," she said.

They parked and got out of the van quickly to enter a back door. Mason tossed the key to a guy standing inside in all black. He went around them and pulled off into the night with their getaway car. Sev didn't like that his exit strategy was gone. They entered a long hallway, and Maia spoke into Mason's ear. Music played from the front, and Sev couldn't hear over it. Could barely walk straight from the floor, moving with it.

The room opened. Loud bass vibrated the walls. A man in a light pink suit and top hat played the music from a large table set up in front. The word Resurrect was in bright neon behind him. The walls were black with textured, vibrant paint splattered. The floor gleamed with metal flecks. It was like walking on tiny gold coins.

Sev assessed the room. His eyes roamed the mates inside. Each had masks or paint-covered faces. Most were dancing and thrusting their bodies on each other. The ones who weren't were in dark corners, either talking unsuccessfully or swallowing each other's tongues. He tried to imagine Mason here without him and failed. Why would he come here?

Mason grabbed Sev's hand, and he flinched. Mason nodded once at him and looked down at their hands intertwined. Said something to him, but he didn't catch it. A spray misted his face from over Mason's shoulder, and he closed his eyes. Not fast enough. Mason let go of him, and Sev opened his eyes to him, holding a petite man up by the throat. His toes dangled inches above the gold-speckled floor. Mason's eyes were deadly. He spoke into the mate's ear, and Sev heard every other word until the last sentence.

"Tell me what it was, or I'll rip your fucking throat out right here." Mason gripped him tighter and he was starting to turn blue. A few mates turned to look. They were creating a scene. Sev didn't want to be recognized.

He tried to grab Mason's hand. Couldn't find it. Which was suddenly hilarious. Sev chuckled, which bubbled into laughter. Closed his eyes to stop the scene unfolding in front of him. Sev opened his eyes, and Mason was holding Sev's cheeks in his hands. Such soft hands. Warm.

"Pretty eyes," Sev whispered to him. Somehow, Mason heard. The rider's smile widened, and he shook his head.

"You're gone, aren't you?" Mason asked.

Odd question. Could Mason not see him?

"No, right here," Sev said. He tapped Mason's nose with his own and giggled.

Mason went wide eyed at the act. Then a smile overtook his face.

Mason waved at Maia, and she disappeared back into the crowd. "It'll wear off in twenty minutes. Okay? Can you even understand me? Fuck," Mason said.

"Never done that. Shouldn't do that here," Sev mumbled and raised his hands to rub his itching eyes. Mason grabbed him in time. "Right. Makeup. Strange substance."

"Let's get you out of here," Mason grumbled. Sev glared and held his ground. Then pouted. Mason motioned to the door. He wanted them to leave? They just arrived. Everyone was having a great time. Why did he want to ruin it?

Sev pulled him toward the crowd. Mason raised a brow. Sev yanked again and whined. Mason allowed him to lead.

Sev pushed mates out of the way until they were in the center of the dark room. The lights flickered above them, and people brushed up against their backs and arms. Mason wrapped his arms around Sev, and then they were moving together to the music. Sev looked to the group next to him. He always learned best that way. Mason grabbed his jaw and forced his eyes back to his. He smiled at him, and Sev let go. Mason rested his forehead against his. Their paint rubbed together smoothly.

Sev could feel the drug working into his system. He felt lighter. Like liquid. Flowing freely around the vibrating room. Mason's hands were on his body, and he didn't feel threatened or trapped. He felt whole.

Sev didn't think. He just acted. He pressed his mouth to Mason's and felt him jolt with shock before they stopped moving. Mason pulled Sev closer so their chests met.

Mason ran his hand up and down his back. A comforting touch. He was trying to keep him calm. It was working. Sev let Mason teach him how to move on the floor as they kept their mouths locked.

A new beat began, and people started jumping around them. So, Mason taught Sev how to do that too. Sweat trickled down his back and forehead, and Mason's paint was starting to smear around his mouth from kissing. Sev couldn't help his grin. The drug was wearing off, but Sev still felt like a drifting feather. He couldn't explain it. He'd never experienced anything like it.

Sev looked around the room again at all the mates laughing and dancing. And here he was in the middle of it. And Mason's eyes were filled with light. His smile came easy, and Sev pulled Mason's lips down to his own.

He didn't care that it was forbidden or if someone recognized him at that moment. Right then he wanted to kiss Mason. So he did. Without regret or any walls up. He ran his hand under Mason's shirt and felt his hot skin under his fingers. His back so smooth without any divots or raised lines from years of training under Superior. Sev gripped him tighter. Mason let him explore his body and kept his mouth busy on his. Eventually, he moved to Sev's throat and nibbled his skin there. Sev jumped, and Mason laughed into his shoulder.

Sev glanced up at the balcony. Mates sat at the bar that was open to the dance floor below. On the opposite side were private tables sectioned off. Harder to see. Curtains cascaded around them that hung from the ceiling but were open to the dance floor. His focus was stolen when Maia closed a curtain behind her and the mate he was after. Jameson.

Jameson reached up and brushed Maia's cheek with a gloved hand.

Sev stilled, and Mason followed his eyesight.

"She'll take care of it," Mason said in his ear.

He was about to flee up the stairs to handle him when Maia turned the man around and placed her hands on his shoulders. She leaned in to speak, and then quickly, her hands moved to either side of his head. She snapped his neck. He fell to the ground. The curtains swayed as she fled.

The lights flickered bright white twice, and Mason tensed. He looked up and Maia motioned to him from the bar. Mason grabbed Sev's hand and pulled him to the front door. They left Resurrect and climbed into the back row of the van parked at the curb. Maia hopped into the driver's seat as the brothers from Wrath got into the second row. Patrick dipped the brim of his cap at Sev as a way of greeting. The corners of Sev's mouth lifted into a soft grin. Jameson was done.

"So?" Mason asked them. Sev kept quiet. The drug had left his system. Still didn't trust his tongue yet.

"It was successful," Maia said.

The blond on the left turned to speak to Mason when his eyes landed on Sev. "Who the fuck are you?"

Mason growled and put his arm behind Sev on the back of the seat.

"None of your business, Reid," Maia said simply.

"Guy looks wrecked," he said. His hair was in a knot on the top of his head. A bright green tattoo of a lion covered his forearm. He wore a bright T-shirt. Was he inside Resurrect, too? Dressed like that, Sev didn't think so.

Patrick laughed, and Sev acknowledged him better to let him know he appreciated his silence. He was pretty sure he got his message. He snapped in front of his brother's face.

"Wildly curious about shit that don't got nothing to do with you."

Reid grumbled next to him and crossed his arms as Maia reached a stop sign. She looked in her rearview at the men in the car.

"Keep talking about him, Reid, and Mason is going to cut the skin from your ankles to your chest," she warned, and the blond looked at Mason. He shivered and focused on the road beside him. Maia laughed and crossed the intersection. Sev wished he'd seen Mason's face to scare a rider like that.

sixteen

Mason pulled Sev into his bathroom to wipe the remaining paint. Sev appreciated that. Didn't like the feeling at all.

Mason crossed the room to the closet and opened the door slowly. He pulled down a safe and placed it on the bed. Tiny. About the size of Sev's keyboard in lab two.

Mason opened the top drawer in his dresser and popped open the false bottom. He revealed a thick gold key and tossed it to Sev. He caught it with one hand and waited patiently.

Mason let out a sigh as Sev swiveled the box toward him and opened it. Lavender hit Sev hard as Mason grabbed the stack of envelopes inside.

"We lived in Sunset Cove for a long time before we left. The thing is...we didn't get here the normal way."

"What do you mean?" Sev asked. Mason took a hard breath. All the envelopes in his hand were blue. Tied together with a rubber band. Snapped it as he spoke.

"We broke in. Our dues are fake. Our arrests are fake. We're not real riders. We just entered to get Superior's attention. A friend hacked into the database and added us in. There are security measures to keep from escaping out of the Valley, and almost none for getting a mate inside."

Who would enter the Valley on purpose? Who would want to be watched constantly by Guard or Superior? Be killed in the street like a stray dog. Or to enter a deadly motorcycle race and kill your peers. "I don't understand."

"Gage, he's the one we write letters to in the Cove, is friends with the Superior in Graves Valley. He heard about Superior Ashbury planning to create a new Guard. A new army, as he keeps calling it. So, we came to get information. To join."

"You're spies," Sev said.

Mason nodded. Waited for Sev to catch up.

"What about Jameson?" Sev asked.

Mason smirked. "All part of the plan. He was the first one to work with Superior on the new army. Superior paid him to kill the Guard that were trying to leave or weren't trustworthy."

"Maia seduced him to get intel?" Sev scrunched his nose. Her tongue was down his throat the first time he'd seen the man.

"Listen, I don't agree with her tactics, but they certainly work. Jameson spilled after a week. Wanted her to join him. So that's how we entered the running of the army. That's how Superior learned about us. From joining the race and then through him," Mason explained. He held out one of the envelopes. Sev raised it to his nose and almost gagged.

Mason laughed. "Gage is...eccentric. Hopefully, one day, you'll meet him."

"He's your—" Sev stopped when he realized what he was about to ask. He didn't want to know. Mason shook his head.

"He's my friend. But, his boyfriend," he hit Sev's shoulder with his arm and flashed his teeth, "is amazing, too. Anyway, now, they're back in Sunset Cove."

"They got out?" Sev was wide-eyed as he focused back on the envelope as if it held all the secrets of the Valley.

"They won the race." Mason grinned. "Gage and Josh, and his cousin, Aster. When Drake Matthews became Superior there."

"I've heard rumors," Sev said quietly.

He'd seen the photos and videos of Superior Matthews over the last year. Every day in town and on the news, he would see him violently killing in the race or punching Guard.

"He's not like his grandmother." Mason closed the lid of the safe and set two more envelopes on his bed. He went back to the closet and returned the safe. "Superior wants everyone to think he's exactly like her. But he's not. He's trying to get rid of the races. Trying to help mates. He's trying to be better. His friends help. Some live at the manor with him. They all run the Valley together. All of them."

"That's impossible." Sev wouldn't believe lies told so boldly.

"I'm sorry I believed all the rumors about you before we met. That you were a robot who couldn't speak and lost his mind to the disease."

"That's what Superior wants all the mates to believe," Sev said.

"Then why can't you believe the same about Drake?" Mason asked.

Sev put his hands behind his back. All the videos and photos he'd seen of himself playing for the town so the mates would fear him.

"I figured you wouldn't believe me. It is hard to believe. I don't blame you." He returned the key and walked back to the bed. Handed Sev the letters. "Read them. Sorry in advance." He rubbed the back of his neck. "I didn't think we'd get this far."

"What?" What did that mean?

"Just read them," he said. Mason stood and headed to the bedroom door. "I'm going to make us some food. Take your time."

Mason walked into the hall and cracked the door to give him some privacy. Sev looked down at the letters in his hand and opened the first one. The black ink stared up at him. Mason opened a few cabinets in the main area of the garage. The sound echoed in the high ceilings. Sev sat down and read the first one carefully.

M.

Keep another gay secret like this again and I'll slit your throat. I deserve a full description and how many inches. And you know I'm not talking about his height.

Sev turned pink at those words. He'd told his friend about him? Was this about him? He couldn't assume.

Just remember, a forbidden love is the most appealing. Sexy. Just be careful.

Made a group of friends though. You'll like the Kiddos. Some call me Papa. Which as you probably guessed, I'm a huge fan of.

D is ready to meet up. Preparing a group to come with. Probably just E. Maybe N, but I can't imagine he'd be much help. He's kind of a wimp if you ask me. But I don't know him well enough. Left too soon for full introductions and battle wounds. We're still trying to figure out how to video chat between the Cove and the Valley.

We're ready whenever you are to get the two of you out. I promise it will be legitimate. We might've been able to mess with the journey going in, but going out, that's a different story. Guard here have photos of the wanted sent to them.

G.

Mason was talking about him. Giving details. Sev didn't understand how this mate was so close to Superior. Spoke about him like a friend. If he could get him out of the Valley, why was he still here? He could leave. Sev tore into the next one like his hands were on fire.

M.

You sneaky bastard. A maze? Clearly he has no idea how your photographic brain works. How many freckles are on his nose, M? SIGH. How romantic. Hope I can meet him.

D says maybe three weeks and he'll be ready. Wanting you and not sissy seems suspicious. Glad he came to his senses and took you both.

Enjoy this photo of me and J on our back porch. Waiting on the sunset with iced tea like the two homos we are. See you soon.

G.

Sev held the photo in his hand and looked at the two men. Bright blue hair on both of them with lipstick and eyeshadow to match. One had his hair sticking straight up on top of his head, and Sev kind of liked it. He was thin, while the other had a round face. What he was in awe over were their smiles. He'd never have that. Never have a smile to relate back to theirs.

           M.

*So you're fucked HAHA Thanks for the intel. Maybe we can stop
the fight before it even starts. I know you think Superior wants
to take over Graves Valley. But if he massacres all of the mates
there, who will he have left to control? I'm not sure about this.
Know anybody on the inside who could get us through the cracks?
An attendant maybe?*

*M said you seem sad. She said you won't speak to her about it. Is
it the boy?*

*Tell L I said thank you. It could not have been easy. Can't wait to
see him.*

           G.

Sev placed the letters on his pillow. Mason was a spy. Telling another
Valley and their Superior about what was going on. Telling them about
the war Superior wanted. About *him*.

Two sides of a coin. And Sev had a hand on each.

Mason came back in and shut the door behind him. His silk shirt
shined in the light as he walked.

"I have to go," Sev said.

"You don't have anything to say? Nothing?" Mason asked. He placed
a plate with two sandwiches on the dresser by the door.

"You're putting yourself in the middle of a war instead of letting your friend get you out of here. Superior could've killed you multiple times by now. Including the races. Get out. Let your friend get you and Maia out. What's wrong with you? Why would you stay here?" Sev seethed.

Mason chuckled. "You read the letters. You can't figure out why the hell I'm here? I'm *waiting* to get out. I have two tickets with a blank space for the name. Just Gage's money. If we win, that means we could have two others join us in our freedom. Don't you get it?"

"You have all the information you need. We could send letters to you if we find out more. Skip the race and get out. Tomorrow." Sev was exhausted. Why wouldn't he just leave?

"You could come with me," Mason said.

Sev stumbled back. His eyebrows scrunched. His lip quivered. "What?" he whispered.

Those amber eyes on his. Mason wanted Sev to flee Ashbury Valley. With him?

Sev couldn't leave. Superior would find him. Find Mason. Hunt him for sport. All Superior craved was a challenge. Could Sev watch Mason leave without him though?

He would have to. It would be a privilege to watch Mason leave. Get out. Be safe. It didn't matter that Sev would suffer. Didn't matter how it would crush him. Body and soul. He understood more now. His feelings for the rider. That suffocating feeling in his chest.

"Come with me," he repeated. "Leave this place. Get away from your Superior and see the world outside of these walls. It's beautiful out there. Trees and flowers. Sunsets. Iced tea."

"Stop." Sev held his hand up. Dropped his head. He could never live that life with Mason. Never. Sev's purpose was here. Beside Superior. "We could never have the life your friend has. Never."

"If you even try to speak the word forbidden, I swear."

"Mason, it *is* forb—"

Mason crushed his lips to Sev's. Wrapped his arms around his body and wouldn't let him go. Sev pushed all his duties and responsibilities away and let himself feel his mouth on his.

Sev fisted Mason's shirt and pulled him closer. Mason ran his hand up Sev's back under his shirt, and a moan slipped from him. The electricity Sev felt on his bare skin from his touch had him seeing stars.

Sev realized Mason could feel the scars from his lifetime in Superior's grasp. Instead of pushing him away, he wanted more. Wanted him to feel every single one and kiss them all away.

Mason bit his lip hard and then massaged it gently with his tongue. This was nothing like their first kiss. This was feverish. Frantic.

Sev wouldn't be able to stitch himself together after this. He knew that. Yet he couldn't stop. Everything he had endured led him to this moment. And it was worth every injury.

Sev stepped back and tried to catch his breath.

"Seventeen," Mason said.

Sev put his finger to Mason's lips to quiet him. "Don't. I'll help you. Lynch and I. Do what you have to. Get out and get as far away from Superior and this place as you can." Sev spoke so softly he wasn't sure Mason heard him until his eyes started to fill.

"Come with me," Mason tried again.

Sev could feel the pull to him. Felt it in his bones. The strings that webbed them together. It wasn't enough. Superior would come after him.

"You don't know my demons, Mason. And I have too many to bring you along."

Mason nodded reluctantly. Accepting his fate.

Sev left him standing there and passed Maia going up the drive. He wouldn't dare let her see his eyes full of unshed tears. He was weak. Breaking. And he'd do it all over again for that last kiss.

seventeen

Another ticker beep, another tossed Phophilac dose. Sev spent the following seven days in his lab or training with Lynch after the riders left. His punishment was still on-going for taking the sword for Mason. At night he took time to write out memories. The fuzzy ones. The fake ones. The true ones. All of it.

Lynch and Sev's relationship had taken on a new level. Sev could depend on him. He leaned into it. Still couldn't rely on his own memories. Had to figure that one out. He trusted the Lynch that was in front of him today. Didn't mean he had to trust the Lynch from twenty years ago. Could certainly ask for his side of the story though.

When Sev told Lynch about the letters and what he wanted help with, Lynch hadn't faltered in accepting his role to assist. Be a traitor. Treason. Fight Superior and lie. So the twins could get Superior Matthews inside. They would risk their lives for it. End the Championship. Stop killing each other.

Sev met Lynch in the library on the day of the third race. His creatures were ready. His Parklings had been fixed, and the stadium prepped and ready to go.

"Plan?" Lynch asked.

"No plan yet."

"You told him why you were ignoring him?" Lynch went to the desk and straightened the loose papers into a neat pile. Sev walked the perimeter of the room and checked the cameras. Red blinking light in the corners. When the room was ready, they stood together to the left of the door. Waiting like dogs for Superior. Only difference was they kept their tongues in their mouths.

"No," Sev said.

"No?" Lynch shook his head at him. And Sev didn't block the slap to the back of his head.

"What the hell?" Sev snapped at him.

"That's for being a moron." Lynch had his pointer finger in his face. His voice getting louder. Words coming out faster. "What's wrong with you? So he thinks you're a dick who ignores him and all his advances and—"

"I don't ignore his advances." Now they were nose-to-nose.

"—now you're just going to stick both our necks out for him—"

"We both know it's forbidden. We will never be able to be togeth—"

"—so we'll probably both die for this kid to run off and fall for some other fuck in the Cove that ain't even you!"

Sev sucked in a breath. His chest tightened. Mason would eventually move on. He knew that. It was inevitable. He wanted him to be happy. That was something he'd never be able to give him. So he'd sacrifice his own happiness for his. Sev would stay right here with Superior. Lead him away from Mason. And Lynch was right. Superior would kill Sev eventually. That was his price to pay for falling for a rider.

"I don't understand you, buddy." Lynch sighed and lowered his voice to just above a whisper. "Just be with him until you can't. Wouldn't you rather feel how he feels, before you throw yourself in front of a bullet for him? You're in deep. No matter how much deeper you go, the outcome is the same."

"Wouldn't that make it worse?"

Lynch smiled. "Cause you won't miss him if you don't kiss?"

Sev blushed. Lynch barked out a laugh. Sev was about to defend himself when Lynch patted his shoulder.

"Save it. I'm glad."

"Glad? You want me to be killed for having relations with a rider? He'll be murdered. You'll be murdered. You want that?"

"Not necessarily. But I'm glad you're living." Lynch winked at him.

Superior would be coming to fetch them any minute. But the memories Sev had begun to write out were weighing on his mind. Now might be his only chance.

"Lynch," Sev started. "Will you tell me about when you brought me here?"

Lynch chuckled as he adjusted the cap on his head. "Finally ready to hear?"

Sev nodded. He didn't feel very ready. Just needed to know the truth.

"I met your parents a few years prior. Awful couple. Terrible to you. Do you remember them?"

That was unexpected. Sev remembered laughing with them. Tossing a ball back and forth in a yard of green grass. Remembered long nights by a fire. Even games of tic tac toe in the driveway with chalk. Were they not real? Those weren't hazy.

"They didn't want a child. They were more interested in sniffing powder than feeding you dinner. Eventually, they agreed to give you an opportunity of a lifetime: be Superior's Second. Did you know your father was a boxer? Loved to fight on the streets for cash. It wasn't hard to convince him. I told him you'd be the best fighter there ever was."

"Well, you weren't wrong about that," Sev mumbled. His parents didn't want him. Had no use for him. Gave him up. "You took me away from people who didn't want me?"

"You thought I took you away from a couple who loved you?" Lynch was wide-eyed at the accusation.

Sev nodded. "Superior made me remember differently."

"I see." Lynch rubbed his jaw. "No, Seventeen. They did not want you. I wouldn't be able to stomach taking a child from a loving home. I figured you had a better chance here than you did with them. I might've been wrong. But you've definitely had an exciting life, ain't ya?"

Superior opened the door, and they took position.

Six Guard stayed in the hall before attendants flooded the room to present breakfast to him. He waved them away and headed straight for the car. He was excited for race day, it seemed.

When they got to the arena, Superior made sure to invite the mates to his mansion again. He had a huge smile on his face as he sat back down in his seat. When all the riders lined up on the track, a team caught Sev's eye.

He hit Lynch's boot with his own and pointed them out. Lynch whipped toward him when he saw what Sev had.

Impossible. Four men in light blue leather jackets and black gloves. Team Neptune.

Superior turned to smile at the two of them. "Thought it was a blood-bath, did you?"

"Yes, sir," Lynch said. No use hiding his shock.

Guard stood at the start line and held a Zap in the air. One team in black with gold stripes had golden helmets raised in the air, getting mates in the stands to cheer for them.

"Chariot! Chariot!"

Sev had seen them around but never knew their name. Didn't care enough to. Their bikes stood out more than the others. Thin and long. Three wheels down the center rimmed in gold. The handlebars were golden and shaped like a lowercase W. The team next to them all had bleached hair down to their shoulders and pearl-white leather jackets. The two teams clearly knew each other. Talking back and forth with smiles. They seemed to be working together. Motioning too much with their hands.

Behind them, Wrath revved their engines next to Knuckles. Bullet flipped his helmet closed as the Guard shot the lightning bolt straight up.

Immediately, a mate in gray kicked a rider going over the first pit. He sank into the spears sticking up, and the pole entered his body in several places. Blood dripped down the metal for the rest of the race.

First death of the third race.

Sev wanted to cheer for his team in blue. Mason got to first place beside Bullet. They were neck and neck for the first two laps. Dodged every fireball and each Parkling that tried to hit them. Neither of them tried to push the other away or into a pit of smoke or fire. Sev was surprised. Maybe they had come to an agreement.

Superior stood to watch when Team Neptune rounded a corner and had to face Sev's Ogle. First one was grabbed by their legs and spun into a thick web before it threw the rider back out onto the track. The rider screamed as another ran over his ankle. As he lay there, the web started working. His jacket began to smoke, and he thrashed in the dirt. Acid ate at him until there was nothing left.

A rider in yellow dodged the line of bones lying in the track. Made a mistake when he curved toward the beast. The Ogle craned its neck and swallowed him whole. Rider didn't stand a chance.

The team in white passed Mason and shot at him from all sides. One stuck in his forearm. Sev held in a gasp as he pulled the spear out in one fluid motion. He shook his head, and Sev could practically feel the pain in his own arm.

Just before the pit, Bullet passed them all and pushed the first one into the spears using his metal hand.

Bullet distracted them enough for Mason to get around them. Before jumping over the next pit, he stomped on his brake and teetered on the edge for a minute before sliding backward down the ramp. Riders yelled at him for being in the way, but he kept his focus. He hit the accelerator, and as he was over the pit, he dropped a smoke bomb. The next two riders in gray went up the ramp blind. They rode straight into the spears, not knowing where the track stopped, and the crater began. They wouldn't be messing with him again.

Finally, the Belvedeer Sev had worked on for months would make its debut. As excited as he was to see it in action, he feared for his friends. It was twenty feet high, with large antlers extending fifteen feet wide. Legs like wet spaghetti. The thorns that shot out of its body were dosed with venom. The large black bead eyes were what attracted a mate's attention. They slid back and forth, slowly tracking each rider's movement before it attacked with precision. The first rider was knocked off their bike with an antler. The mechanical animal grunted and huffed as it went for the next one. A rider in gold yelped as it flew across the gravel and landed on his back. The Belvedeer stomped on him with its hind leg.

He never got back up.

Team Chariot stayed together side by side as much as they could. Pushing riders out of the way to get around them. One shot a fireball at the Ogle, but it was a mistake. The Ogle wasn't paying attention to him until he pulled the trigger.

He died instantly.

Superior clapped as Knox seized first place and stayed there. Bullet crossed in second, and Mason was third. The riders watched as Maia went over the last pit. A rider in pale yellow with orange flames on his back shot a spear at her. It went straight through her side, close to her hip. She screamed inside her helmet. Started to press on her brake before changing her mind and hitting the gas at full speed. She rammed her bike into the side of the rider who attacked her, and he flopped on his side. Maia crossed the line, and Bullet stepped toward her before he stopped. His fists were at his side. Breathing hard. Sev could see his chest heaving up and down from his seat in the stands. His teammates were around him, watching the scene unfold. They were all smiling. Not Bullet.

Mason ran to her side and pulled her helmet off. Held his hurt arm to his chest. Sev couldn't hear what they were saying back and forth. He could see she wasn't in good shape. Superior beamed beside him.

"Well, seems that the warrior of the year, is no longer able," Superior said.

"Right as always, sir." Sev stood, and Superior followed him out to the car with Lynch. The entire ride Lynch had his eye on Sev in the back seat.

He should've gone to help. Would have taken a syringe to her. Antibiotics. He wondered how full his tub of Elastaderm was. Had he used the last of it on his leg last week? Where would Mason take her? Home or the hospital?

Suddenly, Lynch was opening Superior's door. They were back at the mansion already.

"Attendants are requesting Sev's assistance downstairs, sir. Preparations for the party tonight," Lynch explained.

Sev didn't understand what they could possibly need from him. Superior turned to his balcony, and Lynch sent a wink in Sev's direction. Oh.

"Check security while you're down there, Dragon," Superior added.

Sev responded with his normal agreement and ran to his lab. Scanned his eye to enter. Grabbed what he needed before heading to the garage. Didn't bother parking behind the trees or down the street. Almost drove into the doors of the place. He jumped off and ran inside.

Maia was on the floor, blood poured out of her side. Her face had paled, and her arms shook. Beads of sweat covered her body.

"Sev?" Mason looked up. His arm still clutched to his body. Blood dripped from his wound.

Sev kept focus. Ran to Maia. Patrick and Reid were on one side, and Mason was on the other. She squeezed her brother's hand. No tears fell. She bit her lip and yelled when Sev lifted her shirt up. They had tried their best. She needed stitches.

"I need a needle and thread," Sev said to Patrick. He jumped up.

"Do you even know what you're doing?" Reid asked.

"I used to help the doctors in the lab," Sev explained quickly. He took the gauze off her side and cleaned it as best he could. He used the rest of his Elastaderm. It wasn't enough. Patrick came back with the needle, thread, and a thick brown liquid in a bowl. He peered up at Patrick.

"Sterilizer," Patrick said.

Sev nodded. Went to work. She yelled, and Mason winced as she gripped him tighter and tighter. Tried her best not to move. Sev had never worked on a conscious patient before, so he appreciated that.

When he finished, he tried scraping the last bit of Elastaderm out of the tub. He rubbed it on the worst spot, and Mason grabbed the empty tub from his hands and threw it away, so he'd stop trying to get more when there wasn't any.

"Will she be okay?" he asked. Sev looked at the gash and then up at her face. Color was slowly coming back.

"She'll be alright. Just needs rest. Do you have any antibiotics?" he asked.

Reid got up and went to the bathroom at the back of the garage. He came back with six various sized bottles. Sev grabbed one and read it twice before giving one pill to Maia.

"Take this. Every two hours. I'm not sure if it will help. Can't hurt," Sev told her. Reid came back with a glass of water, and she sat up slowly. Mason helped her stay upright as she swallowed the pill and then the water. Her hair was matted to her back and forehead. Mason helped her stand and then got her in bed.

They entered the door beside Mason's bedroom. Reid helped Patrick clean up while Sev started with the blood on the floor.

"She wants to see you." Mason poked his head out. It wasn't until Sev looked up that he realized Mason was talking to him.

He stiffened and slowly shuffled back to her room. Smaller than he expected. Her sheets were a dark shade of green. And a dresser in the corner was covered in books. Her closet was overflowing with fabrics. Shirts and dresses stuck out in all shapes and shades of dark colors. He expected nothing less there.

"Seventeen," she said, and he went to her side. Maia put her hand in his, and he wanted to let go. Forced himself not to. "Thank you."

He didn't respond. Her eyes were glossed and drooping from exhaustion.

"Rest. You'll need it to be in the next race."

"I need it for the party tonight, you mean." She sniffled.

He raised a brow at her.

"You think I'm going to let these men think they can beat me? I'll be there." She smiled at him, and he chuckled. He patted her hand and got to his feet. Maia was asleep before he left her room.

Reid and Patrick were in the process of bringing their bikes inside from the street. Mason leaned over the kitchen sink and looked out the small window. He turned when Sev approached him.

Mason dabbed his clean arm with a rag. Sev grabbed the wrap from the first aid kit and gently began tending to him. Mason kept quiet as he worked. When he finished, Mason swept his fingers down Sev's jaw.

"You came," Mason whispered.

"I knew you would need help."

Mason pulled Sev to his chest. Placed his head on top of Sev's, and a shudder of a breath came out.

"Thank you," he said to him. "Thank you."

eighteen

Sev got back to the mansion just in time for Superior to call him upstairs. Lynch and Sev were to guard the lawn during the party. Bring any information they learned to Superior immediately. They were his spies for the night. And six Guard would be with Superior on his balcony.

"Dragon, I want you close to that team tonight," Superior said. He sipped on his wine before placing a piece of bread between his lips. He took a bite that crunched, and he grinned at the attendant who had brought the tray up.

"Sir?" Sev asked.

"Wrath, of course. The twins, if the girl survived anyway. I guess only time will tell. I need to know what they're thinking. I need to know I can count on them. Understand?"

Sev nodded and receded as he was disciplined to. Lynch walked down the stairs with him in his usual uniform. Charcoal gray with two rows of buttons on either side. Sev matched him other than his pins and the color. Pitch black. Like Mason's hair. Sev shook his head to clear his mind. His focus needed to be on the party tonight. He separated from Lynch at the foyer and headed outside. Sev walked the grounds twice to make sure everything was ready before any riders showed up.

The party started loud and abruptly. And he couldn't find Wrath anywhere. First team he found was Knuckles. Bullet was in a deep red suit. His team surrounded him, enjoying bubbly purple beverages in a slim, clear glass with a lemon slice on the rim. Bullet was the only one with an empty hand. Sev approached the group slowly. One rider had blond waves past his ears and an eyebrow piercing. He wore a red shirt and jeans.

"The mansion isn't a bar. Either dress accordingly or leave," Sev spoke in a firm tone.

The rider's eyes were bloodshot as he cackled.

"You're joking. I won the race today. We're celebrating!"

"Either leave or Superior will deal with you personally," Sev said. The mate's eyes went over his shoulder to the balcony. Sev didn't need to look to know Superior had noticed this mate. His biggest pet peeve was appearance. Everything must be in its place.

The rider shoved his drink at Sev's chest, sloshing to his boots. The sweet berry aroma covered him.

"Guess I'm out," the rider said and stomped like a child to a black car. Two of his teammates joined him and tossed their glasses in the front yard as they left.

Bullet and one other teammate stood. They had soft features and a square frame. Round black glasses rested on his nose. He had dark hair, and it wasn't until then that Sev realized it was dark blue. Even though his was darker, the color reminded him of Mason's friend in the photo. The couple drinking tea on the porch.

"Bull, there she is." The rider slapped his shoulder and pointed across the lawn. Maia stood with her back against the wall of the mansion. An indigo dress flowed to the ground. A slit all the way up to her hip revealed a wrap around her upper thigh. When she took a step toward her brother, the knife held there shined in the twinkling lights around them.

Her hair was pinned to the side and came over her shoulder. Pin straight, it touched her navel. Sev focused back on Bullet, who had a rock in his throat.

"Maybe tonight will be better than on the track," the rider said with a devious smirk.

"No," Bullet barked. Too sharp. Sudden.

The rider scoffed.

Bullet wiped his forehead with the back of his hand. "I mean, that wouldn't be wise. Guard all around." Bullet eyed Sev. Was he looking for help?

Sev straightened and glared at the teammate.

"Thinking of causing a scene at Superior's party would be very unwise. Might want to listen to your captain," Sev spat.

He rolled his eyes and told Bullet he was heading to the outdoor bar on the other side of the mansion. Bullet's head was freshly shaved. A design on the side was done with a razor. A fist to resemble their team logo. Sev wondered if he did it himself or had a teammate do it for him.

"Every rider wants her dead," Bullet said, finding her in the crowd once more. "Only girl rider in the Championship this year. They think she's weak."

Maia laughed with her team and took small sips from the glass in her hand. She favored her right side as she moved.

"And what do you think?" Sev asked.

Bullet didn't answer for so long Sev was sure he hadn't heard the question.

"I think she's the strongest one on the track," he whispered. Finally locking eyes with him. He cleared his throat. Was about to add to his statement when Sev interrupted.

"Understood, Knuckles," Sev said. "I happen to agree."

"Really? Not her brother?" Bullet crossed his arms in front of him.

Sev kept his position. Certain that Superior was still watching his every move. "Her brother is strong. You are correct. She's more ruthless."

Bullet nodded as he tightened his lips. He patted Sev on the back and went the opposite way of the Wrath twins.

Sev found Mason whispering with Lynch near the fountain. Their eyes darted around to make sure mates didn't see them together. When Sev approached, Lynch smacked his shoulder and left. He sprinted up the stairs of the mansion and ducked inside. Mason spun to find his sister and Patrick in a passionate argument. Patrick spun his finger at his ear as he rolled his eyes.

"I'm not crazy! Ask him. Go on, ask Sev," she said.

Sev's ears perked up at his name. They were talking about him?

Patrick waved him over, and Sev hesitated, thinking of Superior. He looked up, and Superior waved him off. He was just as curious. That wasn't a good thing.

"True or false, Dragon Bitch," Maia started. Mason glared at her. Sev expected the nickname now. It was almost endearing. Almost. "The freaky spider thing web isn't made of acid but has acid inside it, and then when it shoots, the acid comes out."

They all waited for Sev to confirm. It was the first time a mate knew he had created the creatures, and instead of trying to murder him, they were curious.

"Close enough. Once the web connects with anything warm-blooded, it releases the acid into the tubes of webbing. Which then melts the tube, sticking itself to the object," Sev explained, and they all looked at him without blame or disgust.

A rider came up behind him. "What about the trees?" He had a neon green suit with diamonds in his ears. Clearly fake. No shine.

"The Parklings work in different ways, actually. Some aim for warm bodies, like the webbing for the Ogle. Uh, the spider thing, as Maia said." He paused when a few riders laughed around him. More gathered around to hear his response. "Others lock onto your bikes and aim above. A few calculate weight. In that case, you'd be grateful to weigh less."

Sasha joined the group and waved to Sev from behind Mason. His beard freshly trimmed, and his suit a shade of deep purple. His tie was loose around his neck, but at least he was in dress code. Bullet came up beside him. Like usual, he stuck to the shadows.

"You enjoy killing all of us?" The rider from Knuckles came to the front of the group. His glasses and blue hair stood out from his other mates.

"No," Sev said. "But it's part of my duty to Superior. To make the Championship a challenge. Not just a track."

"Sure does make it fun." Patrick smiled.

"Fun?" a rider spat with disgust.

"You don't enjoy the near-death experiences? Makes me feel alive!" another rider joined in. Sev turned to see it was Jorge. A smile spread on his face. "I say to hell with Superior for making us think you weren't just like the rest of us."

Sasha smacked his arm. They all knew the consequences of talking like that about Superior.

"I'm not about to thank the guy. But he sure does know what he's doing. Remember that one years back with the feathers and orange eyes!" A rider shivered, and the group started to throw out more creatures they recalled.

The time and effort Sev put into every invention was being noticed. Every Rider had another to add. Details he himself had forgotten.

"Imagine what you could do if you got out of here," another rider said, and the crowd went silent.

Sev found Mason. Looking at his shoes at that comment. Sev was about to slip away when Bullet pushed through the crowd.

"Nobody is going to pay his dues. He's got four times the amount of any mate here."

"Superior adds to your dues?" The rider in green gasped.

"I'm a mate like any of you," Sev said.

"We know about the trials. You didn't commit a crime to get inside," Bullet said.

"And all of you did?" Sev asked the crowd. "All of you committed crimes to be here today? Nobody was born inside these walls?"

Mason stepped toward him. His suit hugged his chest in all the right areas. A small black flower was in his pocket. Sev wondered why it wasn't blue to match Maia's dress or his suit better.

"Even if you had committed a crime, I can promise you one thing: you're not a mate like the rest of us. Nobody can do what you do." He slapped his upper arm in a friendly manner. The other mates joined in and agreed. They started swapping more stories of how brutal he was. A trained killer. But forced to be that way.

"Seventeen!" Lynch called out to him.

Reality pulled out from under him like a rug. He resumed position.

Lynch pulled him to the mansion and brought him to the kitchen.

"Thought you needed a save," Lynch said and sat him down on the attendant break chair. If Sev was being honest with himself, he wasn't sure he needed saving. For once, it seemed like the mates around him didn't want to slit his throat.

The party went on for hours. Sev walked the perimeter twice before Bullet waved him over to his bike. It was just out of sight of Superior. He lifted the seat and rifled through some items before pulling out a beat-up piece of paper.

"Sign," Bullet said. Handed him a pen with his other hand.

Sev stared at the beneficiary form. His eyebrows furrowed. Forehead wrinkled. Only one name was on it so far.

"Patrick?"

"He signed it a very long time ago."

"Why me?" Sev asked and signed the form as he spoke. Bullet held it to his chest when he was finished.

"Got nobody else." Bullet shrugged. "I figure if you don't want it, you'll give it to others."

"Maia."

"I said others," Bullet corrected.

"Heard you," Sev said.

"Hey, Mase wanted— what's that?" Maia came running over, and Bullet shoved the paper into his compartment again before he sat on his bike.

"Nothing," Bullet said.

Maia eyed Sev before turning back to Bullet. Her dress had a swoop neck with thin straps holding it up. Her chest was normally hidden beneath layers of leather, but not tonight. She showed her skin proudly. Sev was jealous of that.

"Why hide it then?" she asked.

"You were saying?" Sev stepped toward her and returned his hands behind his back.

"Mason is waiting for you. By the entrance to the maze." Maia focused back on Bullet. "Why can't I see? Because I'm a woman?"

Bullet rolled his eyes at her dramatically. "Because you're a rider not on my team."

Sev cleared his throat. "I gave assistance to your brother. I offered similar to Bullet."

"Why?"

"I'm not allowed to talk to Sev, but you are?" Bullet crossed his arms over his chest, and she mimicked him.

"You are infuriating," she said.

Sev took her arm gently and led her away from the rider in red. She tried to get out of his grip but gave up. Once they were farther away, she added, "you too."

"Beneficiary form," Sev said. He wasn't sure why he felt the need to be honest. The hurt in her eyes at her presumptions of Bullet made him want to confess.

She stopped walking, and Sev released her. Bullet revved his engine before leaving the party.

"He had you sign his form? Why?" she asked.

Sev stayed quiet. He had told her enough. By the time they got to the entrance of the maze, she spoke out again. "He thinks he doesn't have anyone else."

Sev noticed the phrasing she had used. His assumptions of Maia had been correct.

Why the hesitation though? They were both riders. It wasn't that uncommon to be with a rider from another team. Was it because his team seemed to despise the Wrath girl? Or was there more to it? Sev wished the only difference between Mason and himself was a different colored jacket.

Sev met Mason at the maze. He strolled behind him and made two turns before Mason slid a small clear bag of little yellow pills into his pocket.

"For the next few weeks," Mason said.

"Thank you," Sev mumbled. "I realize I haven't said that. I want you to know I see all you've done. Risked for me."

Mason kept quiet. They knew the outcome. Sev was staying.

Sev looked up at the sky above them. Like Mason had done the last time they were inside the maze. The stars were bright tonight. Almost a full moon. Fires burned nearby. Sev could taste the ash on the back of his throat. He lowered his eyes back to Mason's. Sev wanted to ask about Maia. All that mattered was that she survived. Mason survived.

"We have friends inside. I'll continue to send pills so you don't go without," Mason promised.

Sev studied the flower in Mason's pocket. Mason handed it over. Sev brought it to his nose. He still wasn't used to having such strong senses. Mason lowered Sev's hand until the flower was in front of Sev's uniform.

"I was correct. A perfect match." Mason winked before he left him speechless in the hedges.

Sev showered after the party and got settled in bed when he remembered the Prophilac result. His computer would be done the diagnostic by now. He jumped out of bed and ran to the next room. He signed in and started to skim the page.

Prophilac causes low blood pressure. Over time can cause your blood vessels to narrow. Which meant as he continued to take the drug, his heart was getting less blood and oxygen. How damaged were his lungs and heart now? It also caused purple in the iris of your eyes. He knew that firsthand. It was how Mason figured it out so quickly. Sev read fast and deleted the results so he would leave no trace.

He sat at his desk for a minute to calm his racing mind. Superior wanted to control him. Wanted him to suffer.

Wanted to break him.

Sev went down to the basement, quietly walking the halls in his T-shirt and boxers. After the party, nobody would be around at this time of night. The secret halls were empty as he entered the medical rooms. The ones he remembered helping Bullet in. His spine and his hand. All those years ago.

He turned on the machines and started the scans. First his heart and then his lungs. At least at the mansion, there was only one machine he had to stand in front of for two minutes. It scanned his entire body and sent the images to his computer instantly. He logged out and made sure the room was clear when he saw the syringes and tubes of blood samples. Quickly, he sat and pulled six vials. He always hated watching them fill. Never minded the feeling.

Sev practically ran back to his lab. He looked at each scan carefully. Would have to get a doctor to look at them, too. There was definitely damage to his heart and lungs. Just not sure how severe. He dropped his head to his chest. Took a deep breath. What if he didn't have long? What if it was too severe to fix? He'd been taking Prophilac for almost twenty years. Two decades of pushing his limits. Sev thought back to the other pills and shots he took from Superior. Were they to keep him alive or to make him worse?

All about control. He was just a pawn in Superior's chess game.

What if he only had a few years left? If he only had one year left, did he want to stay in Ashbury Valley or spend it fighting beside the twins? He cared more about Mason's safety from Superior than his condition. He knew if it came down to it, he'd stay in the Valley if it meant he could save him. As long as Superior was alive, Sev would be beside him making sure his focus was away from Mason.

In the meantime, he'd send his results to a doctor and get a real answer. His scans and his blood work. Maybe he'd be able to get a couple solutions, too. Problem was he couldn't trust any doctors in the Valley. Maybe one of Mason's friends would know someone?

nineteen

Only one place was set on the long table when Sev entered the room. Ready for Superior to enjoy his breakfast of assorted meats and crisp ripe fruit. A thick green drink waited for him at the head. Lynch picked a hair from his shoulder and adjusted the hat on his head before he placed a toothpick in his mouth. Sev kept his mouth shut. These days, he had more to worry about than Lynch's terrible habit.

Superior walked in, and they straightened up. His blade had blood dripping from its tip. His hair was ruffled, and his lip curled up. It would be a rough day. Lynch tightened his stance.

"Dragon," Superior said.

"Sir," he responded as he always did.

"You'll be at my side today. Lynch, you'll lead the training. Think you can handle that?" Superior asked.

Lynch responded quick and stayed in position.

Superior snapped his fingers, and an attendant came with a towel to wipe the blood from his face and hands. The splatter was significant. Must have been more than one.

The three of them walked out to the training field and found the twins, Yuri, Bullet, and Sasha, waiting. The sky was cloudy. There would be rain later. Sev thought of the jars of lightning and wondered if Patrick did that every storm.

Superior turned to one of the attendants and waved her to the riders. She held a black bucket in one hand. An oversized hood hid more than half of her face. Sev couldn't even tell how old she was. She was too covered. The attendant raised the bucket above her head and walked to the target.

"Where's Jorge?" Yuri asked. Sev knew before Superior spoke. The blood from his steel.

"Dead. Any other questions?" Superior answered.

Bullet panned to the twins who were still. No reaction. Did they know? Was it because of the comments he made at the party?

Yuri's face paled. "Dead? I just saw him last night!"

"Don't make me repeat myself, rider," Superior snapped. His voice boomed in the field, and an attendant flinched. Even from feet away. Sev remembered when he'd been jittery like that. Those days were long gone. So far in his past, he couldn't even recall what it was like to feel fear like that.

Sev remembered Jorge from the first meeting. Pressing down on the hand test like the rest of them. His bright orange jacket. His messed up smile as he congratulated the twins on every accomplishment. And now he was gone.

"A traitor will always be found. And be slain. Either by me or the Guard. My Dragon doesn't hesitate. Do you, Dragon?"

"No, sir."

"He'll push through blood and bone to get to his target. Because he doesn't question his Superior. Do *you*, rider?"

"No, sir." Yuri shook his head. His braid swayed behind him. His eyes were glossy as he made eye contact with the rest of the riders around him. Bullet patted his back when Superior looked away. Yuri stiffened, and his face hardened. He regained his composure.

"Now, let's get to the good stuff, shall we?" Superior sat in his usual chair. Attendants came and filled a glass with wine.

Lynch led them through a series of basic skills and techniques he used during battle. Stand your ground. Make every strike a lethal one.

Superior listened close as he spoke. Sev stayed silent. That came easy to him. He could design creatures from top to bottom in his head without pen and paper. His mind was his castle. And he used every room.

"Dragon, you listening or drowning in your ideas of mayhem?"

"My apologies, Superior. Drowning as you said." Sev had zoned out, watching Mason stand across from his sister as they dueled with their new techniques. He needed to concentrate.

"Shall we?" Superior asked and stood. Sev followed him. Knew what came next. He locked eyes with Mason at the last second to warn him.

Superior spun, his sword in his left hand and his gun in his right. He smirked as Sev lowered to his knees and prepared himself.

"I remember my father raising me on this game. Such a great warrior he was. A Superior from the east. Legendary. He only achieved two Valleys, though. Sad." Superior loaded the gun as Sev watched him silently. "As you know Dragon, he's my inspiration. His death made me who I am today. A better fighter. A better leader." He paused to lift the gun to Sev's chest and closed one eye to get his aim correct before taking three steps back from him. "Flinch, you'll get the shrieking dart."

"What's that?" Sasha asked. Rubbed his eye as a tear slipped out. He hadn't expected Jorge's death either. Stroked his beard as he waited for Superior to answer.

"A shrieking dart paralyzes you for two minutes from the neck down. My Dragon designed it for me. Quite useful in an unexpected fight." Superior smiled down at him.

When Sev raised his head, Superior furrowed his brow. He locked eyes with him, and Sev knew he was fucked.

Superior bent down and grabbed the back of his head. Pulled him forward. Nose to nose.

"Dragon!" he shouted.

"Sir," he responded. Refused to look away. His fists at his sides.

"Your eyes are green," Superior said.

"Have been since birth, sir." Sev squinted at him as he responded in his usual tone.

"Don't fuck with me. You stopped taking your shot."

"I take it every morning, sir." He glanced down at his ticker. The minutes still rolling.

"What are you taking?" Superior headbutted him, and Sev felt his skull split in two as he tried to stay upright. His head pounded as he put effort into keeping his eyes open.

"Sir," Maia said. Mason grabbed her shoulder to stop her. Bullet stepped closer to the twins. Positioned himself in front of them.

"What are you taking!" He punched Sev's right side. Sev coughed and gasped for air. Mason yelped somewhere behind Superior.

"Sir!" Lynch spoke up that time.

"Leave us! Training is over for the day!" Superior yelled and snapped his fingers at the attendants to clean up.

No training would take place here now. Superior stood over Sev and waited for the riders to leave. Locke pushed Sasha and Yuri forward toward the mansion, muttering that it wasn't any of their business what went on. Bullet was the last to leave behind Maia, pulling a pale-faced Mason behind her. Bullet slapped his shoulder, and it seemed to work. Mason had tried to intervene. His sister was smart. Sev risked a slight nod to Mason before facing Superior.

"You think you can get away with it under my roof, Dragon?" Superior growled at him. Grabbed his gun. Pressed it to Sev's thigh. "What are you taking?"

"Only the shot you give me, sir," he lied.

He'd die before confessing the truth.

Superior ordered an attendant to bring him one of the shots. Sev tensed. Mason warned him about the new drug. *And if you ever had to inject yourself in front of him, it won't kill you. Might make you rage a bit and give you a killer headache.* Seems he was about to find out.

Minutes passed in silence. Superior's gaze didn't leave him. An attendant placed the small box in his hands. He opened it carefully, marveled at the drug. Superior jabbed the needle into Sev's skin, and the purple medicine coursed through his veins. The feeling like an old friend. Superior went back to his chair to watch from a distance.

Sev's vision went out. Not just blurry. Black. Complete darkness. Until suddenly, it was all too clear.

Superior changed his past. His memories. All the pain he endured. Suffered. The training. Killing. The inventions.

His hatred for Superior flooded his entire existence. His arms started to convulse first. Then, his legs. He barely had time to sit up before he vomited in the grass.

Superior laughed and sighed at him. "Dragon, lie to me again. I'll kill you. How mad are you right now?"

Sev stood so fast his brain had to catch up. His hands wrapped around Superior's throat as he reached for his sword. Sev snapped Superior's wrist without a second thought. The chair knocked out from under him. Sev pummeled Superior's face with both fists. Alternating between them. Dirt flew around them as he struggled to get away from his Dragon. Sev's eyes burned from not blinking. All he could see was red.

Superior tried to push him off, but he was too far gone. No matter what he did, Sev wouldn't stop. He grabbed his gun and shot Sev in the leg. He felt a jolt of coldness wave through him. He kept swinging. Superior bled from his nose and lip and cheeks as Sev kept going.

"SEVENTEEN!" Superior boomed.

Lynch ran with Bullet, Maia and Mason at his heels. Bullet grabbed Sev from behind and held him back. Maia tended to Superior's wounds with Lynch. They were trying to avoid an attack themselves. Mason helped wrestle Sev to the ground.

"What did you do to him!" Mason shouted at Superior.

"He needed his medicine! I gave him his shot!" Superior pushed Maia away when she was done with the ointment on Superior's cuts and bruises and his wrist.

Sev thrashed under Mason and Bullet. His shoulder popped, and Mason screamed.

"Sev, please stop. I'm begging you." His voice wavered. "Please. You're hurting yourself."

Bullet pulled Sev's arms behind his back and tightened his grip. Sev growled like an animal as he fixated on Superior. Mason grabbed his cheeks and forced Sev to focus on himself. Sev peered into his eyes and saw his own staring back at him. The purple faded in and out.

"Sev, snap out of it! It's the rage coming through. Push it out. Push it away. You got this. Calm down. Deep breaths." Mason talked him through it. The maze came back to him. The white flowers floated behind Mason as he spoke. Their storage room kiss lifted to the top of his memories. Sev stared at Mason's mouth. Was it real? Was any of it real?

"He's a fucking monster!" Superior yelled as he raised his sword.

"You made him this way," Maia said and held her own sword up to stop him.

Mason kept his focus on Sev. His fury still waved through him like a whirlpool. Bullet kept his arms tight.

"Breathe, buddy," Lynch said over his shoulder at Sev. He pulled the cap on his head down. It was barely on from running to his aid. Lynch lifted a toothpick to his mouth before joining Maia's side with his own blade.

"I got you," Mason whispered to Sev.

Superior lunged at Maia and Lynch blocked his sword from even touching hers.

"You're done. All of you," Superior snarled.

Sev coughed and took steady breaths as he focused on Mason. Worry covered his features. Bullet tapped his arm, and Sev put one hand on Mason's shoulder to prepare for the pain. Bullet worked fast and popped his shoulder back into place. Sev screamed out, and Mason trailed his fingers into Sev's hair to calm him. Sev pushed away from him to get up. He needed to be ready for this fight.

He wobbled before he got to his feet and groaned as Mason helped him stand. The spot Superior shot him was now sore. When Superior snapped his fingers at an attendant, Sev turned to the girl.

"Don't move," he said, and she froze in fear. Her hood fell back to reveal her face. He recognized her. The one he growled at before the first race. She spilled on his boot.

"I am Superior!" His shout reverberated off the trees around them.

Sev leaned on Bullet to stand up straight, and Mason let go of him. "How long did you know there were alternative drugs I could take? Ones that wouldn't make me rage out like a lunatic. Ones that wouldn't make me feel like I lived in a glass coffin. The limits I tested on myself the last twenty years are unimaginable." He stopped to shake his head and make his eyesight come back. Mason held his hands out to steady him.

"You." Superior aimed his sword at Mason. Maia pushed her brother back, and Sev tugged him further away. Bullet drew his blade beside the men with a grunt.

"Hey," Maia said. As soon as Superior looked her way, she shot him in the gut with his paralyzing dart.

"What the hell!" Sev yelled.

"Sweet dreams," she whispered as he hit the ground. She pressed the release on the Memory Bomb Sev had given her and held her breath. Lynch made sure everyone was clear of the smoke.

twenty

"We modified the bomb you gave me. He'll be asleep for two hours. We gotta go," Maia said to Sev.

She pulled out a small black phone from her boot. It looked nothing like Sev's phone. Hers was thick and long with three buttons on the side. She turned it on and dialed as Mason grabbed for Sev. Checked him for injuries. Made sure the smoke didn't get in his lungs.

"Are you okay? What do you feel? Can you see okay?" Mason asked. His eyes tracked him up and down.

"I'm fine," Sev choked out. His head spun. Mason brushed his thumb over his cheek, and Sev blushed.

"Don't," Sev whispered.

"Shut up." Mason chuckled. Maia led them toward the trees. Mason grabbed Sev's hand and pulled him along.

Lynch went to the attendant and spoke to her quietly before running to catch up to the riders. "He'll be here soon to take Superior to his room. She won't talk. I'll talk to the men tomorrow. I'll make sure we're all on the same page in front of Superior."

"We're getting Drake inside. Right now," Maia said.

"Drake?" Bullet asked. Maia bit the inside of her cheek. Bullet coming with them was clearly not part of their plan. They headed for the woods on the edge of the property. The sun leaked through the branches to light their way.

"Sorry for the bomb we just dropped," Mason said.

"We knew it was coming. Just didn't think Superior would notice." Lynch sighed.

Of course he would notice. Superior was around him twenty years. Punished Sev for not having all of his buttons clasped when he was ten. Yelled at him for specs of dust. With Superior, everything had a place. And everything must be in its place.

"I'm a fool." Sev shook his head.

"No. He's just a tyrant asshole," Mason snapped.

"Listen, buddy, we've got a lot to discuss. All of us. There isn't time. Just know we did what we did for you. To help you," Lynch said.

Sev didn't understand. Too many moving parts. He didn't know their plan. Didn't understand what Lynch meant. What had they done for him? His head still hurt. His lungs burned as he tried to keep up with them. Twigs and leaves brushed his arms as he struggled to run in a straight line beside Mason. Bullet eventually put his hand on Sev's good shoulder to help him keep it together.

"Yo D." Maia raised the phone to her ear. "Meet you there. Five. Yeah. Listen." She looked at Sev behind her. "Uh, never mind. You're gonna freak." She laughed. "He's with you?" She started to run faster. Lynch sped up and hit Maia's shoulder. Pointed at the Guard wall.

A square piece, about the size of his fist, stuck out as Sev approached. Lynch put his hand to the small square, and a scanner popped out.

"Sev," Lynch said.

He had never been out here. How could his print work? Lynch grabbed his wrist and forced his hand to the scanner. Voices whispered on the other side. The wall raised enough to see four dark covered shins and bulky boots. Sev stared at his friend for a moment. More and more questions began to arise. How long had he been working with the mates against Superior?

"Drake?" Maia asked.

"G?" Mason called out.

"Mase!" Sev heard someone respond. His stomach tightened at the tone. Excitement. A smile played on Mason's lips, and his eyes lit up.

A man rolled through the opening and stood fast. His bright blue hair stood on top of his head four inches high. Sev recognized him from the photo. Gage. He smiled at Mason and then at Lynch before he froze. He was looking at Sev. Took a step back.

Three more people came through the opening. Two girls about the same height. One had dark skin and leather pants with long hair in a braid over her shoulder and a scowl. While the other had auburn waves blowing around her face. She wore jeans and a matching black leather jacket to the other girl. The logo looked familiar to Sev, though he wasn't sure why. A burning tree. This girl was a rider?

Sev eyed the man last. Short dark hair, bright eyes, muscular and a set jaw. He was all dark, mysterious and way younger than Sev expected. This was their Superior?

Team Evolution captain. He'd seen the logo on the screens around the Valley.

Their Superior noticed Sev and grabbed for his belt. Before Sev could react, Mason had the man's arm in his hand.

"What the fuck is he doing here?" he snarled at Mason. His eyes not leaving Sev's, but his words were for Mason.

Bullet stayed behind them. In the shadows. He looked all around them and the tree line for any potential threat.

Sev stiffened. He felt his brain trying to fight the Prophilac again. The rage bubbled at the potential fight.

"Drake." Mason paused and let his arm go. "This is Sev."

"Sev?" Gage asked. He had never heard the name. That was sure. His eyes scanned Mason and Sev several times. Mason blushed.

"No." The brunette gasped. Drake glanced at her before looking between the boys.

"Wanna clue me in, babe?" Drake said.

"D," Maia chimed in. She motioned swiftly with her hand at Sev and then to her brother. "I told you you'd freak. And I told you we made some interesting friends over here. I warned you Mason had a fucked up situation going on."

"Sev is the guy!" Gage screamed. His smile widened and bolted to Sev. Wrapped his arms around him. Sev grunted from the blow and winced from the physical contact.

"Cool it, Gage," Mason whined. "Sorry. Told you he was a character."

"Hello," Sev said, and Gage hugged him again.

"Oh my, you are too cute. Tell me everything. Immediately. Are you really a merciless killer? With this face? I can't imagine it." Gage talked so fast that Sev had to read his lips to catch every word that spilled out.

So Gage *had* heard of him. From Superior or Mason?

"Gage, please. More important shit going on..." Mason pointed towards the group.

"Yeah, okay." Gage rolled his eyes and whispered to Sev, "Later."

"This is Bullet." Mason introduced him and Bullet stepped forward, taking in all the new faces.

"Hey there, cutie. What team are you from?" Gage asked.

"Knuckles." Bullet cracked his human fingers with his metal hand. Gage's eyes went wide at the non-human hand. For a rider, he seemed on edge.

"Quit scaring my friends." Maia chuckled. He went back to the shadows and watched the area around them.

Gage went over to Lynch and pulled him into a hug. Sev had never seen Lynch smile that big before. Tears in his eyes.

His story. Sammy, his brother. The Guard. Was Gage his nephew? This was how everything was connected. How the twins got inside the Valley. It was all Lynch.

"You serve Superior?" Drake landed his question on Sev.

He paused. "I did."

"It's complicated," Lynch supplied.

"And you are?" Drake asked.

"Drake, this is Lynch." Gage smiled at him.

Lynch stepped forward with his hand out for a proper shake. Drake hesitated before he took it. "I've been with the kid since he was eight. Superior's done a number on him. If I can speak freely, sir?" he asked Sev. Who then nodded once. "Superior brainwashed him. Since he's been on the new drug, he can make his own choices. Before he couldn't even see straight. Everything was for Superior." He paused. "Until Mason."

Everyone's attention went to Sev. His cheeks heated. He put his hands behind his back to find that comfort in his usual ready position.

"Sev is Second. Superior puts everything on him. Everything goes through him. Every mission, every kill, every threat." He took a beat before he continued, "Every punishment."

"Punishment?" The brunette pushed through the group. She crossed over to Sev. "Sorry, I'm Elle. Good to meet you." She smiled at him. He didn't smile back. "I've only heard rumors about you. I apologize for believing them."

"Don't. They're probably true," Sev said.

She chuckled. "So you have a snake's tongue, a gun for a leg and only have one ear because you ate the other?" Elle asked and tapped her leg with her fingers as she spoke. Nervous.

"All true," Sev said.

Mason laughed. The sound echoed off the Guard wall.

"We have no time. Listen," Maia said. "Sev is one of us now. He's got a ton of issues, but we all do. He's also risked his life for us on multiple occasions. Including taking a sword to the gut for Mason. He also helped kill the wrong mate so Gage could continue sending letters to us."

"Knew that was you," Bullet mumbled. His eyes still scanned the area. It was quiet where they were. Unsettling. Not a bird in the sky.

Drake eyed Sev again. "That true?"

Sev nodded. "I care about him."

The Black girl in the back finally opened her mouth. She hit Drake's shoulder. "Dude, this guy is worse than you."

"Shut the hell up, Vero," Drake said.

Sev didn't understand, but Gage and Elle laughed hard.

"That came out easier this time," Mason whispered to him.

"Don't get used to it," Sev said.

Lynch led them all back to the mansion. An hour and thirty-nine minutes before Superior would wake up. Elle handed Lynch a small clear bag with three syringes in it. Different colors. She explained what each did and how to use them and when. First one being the one to make Superior sleep when he woke from the dart and Memory Bomb. He'd have to be confused in order for their plan to work.

"Superior is in lab four," Maia informed Lynch, her eyes on the phone in her hand.

"Listen up, Sev." Lynch pulled his attention away from the boys. "Remember what I said? We all did this to help. You believe me? Us?"

Sev did believe him. Still didn't understand everything fully. He was also exhausted and groggy, and his body ached. But he trusted him.

"I gave you the first pill," Lynch said.

What pill?

Lynch waited a full minute before he continued. Stared at Sev. Assessed him. "The day you met the twins. I made that note. You took a pill that morning. Do you remember? Mason gave you the second one."

Mason gave him a pill in the maze. The first one. What was he talking about?

Superior left him a pill recently. Was that what he was referring to? Was that the morning before meeting the twins? He remembered taking something. There was a note on his nightstand. It wasn't handwritten. It was printed. Superior had always handwritten his notes.

He really was a fool.

Lynch was in on this? His breath came out harder. His nails bit into his palms. Lynch had so many opportunities to tell him. Come clean. Confess. They all lied to him.

Maia took over as she slowed her steps to walk beside Sev. "I thought I'd be able to seduce you like all the other dumbasses in this Valley. Like Jameson. Idiot. I was too angry that day to turn on my charm. Didn't realize I wasn't your cup of tea." She nudged his arm with hers.

Mason pushed her softly out of the way and took the explanation from there. "Maia was the one to realize you liked me. Wanted me to flirt with you to force you to join our side. That's what she's always done." Mason stood beside Sev. Took his hand. "She didn't know at that point I had already fallen for you. When I saw you, I knew all those videos and articles I'd read of the 'Vicious Second to Superior' weren't true. Your eyes told me everything. More purple than I'd ever seen."

This was planned. From the very beginning. Everything. Before Sev had even met them. He'd taken that first pill before entering the library that day. That first interaction with the twins, he had already been free.

"You tricked me?" Sev dropped his hand from Mason's grasp. Deceived him. Lied.

All the conversations in the library and the maze? The training sessions? The letters to Gage? All of it? Was fake. All a game. All deception.

"We were going to. That was the plan. At first." Mason chewed on his bottom lip.

Sev's hands began to tremble. Mason grabbed onto them again and turned him toward himself. They stopped in the middle of the path. Bullet had to swerve to not run into them.

"Listen to me. The plan went out the window after the maze. I told Maia I had real feelings for you. I wanted you to take the pill to join us. To come with us. To get you out."

Had Maia really been on Prophilac, or was that a lie too? He'd ask more questions later.

"What about Lynch?" Sev asked.

"I hoped you'd join my side after taking the first pill." Lynch jumped in from the front of the line as they entered the trees further. Walking faster as the mansion came into view. "You were too far gone, though. Wish I'd met these two sooner."

They were trying to save him? Give him the pill to get him away from Superior. Or get him to be more pliable to kill? His mind raced with all the possibilities. He tried not to let the rage take him in the moment. No matter the beginning, he was alive. Beside Mason. Wasn't the journey worth it? He was off the shots. Could see clearly. Breathe. Experienced so many things the last month because of the pills. To get here, would he change anything?

No.

Sev took another deep breath. Calm. Stay calm.

"We also have known Lynch a couple years now," Maia added. "Not only is he Gage's uncle, he's also friends with Patrick."

Patrick? Ex Guard. On team Wrath. Made sense. He was the one who pointed him in the direction of Jameson.

Maia directed all of them into the library and shut the door behind them. Sev went over to the chairs, remembering Maia sitting in it the first time they met. Ares on the ceiling seemed so fitting. War on their horizon. Now the room felt very full with all of them inside. Maia locked the door so no attendants could enter. Bullet went straight to the desk.

"What on earth are you doing?" Elle asked, coming up to the front of it as he started opening the drawers on the left and emptying them on the top. She looked through some of the papers he spilled.

"Finding the information I need," Bullet said.

Sev went around to his left side and opened the secret compartment on the side. It was empty. Whatever had been there, he'd taken with him.

Maia tore into the top drawer on the right. She pulled out a small black cloth bag, and whatever was inside clinked together. Emptied six into her palm. They were small, white, and hard. Maia lifted one up to the light.

"What the hell is this?" she asked.

"Maia." Bullet grabbed her wrist with his metal hand gently. He took the object from her and added it to the bag. Covered her hand with his.

Closed his eyes before proceeding to empty the items back into the bag. He let her go, cinched the bag closed, and grabbed the notebook underneath it.

"Do I want to know?" she asked quietly.

"Finger bones," he told her.

Maia gagged as he flipped open the notebook.

"What the hell for?" Elle asked as she rounded the desk to stand beside Maia.

Sev crossed the room and started to read over their shoulders. Numbers and letters covered the page. Luckily, Sev knew the code. Bullet put his hand on the page and started to scan.

"How do you know its finger bones?" Vero asked from the chair in the center of the room. Drake sat beside her and Lynch. They were trying to come up with their next step. They needed a plan. Gage scanned the bookshelves. Opened a few and then put them back.

"Fuck," Bullet said to himself. He could read the code? "Fuck!" He punched the notebook, and the desk moved under his force.

"What's it say?" Maia asked.

"Fuck!" Bullet screamed and put his hands on his head as he turned to the window. "There's a chip."

Drake strode over to the desk to see for himself. "Can't just take it out?" He pointed at Bullet's metal digits.

"I have other metal parts," Bullet murmured. His eyes empty as he turned and quickly skimmed the next page of the notebook. Then the next.

"Other parts?" Gage asked and looked at Maia with wide eyes. Then he smiled and gave her a nod. Maia flipped him off, and Vero laughed into her fist from across the room.

Drake looked at Bullet's hand. Then the notebook. "You know about the other army."

Bullet grunted as a response. Sev assumed he meant yes.

"What other army?" Elle asked, bringing the focus of the room back to their increasing problems.

"We're in it," Maia said.

"No." Bullet shook his head and put his hands down. "That's not the real one. You think he'd have an army where mates could have free will again? Leave whenever they want?"

"Like Patrick," Sev said.

"You know Patrick used to be Guard?" the twins spoke at the same time. Mason faced Sev while Maia asked Bullet.

"He's the one who brought me here," Bullet said. He shoved the notebook at Sev. Patrick brought Bullet to the Valley? "Read it." Sev opened it, and Bullet pointed to the paragraph. "Read it!"

"Hey!" Mason stepped up next to Drake on the other side of the desk.

Sev cleared his throat. "Sixty-two right foot, eight zero, thirty-four zero, fifty-two left knee, twenty-two zero, fifty-seven zero, eighty-four zero, sixty-three spine—"

Sev stopped and looked up at Bullet. His eyes glossed and red.

"When you put that piece in, was there a computer chip in it?"

"Yes," Sev answered. He remembered it. Vividly. No haze. Sev remembered back to all those times he helped with hands or a knee replacement. Always a computer chip inside. He never really thought anything of it. Probably from the Prophilac. Thinking back now, though, it made sense. He figured Superior used it to track the mates.

"Fuckin hell," Drake said as his shoulders slumped. Elle put her hand on his back.

"You were in the Medicine Trials," Sev said softly to himself. He started to piece everything together. "Patrick brought you. That's what you said. Not all those children died that day." His head still thumped, but it was getting less and less.

"He's building an army. No limit. No boundaries. I could be Valley's away, and if he activated the chip, I'd come running. Turning mates into soldiers. Without free will."

Superior would have backup accounts and codes. He'd have others on his side just in case something happened to him. Even if they killed him, the soldiers would still be chipped. It just became imperative to remove it. Or destroy the chip somehow. His mind started reeling on the possibilities. Their options. He needed his lab.

Bullet turned to Sev. "You have to kill me."

"What?" Sev said and closed the notebook.

"What the hell?" Vero rolled her eyes from the chair. She got up and joined the group around the desk. Lynch followed her and stood beside

Drake. Folded his arms over his chest and played with his toothpick between his teeth.

"Nobody is killing anybody," Mason said.

"He will activate me. Order me to kill whoever he wants. Know who I'll come for first?" Bullet sneered. "Your sister."

Mason stiffened.

"What? Why?" Maia asked. "Why the hell would it be me first?"

"You're saying Sev put the chip in your spine?" Elle asked. "You can't take it out?"

"Not without an experienced doctor," Sev said.

"I know a couple doctors. But not ones who perform surgery." Elle shook her head.

Sev would have to remember that for later. Maybe he could print his scans and give them to her? Maybe he could get results without having to worry Mason at all. Get a second opinion.

"Why were you the one to put it in?" Drake asked.

"I invent the creatures on the track," Sev said. The group went silent. "Forced to. But it helps keep me sane. Designing new weapons and animals for the track and Guard. Mates, too."

"No way," Vero said. "Dude, that's awesome!"

"Not now, V," Drake snapped at her.

She slid a finger over her mouth and turned it as if she had a key to lock it.

Sev opened the notebook again. Trying to read as fast as possible with the coded words.

"I'm fucked," Bullet said.

"No, you're not," Maia said. "Do you know when he plans to turn it on? All the chips?"

"Before he takes Graves Valley. Right after the fourth race, I would assume," Sev said as he kept reading the notebook. He handed it to

Mason, and they locked eyes. Mason went to the first page and sat down. Quickly flipped to every page and started to memorize each one.

His trick would come in handy today.

Lynch pulled Bullet with him to help Patrick with Superior in the lab as their time was running out. Sev reminded Lynch to delete the camera footage and mess with the time loop so if Superior was suspicious, he could look back on it being empty rooms all day.

Vero went back to the chair. Stepped heavier on one side. The way she maneuvered to sit down. Ideas started to spiral inside Sev, and suddenly, he was back in the workshop in his mind. A metal leg with secret blades and a hidden compartment. Maybe even a section for a Memory Bomb or a Stick Taser. He wanted to ask what materials it was made of.

Maia came up beside him and slapped him on the shoulder. It was unexpected. His body went rigid, and he felt it all over again. Superior's throat in his hands. The chair in the basement. Mason grabbed his arm when his breath hitched.

They were talking, but Sev only heard every other word.

Sev's arm started to shake. Head spun. The room shrunk. A scream echoed. Blood oozed. His head pounded in his skull. Over and over like a hammer in a garage. Like he was creating himself inside his lab. He'd have to put all his friend's DNA into his compartment like he did with the tiger for Mason. Don't hurt them. Don't hurt your friends.

"His eyes are purple," Maia said.

"What's that mean?" Elle asked.

Nobody answered her.

Mason pulled Sev into a hug and wrapped his arms around him. "I got you. Calm down."

He repeated over and over until Sev snapped out of it. When Mason's voice was louder than the hammer. Instead of pushing him away, Sev nuzzled his head into him. He could feel Mason's chest rise and fall with his breath.

"Don't let me rage out again. Please, don't let me, it hurts. It hurts so bad," Sev said. He spoke so quietly. Maia wiped her eyes beside her brother.

Drake cleared his throat so Mason would step back. Drake had thick arms. Big boots. A large frame. Closer to Bullet in size than he'd realized before. But shorter than Mason. Everyone was, though.

"Sev, you're one of us now. We got you." He held his hand out, and Sev took it immediately. They shook, and Drake nodded to Mason before turning to Maia. They went back to planning in the chairs with Vero.

"What were you thinking? I saw you zone out," Mason asked.

Sev peered at Vero. Observed her body language and how she sat down in the chair. How she kept one leg straighter than the other. Mason followed his gaze and still didn't seem to understand. Oblivious. He asked him again, but Sev stayed quiet.

Vero glared at the boys. "What are you looking at, dude?"

Elle snapped her attention to her teammate. "V," she scolded.

"May I?" Sev asked. He walked over to her and bent down in front of her. Mason sat down in the chair behind him. Drake covered his mouth with his fist as his eyebrows shot up.

Vero shrugged. "Sure."

She rolled her pants leg up, and Mason gasped.

"Hm," Sev said. He looked her leg up and down before speaking his thoughts out loud. "Too heavy for you."

"Excuse me?" Vero chuckled.

"Man, your bedside manner is top-notch," Maia said. Vero laughed.

"I could improve this." He tapped her knee with his index finger. She gaped at him as her eyes glossed over.

"You're serious?" Drake asked him. He crossed his arms over his chest. His jacket made that squeaking sound he despised.

"Very. Would you like that?" Sev asked.

"Like that?" Vero chuckled. "If I weren't gay, I'd kiss you."

Everyone laughed. Sev went red.

"I won't," Vero reassured him. "What would you need from me?"

"Measurements." Sev walked over to the desk and had her follow.

twenty-one

All of them chatted in the library to come up with a plan. How to stop Superior from creating his army. How to end the Championship that killed mates every year. How could they prevent more Guard deaths? Mason stayed by the desk and memorized Superior's notebook before positioning everything back where it had been. Superior could not know anyone had been in there.

They had to take Superior down without a complete rebellion or massacre. They had to find out his plan with the soldiers. The chips. How could they stop him? How could they prevent it?

"Think you'll be able to handle a few more days?" Elle asked Sev as he sat down. He wrapped his arms around his knees and kept his boots flat on the ground. Vero sat on the chair across from Maia.

"He can handle anything," Mason said from behind the desk.

Gage stood by the bookshelf and pulled one out. He flipped through the pages and read a couple lines before slipping it back on the shelf.

"Finger bones," Gage said to himself. "An odd thing to collect. Don't you think?"

When Sev fought Knox, they shook hands right before their duel. He had winced. Was he missing a finger? He was wearing a glove. Most riders wore gloves, though. So every mate wearing gloves could be in the army? That formed a rock in the pit of Sev's stomach. The most logical theory was that Superior needed a body part to replace to insert a chip inside.

"In Superior's mind, they probably feel like trophies," Maia said.

"Sev," Mason grabbed his attention, "we'd need you to pretend nothing happened. Can you lie to Superior?"

A year ago? Absolutely not. Today?

"Yes."

"What about kill him?" Drake asked. His muscles bulged under his leather jacket. Sev could understand why mates feared him. How the news easily made it seem like he was a psycho killer like they had done with Sev.

Sev paused to think about his question. He'd killed thousands before. Yet this was tricky. His entire life was serving Superior. Give him anything and everything he asked for without question. Since taking the pills, he could finally think for himself. Sev knew Superior's death would help thousands if not millions. But he also knew the consequences. It would set off a domino effect. They weren't ready for that. At least not today.

Sev paused. "I almost did earlier. But I was raging out. He injected me with my old medication. When my eyes are purple, I can't see. I can't think. I only feel fury. I only see blood. I lust for it. Understand?"

"Purple means run. Got it," Vero said.

Elle sat with her legs crossed in front of her. Drake was beside her with his hand on her thigh. He kept rubbing her leg until she covered his hand with hers. It seemed to ease his tension.

"Why do all of this? The disease. The Medicine Trials. The new army with chips," Elle thought out loud to the group around her.

"Control. The Medicine Trials were the test subjects. The best one would win. To choose a secondhand man for Superior. It's always been about control," Drake answered.

"But Sev wasn't the strongest," Maia said. The wrinkles in her forehead exposed as she shook her head.

"I didn't say the strongest. Sev was the smartest."

"No, I wasn't." Sev shook his head. "I climbed into the dragon's stomach and started pulling every wire I could see. I wanted to die."

Elle grabbed Drake's hand.

"I understand that. Better than anyone," Drake said as he hung his head. Elle squeezed his hand, and he locked eyes with Sev. "Now it's time to fight back."

"I'm in," Sev said. "I'm still staying, though." He turned to Mason. They had already been over this. There was no other option for him. No other way.

"Why on earth would you do that?" Elle asked.

Gage stopped searching the novels and leaned on the shelf behind him to focus on the group. His hair stuck straight up inches over his head, giving him the illusion of height. With his hair, he was almost as tall as Mason.

"Superior will hunt him if I leave," Sev said. "He knows I care for him."

They still couldn't kill Superior. It would be easy. Fun even. But who is next in line? Someone just as bad. With all the codes and information needed for the army. A plan was always in place when it came to Superior Ashbury.

"What do you mean?" Mason asked as he walked over to the chairs. He slipped his jacket off and held it in his lap. Sev wished he could go back to the day they had met in this very spot. Where Mason wasn't constantly in danger from Superior. He sat down beside Sev and put his back to the chair Maia rested in. She ruffled her brother's hair, and he fixed it with a groan.

"The day I ignored you on the field, I didn't speak a word," Sev said to Mason. "Superior threatened to take a limb...of yours. If I leave, he'll know where I am. Who I'm with. He has connections everywhere. Now an army with computer chips he can control. Track. He'd never stop until you were worse than dead. Blind, beaten, and without arms or legs."

"Would he actually..." Gage stopped when Sev nodded.

"I've seen him do it with my own eyes. More than once. Rip an arm off and leave them to bleed out. Or take one eye and put it in their pocket for their family to find them."

"And if you stayed, what would he do to you?" Vero asked.

Sev didn't respond. The silence answered for him. The group all looked at each other briefly before Maia spoke.

"What's he done to you in the past?"

Gage leaned on his knees with his elbows. Drake nodded to him. Telling him it was okay to speak the truth.

"I defeated the dragon when I was eight. The next three years, I was conditioned. I only ate when Superior allowed. Drank when he allowed. Spoke. Sleep was only permitted in two-hour spurts. I was kept in the basement chair room."

"What's that?" Vero asked.

"He'd strap me in, and every time I got an answer wrong, I'd be Zapped. Or poisoned. Or struck. Last time was a result of being late." He undid his ticker to reveal his wrist. The recent wound still red and healing. Elle shivered and covered her mouth.

Sev continued. "He forced me to design weapons every day, inside my mind, and then create them to torture me with. My first invention was the Lightning Zap. Every time my answer didn't sit well, he'd use it on me. I found out recently he messed with my memories. Used Memory Bombs on me. Then inserted false memories. I can kind of figure out which ones are real now. The fake ones are hazy. Real ones are not. No blur."

"Sev," Mason exhaled. He lifted Sev's hand up and kissed his palm. Sev knew it was a lot to reveal. Too much had happened to him to tell them all right now. It didn't feel wrong to explain to them, though. He trusted they were on his side. And he'd do anything to get Mason out of there.

"Go on," Gage encouraged him.

"Eventually, my entire life became Superior. I didn't care about anything but him and his needs. And wants. Whatever order he gave, I would commit. No matter what. Fight, jump in front of cars, drown."

Elle winced. Drake put his arm around her shoulders, and she leaned into him.

"He blocked Superior getting shot with an arrow, pulled it out of his own shoulder and shoved it through a mate's eye," Maia explained.

Drake laughed. "I've done worse."

"You have?" Sev asked. He'd never seen anyone fight like him before. Barbaric.

"Sev doesn't see clear in those moments. That's the rage." Mason shook his head.

Sev shrugged. "What's the difference? I was on the new drug when I stepped in front of you. I thought I would die. Isn't that the same thing?"

"No." Drake chuckled. "No. One is for someone else, the other is being someone else."

"What do you mean?" Sev asked.

"You're someone else when the rage takes control. When you took that blow for him, that's doing it for him. Two very different things."

"Drake's tried dying for me on many occasions," Elle added.

"Yep, me too." Vero nodded. "Damn idiot."

They all laughed. Gage nodded. "For sure. We still love him, though." He pinched Drake's cheek. He smacked his hand away with a grunt.

"Hey, where's Josh?" Mason asked. The room went silent. Mason studied the response. "Gage?" he choked out. His eyes told him. Mason stood. The air left his lungs in a gasp. "Gage."

"Mason. I'm sorry. I wanted to tell you. But...I just couldn't. I'm sorry." Gage's tears came slowly before they began to pour down his cheeks. "He died in the last race. He helped us win. I left with Aster."

Oh no. The letters. Smiles. The back porch with iced tea.

"What do you mean?" Mason said. "You sent me that photo. The two of you, together. When? When did it happen?"

"You assumed he was with me. And I loved that. Probably too much. I'm sorry. I'm sorry I lied. I liked living in that fantasy world. The one where I got the happy ending. And my love came with me," Gage said.

Sev thought of Fantasy Mason. He understood wanting to live in that world. The one where he got everything he ever wanted.

Mason's breath caught in his throat. "Why would you do that?"

"Mason," Maia started.

"No, you don't understand. I've been looking forward to that. Going to the Cove. Seeing Josh. Seeing the two of you together. Don't you get that?" His voice cracked. "You fucking liar!"

"Mason," Maia tried again. More stern.

"No, you're a fucking asshole," Mason snapped.

"Alright. Let's get you out of here." Vero stood and grabbed Mason. Sev led them out and turned to tell Maia they were going to his lab.

Mason followed with ease as he entered lab two. He showed Vero around the room, and she was amazed at all the inventions. Even more than Mason had been.

Sev started his plans for her leg immediately. He input the measurements and plans he had thought of. Typed into the computer as Mason pointed out certain weapons and creatures to Vero. As they got further,

Sev realized they probably thought he couldn't hear them from across the room. They were wrong.

"When you first met Sev, was he all robot like Maia said?"

"Kinda, but not really. It's hard to explain. I understand what Maia is talking about when she says that shit." He shrugged. "He was just so different from what I was expecting. I'd seen him around town. Killing people even. When I entered the library that day, it was as if he was a new person. Seeing the world for the first time. Like he'd just opened a door into a new realm. One where he could see. Feel. His eyes that day were purple, but I don't know, it was something about him." Mason let out a small laugh. "Sounds insane, doesn't it? Love at first sight. With someone you had been trained to fear for years."

"Not insane. I've been through some weird shit. Seems like he cares about you. I mean, the way he saved you is wild. The way he's standing up to Superior for you."

"He's not doing that for me." Mason scoffed.

"Yeah, dude, he is." Vero laughed.

"He's doing that because of all the shit Superior's done to him. Since he was eight. Wouldn't you want to kill him? It's not for me. He's not even coming with me." He shook his head. "And now Josh."

"Sorry he lied. But I totally get it," Vero said.

Mason glared at her. "You get it?"

"If your boyfriend died minutes before you were saved, wouldn't you want to pretend he was there with you?"

Sev understood where Vero was coming from. He himself pretended that he could have Mason. Moments of weakness.

"Might as well be my future." Mason sighed. "He's staying, remember? He won't come. And definitely won't now. Why would he?"

Vero rolled her eyes at him. "So dramatic. Our lives are always life or death. Every day. Just once, I wish we could get a happy ever after."

"Seems Drake and Elle did."

"Yeah, you're right." Vero smiled at Mason. "Assholes."

They laughed together, and he showed her another creature in the far corner.

His laugh made Sev jolt with pain. When they'd gotten moments alone, they were nothing like this. The best day was when they had spent a few hours together in this room. Sev finished typing on his computer and locked everything up under a new password.

Sev put his hands on his head and covered his ears to drown out his future where Mason wouldn't be there. Where his voice wouldn't be heard in the corner of the room. His laugh. His hand wouldn't reach out to hold his.

He needed to get a grip.

Sev jumped when he opened his eyes, and Mason was beside him.

"Didn't hear you," Sev said.

"How could you? You were covering your ears." Mason chuckled. "Vero is meeting us back at the library in ten."

Sev looked around. She'd left the lab, and he hadn't noticed.

The machine was configuring the information he'd entered. Hopefully, by tomorrow, the prototype would be done.

"Sorry about your friend," Sev said.

Mason let out a sigh. "I was a complete dick to Gage. His boyfriend died, and I acted like an asshole."

"Maybe. But he lied. What did he expect?"

Sev looked around at all the creatures in his lab. The room he'd grown up in. Mason held his leather jacket in his hand, and his hair swept over his ear like the first time they'd met. Sev knew he was far from the same man, though. His glass coffin had been shattered with that pill in the maze.

Mason squeezed his eyes shut. "I just thought it would be different."

"You thought it could be us. And now that dream is ruined because it was never real in the first place," Sev said.

Mason looked down at Sev in the chair. "Come with me."

Sev shook his head slowly. "It's not real Mason."

"It could be. Me and you."

Sev stared at him. His cheeks were blushed. Eyes glossy. Adam's apple bobbed.

"Don't say no again. Don't say anything. Let me believe for once that I'll see you every day for the next decade. Please," Mason pleaded.

"Okay," he whispered. Stood from his desk and let the machine continue to work. "Then I'll see you tomorrow."

Sev looked down at his wrist to check the minutes counting down. They had six and a half before they'd have to leave for the library. They could be a few minutes late.

Mason rolled his shoulders and cracked his knuckles as he looked over at one of the creatures on the far wall. He was about to take a step when Sev grabbed his arm. He stared at his own hand as it trailed up to his shoulder. His neck. His jaw. And he pulled him down. Their lips met, and Mason dropped the jacket to wrap his arms around Sev's thin frame.

Sev gripped the bottom of Mason's shirt and yanked it up. Mason ripped it off for him and grinned devilishly as Sev marveled at his body. His dark tan skin gleamed in the light. Mason leaned down to attach their mouths again.

Sev kissed him hard. Like it would be their last. Realistically, it probably was.

Then again, he thought that about the last one.

Mason started on Sev's top button. He jerked away when he realized what Mason was doing.

"Let me see you," Mason whispered.

Sev hesitated before he pulled off his uniform, and Mason lifted his T-shirt. His bare skin wasn't like Mason's. It wasn't a work of art. And yet Mason looked at him like the night sky when they were in the center of the maze. That felt like a year ago.

Mason dropped to his knees, and Sev froze. Mason rested his forehead on Sev's stomach before kissing his scar from the other day. Where the sword entered his body instead of Mason's.

He kissed Sev's body slowly up to his mouth again. Mason swiped Sev's bottom lip with his thumb. "I want this."

"Why?" Sev asked quietly.

Mason cradled Sev's head to his chest. Sev's headache subsided and his calm finally returned. He hoped for good.

The condition forced on him changed the course of his life. If Superior hadn't wanted a Second, maybe he would've met Mason as another rider.

Would he be muscular and fit like him? If he could actually run and exercise, would he? He could now. Would he start?

Would Mason like him like that?

Did Mason even like how he looked now? Breakable. Fragile.

"What do you see when you look at me?" Sev asked. Mason pulled away when a footstep sounded in the hallway. Sev buttoned his uniform as Mason went to the door to listen. Sev grabbed his Zap and handed Mason the longest blade from his thigh wrap.

Sev pulled the door open, and an attendant yelped, dropped a tray, and stared at him as she trembled.

"Apologies, someone else here?" Sev asked.

She shook her head as she gulped. Sev nodded and shut the door.

"This way," Sev said and pulled Mason to the other exit. They crossed to the wall on the side, and Mason eyed Sev. He placed Mason's hand to the scanner. An opening on the floor revealed itself, and Mason chuckled.

"Why'd you do that?" Mason asked as they descended the spiral staircase to the basement.

"So you can easily sneak in and out," Sev responded as he led them toward the library.

"You want me to sneak in?" he asked.

Sev laughed. "I won't tell you not to."

"Why do I feel like something just changed?"

Sev shrugged and turned red.

Mason chuckled. He shoved Sev to the wall and slammed his lips on his. Sev groaned into him. "Must've been your fucking mouth on mine? Is that it?"

"Something like that," Sev said and kissed him harder. "We're going to be late."

"Okay," Mason said, breaking the kiss long enough for one word.

"They'll look for us."

Mason took a step back from him. His pupils dilated. "To be continued."

twenty-two

The entire group walked to the door of the mansion to say goodbye to Bullet and Patrick. They had given Superior the shot. Lynch stayed with him in case he woke up. He would give him the lie they had all agreed on. Superior collapsed on the training field. Heat exhaustion.

While everyone chatted, Sev pulled Elle to the side quickly. He shoved papers into her hand and then a vial of his blood. She folded the scans and shoved everything in her front pocket without question.

"Give these to a doctor. A trusted one. The scans are of a heart and lung," he whispered to her.

She nodded to him, and the corner of her mouth ticked up. "I'm sure I'll be able to whip up some kind of cure for you."

Sev changed his questioning glare to a soft one before he said, "Thank you."

They joined the group again without anyone noticing, and Sev felt a weight off his chest. So much was going on, but he felt like his own condition and not knowing what his real chances were made it worse. Would he even be able to see them in the last race? Would he be able to fight Superior the next time? Or will he collapse? Fade to nothing. Like falling asleep. At least there, he'd see Mason. He always did.

Patrick waved to everyone and opened the door. Before Bullet could take a step, Maia pulled him to her.

"That day after the race…Your teammate was going to hit me, but you took over. You meant to hit me with your fist instead of the metal one, didn't you?"

"I couldn't risk my team finding out I didn't hate you," Bullet said. He chuckled softly and brushed her cheek with his human thumb. He leaned closer when he said, "Take care of yourself. I know you're capable."

He tapped Drake, Mason, Gage, and Sev's fists with his own and waved to Elle and Vero, who stood behind them. Bullet walked out the door and headed after Patrick down the driveway.

"Will you be at the last race?" Maia called after him. No response.

Sev didn't comment on her wet eyes.

Mason led the way back to the Guard wall where they entered. Sev placed his palm on the scanner, and the opening lifted again. The riders were saying goodbye when Mason went to Gage with an apology.

Gage smacked his back and gave him a hug. Gage turned to Sev when Mason said goodbye to Elle.

"Tell Lynch I said bye and that I'll see him soon." Gage smiled before he added, "Glad I met you. Thanks for not killing my friends," Gage said.

Sev laughed and put his mouth to Gage's ear. "Take care of him on the other side."

Gage nodded. "It should be you. I know you think it can't be. I understand. But I hope you change your mind."

"He's safer without me."

Gage pulled away with tears in his eyes. "But happier?"

"He will be. Eventually."

"And you?" Gage asked. "Will you be happier?"

Elle grabbed Gage's arm and told him it was time to go. The four of them crawled back under the wall. The twins walked Sev to the mansion again before leaving him. Mason kissed him softly with a promise of seeing him soon. It was strange to kiss him in front of someone else, but when he pulled away, Maia wasn't even looking. Her eyes were on the spot that Bullet had walked toward. He could see the pain behind her eyes but didn't dare make a comment on it. She hadn't spoken to him about his.

They waited for Superior in the dining hall like usual. Lynch made sure to tell the guys not to speak of the previous day. They were okay with keeping it to themselves. Nobody trusted Superior after Jorge's death and the men from Neptune.

Sev stared at the seat that he'd first seen Jorge in. His orange jacket was such a horrendous shade. Superior walked in, and his blood-red uniform seemed extra fitting that day. His honor pins on his lapel shined brighter. Sev glanced down at the four on his uniform and wanted to rip them out. Should've let that first bullet go through Superior's skull.

Superior snapped his fingers, and an attendant left and came back with meds for a headache. Lynch grinned at Sev. Their plan had worked.

Superior led training that day. Bullet showed up on time but stayed silent throughout the session. Even when he forced Yuri and Bullet to duel six times in a row. He didn't make a single comment. Sev found his eyes a few times and felt they had come to an understanding. He would have to help him get that chip out of his spine. He tried to remember the doctor's name. The one who had put the piece in him. Maybe the name was in that notebook. Maybe other doctors he remembered would be in there, too.

He would help Bullet. He had to.

Maia and Mason dueled as Sasha went against Sev. No match there. Sev won every round. Sasha panted as he tried to get a hit in. Sweat pooled in the center of his chest. He took his shirt off, and Maia scrunched her nose at the sight. Mason laughed at her as they continued to fight each other. Practicing better footwork.

Sev kept his head down and away from Superior's gaze. They didn't want a repeat of yesterday. When they were done, Superior ordered them to run the training course again. He had to make sure they were all better than they were. Sev was convinced he'd try the Hand Press later this week, too. Had to see how much they had improved. Superior was obsessed with growth. His army needed to be better than Guard. Indestructible.

The air was different around the group. Now they all knew this wasn't the real army. They were being used. What was the point in running faster and training harder now? None of it was real. Sev watched Maia as she went through the course at top speed. One person still wanted to be better. He wasn't surprised.

That night, Lynch left on a mission, and Superior called Sev to the basement. He strapped him into the chair. What had he done this time?

Superior circled the chair a few times before locking his eyes on him. Blood pooled on the armrest, and Superior put his hands behind his back and held his position.

"What are your thoughts on Mason from Team Wrath?"

"Good warrior. Lots of potential. Great pick, sir."

"And his looks?" Superior asked.

Sev raised a brow. "His looks, sir?"

Superior circled him again and stopped to Zap him in the back. Sev bit his lip to not yell out. The electric current shot through his ribs.

"His looks, Dragon?" Superior asked.

"He looks good, sir. Fine young warrior."

"Do you love him, Dragon?"

"No, sir," Sev lied.

Superior circled Sev as he spoke. Sev kept his eyes on the door. Focusing on getting out of the chair. Eventually, he'd let him out of here.

"I know the twins are not real riders," he said.

Sev was not expecting that. He didn't falter. Kept his eyes on the door.

"Idiots. Every year, a mate tries to get past me. Getting inside the Valley and entering themselves in the race though, that's new. So that's why I created this fake army. You see, they all think they're one step ahead of me when, in reality, my Dragon, they are so far behind. One way to keep your enemies close, huh?" He smiled at Sev.

"Yes, sir," Sev said softly. "Brilliant, sir."

"I thought adding the girl into the mix would be my ticket to get you close to the twins. I figured a young one with a smart tongue and no fear would be your type. But I've been wrong before. Then I realized it was the boy who fancied you." Superior chuckled and shook his head. "I never put much thought into it before, but then I figured I had nothing to lose. I didn't realize you were so against it all, though. You didn't want either of them."

Sev sighed with relief. He didn't know.

"I am glad. However, I still needed you to be close to them. Needed to know what they knew. How much they knew. Now…I cannot take any risks. Not this close to the end. I know you understand."

Superior went back to the front of the room to grab another weapon from the shelf. Sev prepared before he released the gas into the room. He held his breath as Superior released the Memory Bomb.

His lungs were better now. Stronger. Superior wasn't aware of that. Sev just closed his eyes and slumped forward. Kept his airways blocked until he couldn't hold it any longer.

"Forget Team Wrath. Forget the twins. You don't need anyone other than Superior. Superior of all. Superior for all time. You don't need anyone else."

Sev stayed in the chair another hour before he let him go up to his room. He stopped to breathe in the hallway outside his room. Shut his eyes as he tried to steady his breath. An attendant passed by, and he opened his eyes to stand straight. She stopped and raised her head so he could look at her. She was small. Frail. Young. Light eyes and thin lips. She handed him a napkin, and he took it to wipe the sweat from his forehead.

"Thank you," he whispered.

She smiled at him with cracked lips before returning her gaze to the floor. The attendant walked back towards the kitchen with soft steps.

Superior had planned the army he was training to keep everyone's focus away from the real one. Genius. It had worked. If Bullet hadn't known, they would've never thought that the army was fake. They were training every single day for nothing. What about the others? Sasha, Jorge, and Yuri. Were they training to join the real army? Or were some getting too close, like the twins?

Superior wanted him to forget the one person who had opened his eyes. The one person who had kissed him. He wanted Sev to go back to how he was before. Empty. A robot, as Maia says. Was that his goal with Bullet? Wanted a monster with an actual brain he could control. Or was that his end goal with Sev?

Sev locked his bedroom door behind him and turned to see Mason asleep in his bed. His hair cascaded over his forehead. His shirt rode up to show his midsection. He took deep breaths in and out. Sev considered himself. Bruises and burns on his chest and back. He grabbed his head and closed off his ears again. Silent tears fell as he sank in the dark room.

He shook his head at the flashes of images his brain produced. Mason kissing him. Hugging him. Holding him. Superior. Zap. He flinched, and Mason removed his hands from his ears.

"I got you," Mason said. He pulled him into his arms, and Sev let him.

"Shower," Sev mumbled.

Mason stripped him piece by piece, and Sev winced every few movements. He helped him get in the shower and waited for the water to heat before hanging his head. Sev let his defeat and blood run down his back to the drain as he watched Mason strip on the other side of the clear glass door. His perfectly sculpted body. Mason stepped into the shower and gently scrubbed Sev's arms and chest. Then turned him around to rub his back. His wounds no longer hurt. Just sore.

Mason rinsed Sev again before he wrapped his arms around him. He held Sev to his chest and let him rest. For the first time, Sev wanted to be taken care of.

"He's trying to make me forget you," Sev said. "Don't let him."

"Then let's give you more to remember."

Mason brought his lips down to Sev's.

twenty-three

Today marked the fourth race of the ChaosMotors Championship. Sev got ready fast to meet Lynch and Superior at the front door. Lynch smiled at him before Superior rounded the top of the stairs.

"Good morning, my Dragon. I presume everything is ready?" He combed his fingers through his hair before straightening his uniform one more time. Licked the tip of his thumb before wiping his moustache.

"Yes, sir," Sev said. He held his position as an attendant opened the door wide. Sev went to leave when he noticed it wasn't someone he recognized in the dress. They were a bit older than the usual attendant. Maybe sixteen or seventeen. More muscular. Three dots tattooed under one of their green eyes were in the shape of a triangle pointing down. They winked at him as Sev passed by. Lynch pat his back, and that was the cue for him to let it go. Lynch knew them.

"Think Wrath will win today?" Superior asked.

The test. There was always a test.

"Who, sir?" Sev asked. Lynch looked over at him with wide eyes. Sev kept his focus.

"One of the teams racing today, Dragon." Superior entered the back of the vehicle. Lynch got behind the wheel as Sev slid into the back beside Superior.

"Is that the team you're rooting for, sir?"

"Neptune will win today," he said. The way he said it made Sev's skin crawl. So sure of himself. No other option. He had a tablet tucked under his arm, and Sev tried his best to ignore it. He never brought one before. Why today?

Lynch paved their way to the seats of Superior's choice. He rested the tablet on his lap. A dark screen came up with toggles and levers. Orange and red buttons on one side and green on the other.

"This will be fun." Superior grinned and waved at an attendant to bring him a glass and a plate to munch on. This attendant was the one he was used to. When she got closer, she nodded to Sev. He turned away quick to not bring attention to her.

The riders were getting ready at the line. Sev noticed how many of them wore gloves. Too many. Were all of them in the new army? How did he recruit them? One by one? By force? Choice? Did they willingly lose a finger to be replaced by metal? Were they even aware they were chipped? Too many questions floated around as the Guard walked out in front of the first team. Thick black armor with helmets and glossed bullet-proof shields over the front. Lightning Zaps on their hips and Guard modified pistols.

Guard raised the Zap and shot it in the air. The blue bolt lit up the arena in a flash.

The riders whipped passed him fast as they went up the first ramp and jumped over the spears. The tiger was ready and waiting for them. Teeth sharpened and DNA from all the riders to avoid.

"I forgot to mention something to you, Dragon," Superior said. His eyes darkened on Sev. Mouth tightened. His jaw locked. "Nothing gets past me. Nothing."

What did he know exactly? Sev ran through the millions of ways Superior could kill Mason and Maia and Bullet and all the riders on the track before he even blinked.

"Sir?" Sev said and faced him as the screen turned to one controlling the tiger. He pressed a couple buttons. A screen of all the riders Sev had entered for it to avoid started erasing one by one.

Shit.

"I don't know what you did. But you won't be getting away with it."

Sev froze. The contents in his stomach threatened to come up. Superior was targeting his friends. Mason. Maia. Sev needed to act. Now.

A part of him wished he had a shot of Prophilac to attack him like a bull again. This time he'd get the job done. Cut his damn head off.

Superior brought up a new screen and added the twins to a new project. Their photos. Names. Profiles.

Superior pressed more buttons before sliding his finger to the big red activate on the top left. The creatures glowed red on the screen, and Superior laughed.

"Now they'll be targeted. Your team won't be leaving anytime soon. The only place they'll be heading is hell."

"I don't know what you're talking about, sir," Sev seethed. Breathing hard through his teeth. "You made me forget them. Remember?"

"I noticed your eyes last night, Dragon," Superior said. "Think I'm an imbecile? Lynch, get him away from me before I do something I'll regret. And Dragon, I'll see you later for your punishment. Don't be late." Superior waved to them as he focused on his tablet. The vein on his forehead popped out as he swiped the screen harder.

Lynch grabbed Sev's arm and lifted him from the bench. "Go."

Sev breathed hard as he ran down the steps underneath the arena into the medic area. The sounds of the wheels above made his stomach turn.

Don't die. Not today. All his friends. Mason.

Sev ran faster as he got to the control room. He shut off the Parklings that he'd activated that morning. Went over to the control panel for the

Ogle and shut its eyes off. Went to the panel for the tiger and opened it to find each of the levers torn out.

Superior had thought of this. He was a step ahead.

Sev ran to the end of the hall and watched from the clear glass next to a group of Guard. They stiffened in his presence. Stayed planted though. Held their weapons to their chests like they were supposed to. Had their helmets on tight as they were told. Their boots tied twice. Their pants belted on. If anyone was a robot, it was them.

Sev went around to the other side to watch Mason push another rider into a pit. Maia got side-swiped and hit the dirt as a rider in white came up and around. Suddenly, a rider in red shot a fireball at the white bike, and they missed Maia by inches.

Bullet got her back on her bike, and they took off like cannons.

Sev cheered as Mason gained speed. His smile was gone when Neptune rounded the corner. No helmets. No light in their eyes. They were soldiers through and through.

They had been turned on. Sev could see the white gleam from Superior's smile from here.

Knox hit the gas harder. Swiped his blade straight through a rider's thigh as he went past.

Strength: doubled.

Fear: zero.

They were warriors and nothing else. Exactly what Superior always dreamed of. They were his machines now.

Sev turned to run when an attendant put their palm on his chest. He moved to break it in half until he realized it was the green-eyed one from the mansion.

"Hey," they said. "I'm Fenix. Friends with Gage."

"What?" Wait, what? Gage?

"Drake is here. Plans have changed."

He knew what that meant. They were going to kill Superior. A week ago, Sev would've told them it was a bad idea. But now, Superior had so many on his army. Too many risks. Bullet. Knox. Team Neptune. And all the rest. He couldn't fathom the real number of soldiers in his army now. If they killed him, most of their problems would cease. Assuming nobody else knew the passwords and secrets. The other problem was that they had no idea who was next in line. Who would be Superior if they killed him?

The drain cover Sev used after the first race opened and two people jumped down. Sev turned to see Drake and Vero running at him. Vero wore a huge smile. Drake looked ready to win a war.

"Let's go," Drake said and grabbed Sev's arm.

"Superior changed the creatures. They're all targeting us now. He reversed it."

"We figured he might. Get on the bike. Help where you can."

"What?" Sev asked. "How'd you know?"

Drake shoved a light blue jacket at Sev and put one on himself.

Vero chimed in, "Nate hacked Superior's tablet this morning. Screen capture only. Couldn't get inside from that far away. Elle is in the stands trying to gain access right now. We're hoping she can cut the frequencies from Neptune's chips."

Sev raced beside them, and Fenix waved and ran the other way, pulling the hood back up.

"Who's Fenix?"

"One of Gage's Kiddos. Later, dude," Vero explained and hopped onto a blood-red bike. Thin and sleek with silver lining the wheels. Drake got onto a black one with a clear seat and large handlebars. Sev hadn't noticed his own bike sitting next to his.

"How'd you get my bike here?" Sev asked.

"Lynch," Vero said. She smiled as she threw a helmet at him. He caught it and followed them out onto the track.

"Most of the Parklings are off, and the Ogle is blind. Good luck," Sev said.

"What the hell is an Ogle?" Vero asked.

Sev laughed and pointed at the large creature on the wall across the track from them. He hit the gas and caught up to Bullet fast. He looked at Sev twice before realizing it wasn't a rider from Neptune. He flipped up the helmet visor, and Bullet went wide-eyed.

"Thought you could have fun without us?" Sev said as Vero and Drake zipped past them.

Bullet shook his head with laughter before he pressed on the accelerator harder.

The tiger swiped at a few riders but when Reid tried to pass, it snatched him quick. Chewed off the top half of his body and threw the rest into a pit nearby.

Not Mason. It wasn't Mason. It wasn't Maia. Not Patrick. It wasn't Mason.

Sev finally saw Mason's back tire. He was nearing the tiger again. Once Sev came into view, the tiger ignored Mason and went for him. Sev shot a fireball at it that exploded on impact. Half of its face fell onto the track, and riders had to dodge the debris falling and the large metal pieces sticking out from the gravel.

Mason lifted the shield on his helmet and smiled. "Hey, baby."

Sev rolled his eyes. "You're not calling me that."

They went over a ramp at the same time as Knox came into view. He went around Sev, got in front of Mason, and hit the brake. Mason rammed into Knox's bike and flew over him completely. His back landing in the dirt. Sev swiped Knox and pushed him off his bike. He threw his fist into Knox's gut. He swerved and grabbed Sev's arm. Pulled him forward, and Sev tripped into him. Knox got him on the ground and hit his helmet over and over with his gloved hand. He could hear the metal clang of his pinkie every time he hit. As he stared up at the rider, he could see the blank stare. Nothing inside. No gears turning. Just Superior's soldier.

Mason got up and tackled Knox to the ground, tearing him away from Sev. He stood to help when Mason grabbed a blade from his boot and slit Knox's throat.

Blood sprayed him as Sev ripped him away from the rider. He watched as the light never came back on in Knox's eyes as he died on the track. He didn't deserve that. Didn't blame Mason though. He was just protecting Sev. Superior was to blame. For all of it.

Mason checked Sev for injuries before hopping onto his bike again. He quickly realized the front was too damaged and got on Knox's instead.

Sev searched the track for Patrick and found him near the end around a four-member yellow team and a green rider. At least they weren't light blue.

When he turned back around, he noticed all the yellow members had black gloves on.

Could they all be Soldiers, too?

Sev hit the brake and turned his back wheel to head the other way. He dodged Yuri, who screamed as he swerved around him to ride head-on. Sev shot at the yellow rider who was trying to push Patrick into a pit. He popped his tire, trying to get away. A Guard tried to escort the yellow rider off the track. Instead, he started running full sprint toward them. Gaining speed as they were going up a hill. Sev turned back to see a green rider whack him with a baton on his way past. He hit the dirt hard.

He wasn't getting back up.

Sev helped Patrick fend off the rest of Team Python as the green gained speed. Patrick waved him off, and Sev went around the track a full lap before he got up to Mason. Maia was still in the lead. The Ogle tried to attack but kept missing due to its sight.

Sev's attention went to the stands when there was a brawl in the crowd. The attendant threw the tablet down to Elle who booked it to the medic area.

Superior immediately stabbed the girl in the chest and tossed her into the arena for a creature to grab for dinner. The attendant hadn't lived past her twentieth birthday. Sev remembered her in the hall as quiet and shy. Frail. She had sacrificed herself for them.

Superior was furious as he stomped after Elle. Drake drove his bike right into the medic tunnel from the track, and Elle got onto the back. Drake hopped off the bike, and Elle took over. Drake grabbed a Guard bike from the side of the track and jumped back into the race.

Superior screamed as Elle pressed the right button, and the chips turned off. Roughly fifteen riders stopped in the middle of the track and looked around. They slowed and pulled off to the side of the track, holding their heads.

Sev focused back on the track and trusted his friends to finish what they started. Sev got beside Mason as the arena exploded. He heard the explosion before he knew what was going on.

Clouds of dirt and dust surrounded the finish line. The crowd screamed, and all stood to rush to the edge of the stands.

Bomb.

Mason and Sev sped as they approached the scene. Too much smoke. They couldn't see. Sev tumbled off his bike after Mason. He was running full force toward the center of the explosion.

"Maia!" he screamed.

Could he see her?

Sev ran faster. Mason screamed again as Bullet came into view. He was giving Maia mouth-to-mouth on the ground. Mason slid to put the fire out beside her leg. He yanked his helmet off and threw it when the flame died.

"Come on, you won, fair and square. Don't do this," Bullet murmured as he pressed his hands to her chest. He bent down to give her another dose of oxygen. Then, another round of compressions.

Bullet's side was singed. His sleeve ripped to shreds. His arm had burns up and down where the jacket had charred off.

"Give them space," Sev said to Mason as he went to touch her.

Sev watched in horror as Maia lay dead on the track. Bullet kept talking to her as he used his hands and then gave her another puff of air.

Sev searched the stands for Superior or any Guard who would be responsible. Only mates could be seen. No Guard were left inside. Superior had done this. Killed his friend. Mason's sister. Mason pulled away from Sev and grabbed his sister's hand as Bullet pressed his mouth to hers once more.

Yuri ran to the group and gasped as he threw his helmet. He began a silent prayer with his eyes closed and his hands together. Ten other riders joined him as they came upon them in the dust. Sasha caught up to them and started to speak a prayer out loud.

"I can't do this without you," Mason cried.

"Don't you dare fucking leave like this." Bullet trembled above her as he pressed into her again and again. Sasha's prayer became a group chant from behind Sev. They all watched and waited as Bullet tried harder. He wouldn't give up. They all knew.

Sev kneeled in the dirt beside Mason and placed his hand on Mason's thigh. Maia couldn't die like this. She was strong. Stubborn. Resilient. Couldn't die. Bullet had to save her. Had to. Sev closed his eyes. Couldn't watch anymore. He'd seen thousands of mates die. Couldn't watch this one.

Maia gasped and her eyes flew open. Red and cloudy in the smoke. Bullet's hands shook as he sat back and covered his mouth.

"Maia!" Mason jumped on her with a wail.

"Yo, who the hell blew me up?" Maia croaked out. She pushed her brother off as she coughed into her elbow. Bullet chuckled into his fist.

The riders around them cheered and clapped. She tried to sit up and instantly laid back down. Clenched her eyes shut. She needed to take it easy. Mason placed his hand on hers. Knew she hated to look weak. Maia coughed again and Mason wiped his face with the back of his free hand. Streaks of dirt and tears covered him.

Sev couldn't believe the miracle. He wiped his own tears before he smiled down at the rider. Maia nodded to him once. He got the message. She would be alright.

Cannons erupted, and confetti sprayed all around them. Blue fireworks exploded over the arena, and ash floated.

It was just like the video Sev had seen of Team Falcon winning the race last year. So much blue was around them. And yet, so much death. Pain. Suffering.

The crowd roared. Music blared all around them. Mates ran to congratulate them from the stands as Patrick crossed the line to find his team covered in debris from the bomb. Mason helped Maia stand carefully, and Patrick gave them both gentle hugs. They would have to tell him about his brother.

Sev noticed Bullet walking away. Limping toward the exit. He ran to catch up to him.

"I can help you. We can figure it out."

"Help them. Get them out of here," Bullet said. He didn't stop. His face was coated in dirt and ash. His eyes dimmed. Sev glanced at his burned arm.

"You were wrong, Bullet. You do have a heart." Sev slowed, and Bullet continued out of the arena on foot.

Now Superior was on the loose. And he would turn Bullet's chip on. Sev agreed with Bullet on one thing. For his own sake, he needed to get away.

twenty-four

Mason helped Maia get onto the back of Elle's bike. She fought them the entire time. Kicked. Screamed. Riders were still being nursed at the finish line.

"Where is Bullet?" she screamed.

"We don't know. We'll find him. Get on the bike. He didn't explode in the bomb," Mason said and forced her to stay focused.

"Then where is he?" She turned to glare at Sev. "You let him leave."

"We'll get him later. It's not safe to have him near you right now," Sev explained. Riders were running around with mates in the arena. Trying to get out before another bomb exploded. Nobody knew what to expect.

Fenix waved to them from the entrance of the arena. Drake grabbed Elle and crashed his lips to hers. Sev turned away to give them privacy. Fenix didn't seem bothered. Did they do this a lot?

They were about to leave when Elle grabbed Sev's attention. "In case we...I had someone look at those scans. They'll be just fine. Your friend, I mean."

She was keeping his secret. He appreciated that. Tears filled his eyes. He'd be alright? His lungs and heart. Damaged. Not terminal. All he could think of was Mason. He could spend more time with Mason. "Thank you," he said. She patted his arm and then turned to Drake.

"Don't die," he said.

She winked at him. "See you at Gage's."

Drake led the group to Fenix, and they followed him to the mansion. Sev let them in the basement entrance. Lynch, Vero, and Drake followed Fenix while Mason and Sev stayed in the back.

"She's alright. She's in good hands. Gage has resources in the Cove," Mason said to himself. Over and over. His chest heaved.

"Hey," Sev said. Mason stopped, and Sev wiped his cheek from a patch of dirt. "She's alright."

Mason nodded and swallowed before they caught up with the team. Superior fled to the mansion. Maybe he had a backup tablet.

"This way," Sev said and led them up the set of secret stairs behind a large tapestry.

"Never knew this was here," Lynch said, running to catch up to him.

"You weren't allowed the knowledge," Sev said, and Lynch shook his head.

"Prick."

Fenix got in front of them before opening the door into the hallway. Superior rammed into them, and Fenix let out a sharp squeal. Superior rounded his weapon to Fenix's throat. They rolled to the tile. Mason exploded from the back and bellowed as he attacked. Sev threw a blade to him and he caught it before slamming it to the side of Superior's.

"You tried to kill my sister!"

"She deserves worse. Trying to get rid of my army. I've worked my entire life on this. And you almost ruined it."

"We did ruin it!"

Superior grinned. "You tried." He grabbed Mason's wrist and twisted it. His blade clamored to the ground. Echoed off the walls. Fenix went to grab it when Superior put his weapon to Mason's throat. "Uh uh uh. Don't even think about it."

"Let him go," Sev warned Superior. Placed the tip of his longest blade at his stomach. Ready to spill his intestines on the floor. He pressed into him, and Superior released his grip. Drake pulled Mason behind him. Sev pressed harder, and Superior took a step back.

"Dragon, kill him, that's an order."

"No," Sev snarled at him. Lynch gripped his throwing knife, ready to let it fly. Vero prepared herself beside him, checking behind them for the Guard in the hall.

"No?" he repeated. The sting hit him harder than Sev, pointing his blade at him. Superior cackled in the dark hall. "You think I won't kill you to get to him? Maybe killing you will break Mason just enough."

"You'll never break me. I'll never join you!"

"You will." Superior smirked. "Dragon, last chance or die."

He snapped his fingers, and the door at the end of the hall opened. Guard started marching toward them in rows of four. Their armor fresh and new. He already started his army.

"I'd rather die than watch you breathe the same air as him." Sev glowered.

"No!" Mason cried. Drake stopped him from getting in between them. "Sev, don't do this!"

"Guard." Superior waved them forward.

"Lynch, get him out of here. Don't let him stay inside the walls." Sev didn't take his eyes off the oncoming Guard. Twenty of them came down the hall in deafening synchronized steps.

Superior slipped to the side of the Guard as they kept gaining on them.

"Yes, sir." Lynch grabbed Mason and hauled him down the hallway. Fenix followed after they picked up the blade Mason had dropped. Only their footsteps could be heard. Sev glanced to see Vero and Drake still at his side.

"Death is just a side effect," Drake said and pounded Vero's fist. He held his other out to Sev. He tapped it, and they charged.

Drake punched the first Guard in the side of their helmet, and it shattered. The glass scattered on the floor, and he kept fighting. Sev pulled out his Nin Spin and shot it through three of them in a row before he swung his leg under the last to trip him. He straddled him, pulled the hidden blade from his heel, and slit his throat. Vero grabbed a Guard by the arm, slammed him into the brick wall, and stomped on the back of his knee with her metal leg. The snap of his bone echoed in the hall before his screams.

Superior watched as they destroyed almost two dozen Guard in minutes. Drake pulled Vero to the wall to clear a path. Sev tackled Superior to the ground.

Superior seized Sev's bad wrist, where he knew the fresh wound was. Sev wouldn't falter. He clasped Superior's hands together, placed them on his stomach and kneeled on them. Trapped below him for the first time.

"Coward," Sev shouted in his face. "Who is next in line?"

Superior smiled at him. "I'm not telling you."

"I can figure it out." Sev pulled him up to his feet. They tripped over the mountain of dead bodies, and Vero wrapped Superior's hands together behind his back with a pair of cuffs she nicked off a dead Guard. She undid her hair so it covered her entire back. Only a couple inches longer than Maia's.

Would he ever see her again?

It didn't matter. As long as she was alive. Mason and Maia would survive. They had to. He wondered how far Lynch and Fenix had gotten Mason by now?

Sev led the way to the main office and forced Superior to sit at the computer. He pressed his thumb to the scanner to enter the system.

"You don't know the password." Superior stopped talking when Sev typed it in.

"I'd keep your mouth shut if I were you. Dumbass," Vero said. She grabbed his hair with her fist to force him upright in the chair. He was going to watch every move they made.

Sev got deeper into the system and found Superior's documents. Next in line for the throne, as Mason would say.

He didn't have any children. No blood left. Whatever names were on the document would have to be it. He opened the next file and nearly threw up.

They were fucked.

"Seventeen?" Vero asked. She didn't know his full name.

"See Dragon, I've been training you your entire life for a reason." Superior smiled.

"Change it, right now." Sev placed his blade at his throat.

Superior laughed. "I cannot. Only two ways you get out of being Superior. You're dead. Or you're on the other side of the wall when I die. Seeing as your dues are triple what any other mates is...congratulations on the promotion."

"That's you?" Vero asked.

"Seventeen has been like a son to me since he was eight years old. Isn't that right?" Superior smiled at him.

Sev pressed harder into his neck. His eyes turned to slits. "Change it."

"You'll have to kill me."

"Who's next on the list?"

"Lynch Synder," Drake read aloud. The three of them exchanged glances.

"So, let's get Sev on the other side of the fence and let Lynch take over," Vero suggested. Drake looked over at Sev. He put his hand on the blade, and Sev allowed Drake to take control.

Superior started to argue that he couldn't pay when Vero covered his mouth.

"Listen, Sev," Drake said softly. "I understand. I've been where you are. Quite literally. Choose him. Or you'll regret it the rest of your life."

Sev looked from Superior to Drake to Vero.

"We'll find you," Vero promised with a smile.

"What about Lynch? What if he doesn't want to be Superior? What about Gage being with his uncle?"

"We'll deal with that later. Go. I can't wait to watch this fucks head roll," Drake said. Sev let out a laugh.

"I'll signal. You'll know," Sev said.

Drake nodded. "I'll call Gage. He'll post your dues. No Guard will be after you."

"How will I—"

"Don't think about it right now," Drake said. "Go."

Sev remembered Lynch saying the same word to him the night he went to Resurrect with Mason. Kissed him on the dance floor. Felt light as a feather. Mason forced him to live. Always made Sev feel alive.

twenty-five

Sev ran. Made a quick pit stop in his lab and grabbed his tablet and backpack. He sprinted to his bike at the edge of the property. He knew where they'd go.

He traveled the back roads just in case. Sev hid his bike in the trees and ran for the fence they came through. Fenix's blond head appeared first, and he ran faster. His lungs were stronger than they were a couple months ago.

Sev slid to a stop before ramming into the wall. Lynch yelped, and they stopped. Mason wrapped his arms around him instantly. Tears poured down his face. Sev pushed him off to catch his breath.

"There's no time," Sev said.

Lynch had knowing eyes and pat him on the back. "Finally."

"You knew?" Sev heaved his words as he tried to catch his breath.

"Had my hopes. I've been waiting for you."

"I'll never be able to repay you," Sev told him.

"That I know. Just keep in contact. All of you are welcome any time." Lynch smiled. "Take care of him for me," Lynch said to Mason.

"You're coming with me?" Mason asked Sev. Wide eyed and pale.

"Keep up, would you?" He kissed him full on the mouth.

Sev pulled him through the wall, and they ran. Gage, Elle and Maia stood waiting beside three Chaos bikes. Fenix hopped on the back of Gage's bike with a grin. Maia ran to her brother to wrap him in a hug.

"Where's Lynch?" Gage asked, looking around them.

Sev stopped and raised his Lightning Zap straight in the air. He pulled it, and a green bolt exploded into the sky.

"Shit!" The group hit the ground. They'd never experienced a Zap like his before.

Sev chuckled. "Sorry, forgot to warn you. Had to signal Drake."

Sev explained as they ran to the bikes. Mason got on the blue bike first and Sev wrapped his arms around his middle.

"Hold on tight, baby," Mason said.

Gage led the way to his house. Desert surrounded them. No life. Not even a single tree. No other cars or bikes on the road besides them. They passed a sign to enter Sunset Cove after about two hours. Gage waved, and they all pulled over. He took his helmet off and answered his ringing cellphone. Everyone gathered to hear what was going on.

"Drake?" he asked. His eyes went to Elle. She seemed confused, too.

Something was wrong. Gage nodded and bit his lower lip. He put the phone on speaker.

"Superior is after you. Patrick, he—" Drake coughed and cleared his throat. "Patrick is one of his soldiers."

"What?" Mason turned to Sev.

"Sev," Drake said. "Gage...he didn't make it. Lynch. Superior killed Lynch."

Sev heard the words. It didn't register. Didn't make sense.

Lynch?

"What? What do you mean?" Gage brought the phone closer to his mouth. The shock made his voice crack.

Vero took over the explanation. Her voice came through louder. She'd taken the phone off speaker. "Patrick came in. We didn't know he was one of them. We're still not sure how his chip was turned on. Maybe he's on a different wavelength than the other soldiers. He untied Superior. And dude came hard. Drake fought him. His arm is in bad shape. He'll be alright. Superior took a sword off the wall and came charging at me. That's when Lynch came in. Stepped in front and took the blade instead. Patrick dragged Superior out of there, and we couldn't go after them."

Everyone was silent. Waiting for someone to speak. Nobody did. Mason put his hand in Sev's. He was still trying to process. He couldn't be dead. He just saw him.

Vero spoke again, finally breaking the silence. "He said to tell you, Gage, that he's sorry. He missed out on your entire life. He's proud of you."

Gage handed the phone to Elle. First, his husband, now his uncle. He put his palm to his forehead before sliding it down to cover his mouth as he let out a sob.

He couldn't be dead. No way. There was no way. Lynch had smiled at him. Let him go with Mason. He helped all of them. The past few years. Helped Sev. From the moment he arrived in the Valley, until now.

Sev was reeling. He couldn't imagine his life without him. His best friend.

"And Sev," Vero croaked.

Everyone looked to him.

"Yes?" Sev whispered.

"He said don't forget to live."

three months later

S ev poured three glasses of iced tea at the kitchen counter. Fenix ran after Ace with a baseball bat, and the back door slammed. Sev followed them out to the porch. Large white flowers bloomed around the edge of the deck as the sun touched the hills in the distance.

Gage yelled at the younger two, and they stopped by the table to apologize. Ace had stolen Fenix's hat and refused to give it back. Which led to a chase. Ace threw the hat at his friend, and Fenix caught it with ease.

"Quit acting like children and go fetch me the tablet. We're having a meeting with Drake while you two cook dinner."

"Okay, Papa." Ace gave him a salute and headed back inside the house. He was medium height with bulky arms and thick dark hair on top of his head. His sides were shaved, and a couple hairs were coming in above his top lip. His mustache wasn't full yet. The kid must've been about seventeen, like Fenix.

The two were complete opposites. Fenix stood about a foot shorter with white-blond hair in ringlets on top of their head. Bright green eyes. While they were muscular, they were nowhere near as big as Ace. They slid the hat back on and turned the brim backward before following Ace inside.

Mason kissed Sev's forehead as he sat down beside him. Sev grinned as they clinked glasses. Mason took a sip before winking at his boyfriend.

"Is Vero's leg alright?" Mason asked Gage.

"It's wonderful. She says thank you." Gage had his hair done up in his usual mohawk. The blue stood out more today in the bright sun. His earring hung low with a single blue gem at the end. And his new tattoo on his skin was red as it healed. Three blue dots to match the Kiddos. He was creating his own army of sorts. More of a family.

When Gage turned, Sev saw his other new tattoo. Blue lips on the side of his neck. Gage caught him staring and winked.

"Wrath was blue for Josh. Did you know?" Gage said with a soft smile.

Sev responded with a silent nod. He figured that out after getting to the Cove. All of Josh's items were blue. Now so were Gage's. Sev knew Gage was in pain. Didn't begin to understand. Didn't want to. His soulmate. His uncle. Sev couldn't imagine. Before Lynch, he'd never known someone personally who died.

Sev was glad he remembered to grab the prototype and all the configurations from the computer in his lab before he ran from the Valley. He remembered Lynch helping him train every day when he was Fenix's age. Remembered him riding on a track beside him. Taking the blame on a few occasions. Especially switching with him at the end. Allowing Sev to leave the Valley so he would take his place as Superior.

Instead, he died. Sacrificed himself for Sev and his friends.

Superior Ashbury got out of his cuffs. With help from Patrick. They hadn't known. He had all his fingers. They couldn't trust anyone now. Drake's arm was mangled by the time he'd gotten to Gage's. Elle was furious. Frantic. Luckily, she had a tub of Elastaderm. Or Blue Sludge, that's what they called it here. Now there was a long scar from his elbow to his wrist. Sev knew what that was like. He'd think of that day every time he looked down. Would Drake think of his failures or his successes on that day?

Drake and Vero lost the battle, but they still had a chance to win this war. They needed to figure out the chips. Sev would save Bullet. Had to. He made a promise. He'd keep it. Sev built his own lab in Gage's spare room. He began the week after they had arrived. Needed his own space if he was going to be of any use to them.

When he wasn't home with them, he was at work. ChaosMotors Headquarters was in the center of town, and he had a lot to improve on. He got to use his knowledge on bikes instead of creatures. And he enjoyed it thoroughly. Even his coworkers were alright. Ace and Fenix were test riders there. They would become mechanics soon. He taught them more as the days went on. They were young and easily fascinated. Eager to learn.

Ace came back outside with the tablet and set it down in front of Mason. Gage thanked the boy before he joined Fenix in the kitchen.

Mason got the video call ready before they crowded him to fit on the screen.

Drake appeared after a minute with Elle by his side. She waved and smiled at them before Vero turned the screen to herself. She thanked Sev profusely before Lex grabbed the tablet to say hi. Nate waved from the background, and Drake groaned.

"Done?" Drake snapped at them. Elle put her hand on his scarred arm.

"Down to business. What's our first step?" Vero asked.

Superior Ashbury was still in charge. Patrick took Sev's place as Second. The new army doubled by the day. More and more chips were being made. Bullet in hiding. Lynch dead. What was their first step? Sev didn't know. He took a deep breath. Every other week, they tried to have a meeting, he felt they were going nowhere.

"Where's Maia?" Vero asked, noticing her absence.

"Searching for Bullet," Mason said.

One day, she will find him. Hopefully still alive. Sev hoped she was prepared for either. Bullet wouldn't let her bring him back. He knew Bullet left to protect her from himself. Once Superior turns his chip on, he'll become a killing machine. Nothing would stop him.

Sev allows Maia to search. It gives her a task to ease her mind instead of sharing Bullet's location with her. Sev put the chip inside his spine. He figured out how to hack into Superior's tracker map. Sev could see each soldier's location. At least this version of chips. He couldn't see Patrick. And they weren't sure how many others would be in different versions. Next step was to disable them. He owed Bullet. Understood him. He would help him. Had to. Sev didn't care what the group's next step was. He had his own path.

"She'll find him," Lex chimed in. Always tried to keep the group positive.

"What if he's dead?" Vero asked.

"He isn't," Elle said firmly.

The group was quiet until Gage piped in. "Heard from Aster?"

Vero shook her head. That must've been enough for him because he dropped the subject. Aster was Josh's cousin. And apparently, the girl of Vero's dreams. Once Aster got to the Cove, she fled. Every once in a while, she would send Gage a message to tell him she was alive. Nothing about where she is or what she's doing. It crushed him. Every week, he'd send an update of his own. Always coded in case her phone got into the wrong hands.

They kept the meeting short and ended on a good note. Discussing Drake and Elle planning a meet with another Valley. Superior Frost agreed to their new ideas of a Championship where the contestants wouldn't fight for their lives. They also lessened weapons on Guard and allowed mates to live better inside the walls. Baby steps.

They use Graves Valley as an example. With statistics and graphs Nate made to help Drake plead his case. Nate was good with numbers. Drake explained a while ago how he had taken Nate under his wing. Trained him to fight and how to shoot. While Nate taught him how to win over the more reasonable Superiors with logic instead of using his fists.

They had big plans for the new world they were trying to build. Sev was excited to be a part of it. A part of something good. For the first time in his life.

Everyone went inside to help Ace with dinner. Fenix left on their bike to grab the rest of the Kiddos by the lake. They fought to come home until food was mentioned. Gage made sure all the kids were well fed every night. Something he had struggled with growing up.

Mason took Sev's hand and pulled him down the steps into the yard.

"Are you worried?" Mason asked. "If Superior finds us, we're ready to fight."

"What if it's Patrick or Bullet that comes? With the army? Are you ready to kill your friends?"

"We'd figure it out. Trap them until we could get the chip out."

"That's your plan?"

"Until you figure out how to disable them."

"What if I can't?" Sev asked. Uncertainty crashed through him.

"You will. I know you've been researching," Mason said.

Sev peered at his partner.

"Don't worry. I won't let the others know you're a big softy when it comes to Bullet." Mason tugged his cheek, and Sev glowered. Hated when he did that. "I know you care for him. And my sister."

"It doesn't bother you?"

"Bullet and Maia?" Mason shrugged. "I'll cross that bridge when we get there. Maia didn't give me too much shit when I fell for Superior's Dragon. How can I be upset when she falls for Captain Knuckles?"

Sev nodded. He had a point. Mason pulled him close and kissed him tenderly. Brought his lips to Sev's ear.

"No matter what, we'll get through it together. I got you."

THE END

If you loved *Acheron Bound*, please consider leaving a review! It helps more than you know. Any review, no matter how long, helps get my books in the hands of new readers.

-millie

FIND ME ON SOCIAL MEDIA
millieleighbooks

tiktok

instagram

facebook

about the author

WRITING HAS BEEN A HOBBY FOR MILLIE SINCE SHE WAS A CHILD. YOU CAN FIND THIS QUEER AUTHOR AT THE COFFEE SHOP SHE WORKS AT OR HER HOME LIBRARY. TO GET AWAY FROM THE *CHAOS,* SHE GOES TO THE BEACH WITH HER HUSBAND, KADEN, OR GETS ANOTHER TATTOO.

www.ingramcontent.com/pod-product-compliance
Lightning Source LLC
Chambersburg PA
CBHW032027310726
48972CB00002B/562

9781961382046